I0583143

# Desires
# Of a
# Deceiver

### Barbara Woster

Cover by Ashley Creatives

# DEDICATION

For my family, without whose love and support,
I could never have written this book. I love you all, very much

# CHAPTER ONE

August 25, 1915

*Eagerly awaiting arrival. Stop. Money on*
*way for fare. Stop. Inform arrival date. Stop.*
*Meet at station. Your future husband,*
*William. End.*

With a dreamy sigh, the young woman rolled onto her back, closed her eyes in a moment of languor, the telegram clutched to her breast in wordless desire. She longed for a man that would be sincere in his fervor, sincere in his desire for her.

As if speared with a cattle prod, the woolgathering moment passed, and her eyes flew open, "Prince Charming does not exist, and if he did, he certainly would not be desirous of me," she sneered in self-derision. Still, her lack of desirability could not prevent her enjoying the enthusiastic yearning she elicited in others. She cackled and wondered, not for the first time, whether her rejection—when she finally sent one along—would cause crocodile tears, anger, or perhaps sanctimonious indignation. Would any of them read her rebuff—carefully worded—and feel a sense they'd been duped?

"None has thus far," she mused aloud.

She clutched at the telegram one more time, and a laugh issued forth as she thought about all of those men, just waiting for someone to arrive. Until now, she'd found little to laugh joyously about; had avoided genuine laughter as a rule over the years; especially when her first episode had elicited so negative a reaction.

*"Dear Lord!" Her mother exclaimed, "Tell me you're doing that on purpose."*

Of course, she hadn't been; hadn't realized how ear piercing her shrieks were, but did find its annoyance beneficial when she wanted to drive someone away from her; until it started driving away potential suitors. That's when she learned not to laugh, unless she was alone. The deliberate tamping down of this primary emotional release, developed within her a sadness, a darkness, a desire to seek

3

retribution against all men, her mother,—and one particular woman, for whom she had developed a deep-seated hatred only three months prior.

In this particular quest for vengeance against the woman, she likened herself to the evil queen in "Snow White"[1] whose fairytale world was disrupted by the appearance of the princess, much as her own world had been disrupted by the arrival of this woman—her cousin.

The comparison made her let loose an unexpected cackle, and a bird sitting on her windowsill squawked in agitated protest and soared away. She shot an annoyed look at the retreating blackbird and crinkled her nose in disgust. She hated birds. With a huff at the blackbird, which had settled on a higher branch, still squawking, she reread the telegram, and then laid the cream-colored paper on the mattress. She straightened the crinkled edges amorously until it lie flattened atop the previously read one.

With another wistful sigh, she turned and looked at yet another telegram lying on the other side of where she sat, awaiting her attention. She reached down, picked up the yellow parchment, and scanned its contents.

> *Can't wait to meet new bride. Stop. Fare*
> *adequate? Stop. Sent yesterday. Stop. Meet*
> *soon. Yours, Kendall. End.*

*Such eagerness towards a stranger,* she snorted tacitly, *so desperate to wed me, sight unseen.* "I could be a complete loony, yet you're willing to take me into your home, take me as your wife. All you really want is someone to warm your bed. The same with all of you. What's wrong with the lot of ya?" She continued aloud, conversing with the sheets of paper nestled beside her. "How desperate can men out west really be to place an ad, and then jump at the first response they receive?" She sighed, "How desperate am I to be willing to marry one of you?"

After a moment, she answered her own question, "Apparently,

---

[1] The Brothers Grimm published it in 1812 in the first edition of their collection *Grimms' Fairy Tales*. It was titled in German: *Sneewittchen* (Wikipedia).

very." She snorted again and then laid that telegram atop the first two with the same level of affection as she'd shown the last one. With a bemused shake of her head, she realized how careful she was and wondered at her ignorant and silly behavior. These men didn't know her; would not grant her so much as a by-your-leave should they pass her on the street, yet she treated each of their responses with the attention one would a lover's note?

That small reminder at her lack of prospects was nearly her undoing—again—and she eyed the communications with sudden suspicion and open hostility. She leaned toward the papers, her eyes narrowed and her lips stretched into a thin line of disapproval, "I should wad you all up and toss you into Hell's fire," she whispered. "That's where you all truly belong, but if I do that..." The momentary lapse of insanity passed, and she sat up straighter. Ignorance was bliss, she reminded herself, for all parties concerned; and as these were her only connection with feelings of acceptance, she would treat these pages with the respect they deserved, at least until she collected the money each promised. Then she would relegate them to the wastepaper basket.

A final shudder raced through her, releasing her from her oppressing ruminations and a smile graced her inelegant features. She had read all of the telegrams now. All that remained was the only letter to arrive that morning. She knew from whom it originated, which is why she chose to read it last. This was the only man with whom she maintained open communication. Why she had not rejected him along with the others, she did not know. Something about his prose, although not much differently worded than all the rest, reached deep inside to what in some would be a responsive beating heart. His words touched her somehow, barely warmed her cold interior. If only provisionally.

*My Dearest Iliamna -*

*I wanted to wait until completing the project before announcing it to you, but I fear I have allowed my eagerness to overrule my judgment in the matter. Still, it is my greatest hope that by telling you, you will endeavor to join me sooner so that we may begin our journey as husband and wife.*

*I ramble on. Forgive me.*

*The day I received your first reply to my advertisement for a bride, I knew that you must be the one for me, so casting aside my normal circumspection; I began immediately upon construction of a new house for which I hope you will soon call home.*

*I pray for your mother's speedy recovery every day, admittedly to my own selfish ends, and fervently hope that you will join me before another month passes. I also know that it is a vast presumption on my part, but I have enclosed money for train fare in case my hopes become a possibility.*

*Eagerly await your reply—and possibly a date of arrival?*

*Affectionately yours,*

*Shreve*


"Oh Shreve, if it were me, I would readily be on the next train out of this self-imposed prison in which I reside, but you are not really writing to me, are you, Love? If only you knew. Iliamna would not so much look your way twice—as you would not likely glance *my* way twice. She is far too beautiful and her hand in marriage too eagerly sought after, for her to consider entertaining suitors from such an uncivilized place as Texas. I wish I had the heart to exchange the drawing of her that I sent to you, with one of me; and to reveal to you my true name, but selfishly, I relish your correspondence too much."

With a squeal of anger over the realization that Shreve would never be hers, she tossed the paper onto the floor, "You're an imbecile!" She yelled. "Building a house for a woman that you'll never know! Why do I even bother writing to you?"

She continued to glare down at the paper, her breathing heavy, as if it were Shreve sitting there, and then as quickly as her anger rose, it dissipated, and she fell off the bed, and onto her knees. Gingerly, she lifted the paper and held it to her breast, "Please forgive me. I cannot help myself sometimes. If only I could express why I act the way I do. If only you knew how people overlooked me so readily when Iliamna is in attendance; how readily *you* would."

With a sigh, she stood, gently laying the letter atop the telegrams. She blew the pages a kiss, and then pulled a black lacquer box from her dresser; a box that she'd painstakingly hand-painted with renderings of flowers in bloom and blackbirds lying dead amidst the multi-colored flora—along with a multitude of other fowl.

The euphoria she felt at reading each telegram and Shreve's correspondence slowly faded when she started to tuck them away, for only when she held them did she feel beautiful and wanted. A tear threatened to break free, but she slapped herself hard across the cheek to prevent it doing so. She would rather die than allow herself to feel sorry for her circumstances.

"I will see you all again soon," she whispered, picking up the papers and laying them inside on the red-velvet interior. She would pull them out only once more, when it was time for her to go to the Western Union offices and collect the money each telegram promised would arrive for her and then to write one final return telegram expressing her sorrow over not being able to join them after all, due to familial distresses. Once she tended to the rejections, each telegram found its way into the nearest trash receptacle.

For now, tucking them away closed the lid on her fantasies, enabling reality to invade, reminding her that it wasn't really *she* these faceless men were interested in; only words on a page and a drawing she'd done of a woman that wasn't even a good likeness. *Perhaps because it is not my face in the drawing*, she smiled grimly.

With a concentrated effort, she shook the depressing thoughts from her mind—again. After all, it did not truly matter that it was not her face in the drawing, because each correspondence was addressed to her, by proxy. It may have been her cousin's name on the communications, but each was for her and her alone. *She* was the one men wrote to with fondness; it was her words written to them that they cherished. It was to her they proposed. Her, not Iliamna, and that was enough—for now.

Of course, because of her deceit, it also fell to her to make daily trips to the telegraph office to ensure that she was the only one to take possession of any telegrams that arrived. The same with the post office. It was a daily exercise in worry that someone other would get there ahead of her and give the correspondence to Iliamna. For every successful excursion over the past three months, she felt invigorated to plan just a bit more of her own Snow White fairy tale. A story with more depth than just simple deception; it was a story in which unsightly would ultimately triumph over beauty. She would see to that.

She sighed, tucking her letterbox inside the dresser and retrieving another, less ornate box, "Before I answer any more ads, let me just see if I have enough to set my plans into motion; especially as my plans have an expiration date."

She added the money that Shreve sent to the bills inside the box, and then started counting. With a sigh and a grin of satisfaction, she tucked the bills into her reticule. The accumulated funds would prove sufficient, she was sure. She then placed a kiss upon the black ink and tossed the newspaper into the wastebasket. There wouldn't be a need for her to answer any more ads for now. Humming a happy tune, she bounded down the stairs towards the stables.

"It's time to go for a ride," she murmured as she exited the house. She saw her father's chauffeur waxing their auto beneath some nearby trees and called for him to bring it around for her. He complied, but instead of remaining in the driver's seat, he climbed down and held the door open with a slight bow. Normally his disinterest in driving her annoyed her, but not today. Today she wanted to be alone; didn't want any knowing where she was headed, or what her plans were. Still, it was rude of him not even to offer. If he were her driver, and not her father's, she'd dismiss him straightaway.

With her nose elevated, she climbed aboard, placed the automobile into gear, and headed down the drive. When she reached the main street, she turned toward the wharf, and went in search of trouble, knowing that if she went far enough on the outskirts of the city, she'd find it.

# CHAPTER TWO

"A woman traveling alone in this part of town is very unusual," a man whispered to himself, as he viewed the woman approaching him in her Ford Model N Runabout[2].

Alana slowed the older automobile. She was embarrassed to be seen in such an outdated car, but she didn't have a car of her own. When she did finally rid herself of her cousin and was able to save up money for her own vehicle, she would purchase her own automobile, which would be easier, thanks to Ford building his working man's vehicle. The Model T wasn't her ideal, as was the Model S, but she couldn't afford to be too choosy[3].

The man's grin widened when she stopped her vehicle in front of where he stood, and Alana turned her head aside in disgust of his stained teeth; very few of which he had remaining. The smell from his mouth and his body—even from a short distance—made her stomach heave, and she pulled her handkerchief from her sleeve and placed it over her nose and mouth, breathing deeply the delicate scent of perfume to dispel the odors, "And people find *me* disagreeable," she murmured.

She parked in the shadows, and remained there after climbing from her vehicle, in order to prevent someone noticing her; but while the shadows provided a small measure of safety, she could not shake feeling slightly insecure. She was definitely out of place among the rusty warehouses, rotting fish smells, and slick-oily docks. By no man's measure, was she a looker, but she dressed nice, smelled good, and looked clean—a stark contrast to this particular locale. With a deep breath, she brushed aside her feelings of unease. There was a purpose here, which she needed to accomplish sooner rather later, so that she could return to civilization.

---

[2] Ford produced the Model N Runabout from 1906-1908. This was the seventh in a series of letter cars produced since 1903; each with a manufacturing lifespan of one to two years (henryford.org).

[3] The Model T—the Tin Lizzy—was manufactured by Ford Motor Company between 1908 and 1927. It was the most inexpensive, most popular, and extended manufactured vehicle by his company at that time (history,com).

With a glance about the area to ensure that no one was around who might recognize her, she straightened her shoulders, threw her nose in the air, and stepped from the shadows of rapidly waning daylight into the light cast by the electric street lamp, which had only just flickered on.

The man she determined to approach was having his own thoughts, as he waited for her to speak. He ran his gaze from her shiny buckled black boots, to her rather disappointing cleavage peering above her dress, thoughts racing through his mind on how to get her behind some of the nearby crates in order to enjoy some pleasurable release. Those musings ceased abruptly when she stepped from the shadows.

Much as she'd cringed when she approached him, he cringed now. *She's more homely than the men I work with,* he thought, with a shudder of repulsion. After a moment more, he decided that he wasn't yet desperate enough for a woman and determined to scare her off as quickly as possible.

"It ain't safe for you to be traveling alone down here," he said in his best intimidating tone, but she didn't so much as blink. Whatever she wanted down here—especially if she came in search of a specific type of intimate company—he would steer her in someone else's direction. He had his limits on what his women should look like.

When she finally deigned to address him, he wondered what he'd done of late to make God want to punish him by sending her his way.

"I'm not traveling alone," she assured him, and he flinched—not at *what* she said, but rather the tone of her voice. *Well, she may be upper crust,* he thought, *but her voice is definitely lower ditches—similar to her looks. No wonder she's slumming. No one in her own neighborhood could tolerate her noises. Still,* he thought, not paying much attention to what she was saying, as he was suddenly having second thoughts as to his need for a soft body, *she ain't all that bad below the neck; and she does have a nice smell about her. Maybe a gag and a potato sack over the head would make it easier for my pecker to make an appearance.* He was thinking about finding a way to lure her into a very dark alley, when what she was saying registered and his brows knitted in confusion. He looked around, but could see no other people near the two of them; had not seen another automobile approach.

*Perhaps her mental state is on par with her looks and voice*, he thought, *not so great.* That was the only way to explain her lack of a chaperone and her obvious lack of fear. Still, mental or not, ugly or not, nerve-grating voice or not, she was still female and he decided that he *was* aching for a bit of female. He took another quick glance around, not because he craved to be alone with her, but because he did not fancy someone attacking him from behind, especially if the companion she intimated traveling with her was as ugly and crazy as she was; however, his inspection of the surrounding area discerned nothing, no one.

"I don't see no one else, Missy," he said softly. "Perhaps you travel with ghosts."

"No!" She cackled, and he winced and took an involuntary step back. "I travel with steel." A slight movement near her waist caught his eye and his gaze widened. Where that wicked looking blade came from and when she managed to aim the tip toward his belly, he didn't know, but his first reaction was to snatch the weapon from the stupid twit and shove it down her throat, which he knew he could easily do, but he stopped himself from acting on his impulse. He'd never harmed a lady in his life, even an ugly one, even if this one did deserve retribution for pulling a knife on him. Maybe he could carve her a better face. He grinned, but it was not because he considered the situation humorous, for he did not. Still, he did want to get even somehow, so he decided on an insult, "Lady, you don't need nothing else but your voice to keep men away from you down here. Now what do you want, and keep the explanation brief."

She hissed at him—like a cornered cat, which made him wonder what sort of woman this really was. She traveled alone and seemed to have little fear and that, alone, made his nerves jump. Not that he was afraid of no woman—usually—but when she hissed and he really looked her in the eyes for the first time, something in those depths caused his skin to crawl. He had to force himself from retreating to the closest saloon and downing half the liquor stock. He understood now why she could walk the docks at twilight undisturbed—she was Lucifer's daughter, and he was convinced she would look like him too—a fact he'd see firsthand, when he finally met the Prince of Darkness after he died. He crossed himself quickly.

If she did not happen to be related to the devil at present, he truly believed that the king of the underworld would willingly adopt her, for there was definitely something evil displayed in the depths of her gaze. One top of that, she was not playing with a full deck of cards. In fact, it appeared she was missing nearly the entire deck.

"It's nice to know I have your attention," she said.

"Oh, that you do," he cringed.

Alana's gaze narrowed, but she kept it level on his, "I need to know if you are for hire for a job I need doing."

The man shook his head rapidly. He may not be a good man, but he'd promised his momma when he was little that he'd never crawl into bed with the devil—or his daughter. He shook his head more intensely.

"Do you know of someone that I might hire?"

It took a minute before he was able to shove aside his nervousness and answer. When he did, he had to clear his throat and start again when his words initially emerged on a croak. He sniffed deeply and wiped his hand across his face, and tried again, "What you looking to have done?" He sincerely did not want to aid this girl, but he was suddenly fearful that if he did not, she would cast a spell upon his manly parts and turn him into a eunuch. She was no doubt wicked, and he happened to like his boys to stay neatly tucked inside his britches. He crossed himself again, determining that he'd attend Sunday services this week. When she finished explaining what she was there for, he shook his head and sighed deeply.

He'd done his share of bad things, which was why he ended up where he was now, living in squalor in a bad part of town, but a girl dressed in such finery, who obviously had a life of ease, shouldn't have thoughts like the ones she was describing. It just did not fit. She should be living in the dredges along with the rest of the scum of the earth; not living high off the hog like a lady, even if she did look like said hog. Still, it was not his concern what she did or who she did it to, just as long as she left him alone. He'd point her to someone, just so he never had to see her again.

"I know of a man who might be able to help you," he said. "Take yourself on down to the Silver Palace and ask for Gitano. He should be able to help with your particular needs."

"I'll do that," the young woman said. She reached into her

reticule and pulled out a silver dollar. "Here, for your trouble."

"No thanks," the man said, backing away into the shadows. "This bit of information is on me."

"As you wish," the young woman said and turned away.

The man hid in the shadows until she had climbed back into her vehicle and drove away, and then he stepped back into the light of the street lamp, bathing himself in the warmth, hoping that the small amount of light washing over his cold body would erase the shadow of evil that lingered in the dark.

# CHAPTER THREE

Iliamna Dearborn stood on the balcony overlooking the manicured garden and drew in several, short, incomplete breaths. She'd never worn a corset because her mother never saw the sense of them, but her aunt had given it to her and insisted she wear it. She'd tried to tell her aunt that corsets were not a fashion requirement any longer—at least that her mother had said—but her aunt was old-fashioned and had refused to transition to a girdle, or to even try some of the brassieres being worn by many women of her acquaintance.

"No, as long as you're in my house, you'll wear a corset", her aunt declared, and now she was standing here on the balcony simply trying to breathe. "No wonder these things lost favor," she whispered airily. Her first breath escaped on a whoosh of air along with a prayer, not that God could answer her prayer, for it had to do with the return of her her mom, and their home in Virginia. There, she was free to dress as she pleased, could even persuade her mom to allow her to try the latest fashions. Here, she had to deal with her aunt's antiquated ideals.

Mother had never required her to wear this uncomfortably confining contraption, even before they went out of fashion; but so much had changed since her parents' passed away: her clothing, her circumstances, and her home.

Of course, this was not her home. This was a place to dwell— and miserably at that. She felt sadness grip her heart again, but pushed it away, since she knew her mother and father would not like to see her wallow in self-pitying depression, even if it was justifiable in her own mind. Aunt Magdalene would not tolerate it either, but not out of concern for her niece's happiness, but because "frowning makes a woman's face look old, and an old-looking woman is not eagerly sought after". Her aunt's words resounded in her mind and Iliamna shuddered.

She looked toward the horizon and wondered just how far

Sweden was. Perhaps in time, she would be able to afford a trip. She was certain that her mother's family would welcome her with more kindness than her father's sister-in-law had, but finances didn't allow for a long boat trip, and besides, all she knew of her mother's family were from stories told. She could not even remember in which part of Sweden her relatives lived, and no way to locate them should a boat trip become affordable.

She sighed again, a half sigh, which once again reminded her of her circumstances, and that her aunt had forced her to wear a corset from the moment she arrived. "A true lady wouldn't be caught out and about without stays", her aunt chided when Iliamna arrived at the front door—without a corset, of course.

"But what about indoors, Aunt Magdalene?" Iliamna asked innocently, and received a look that bordered on a mental breakdown.

"Good heavens, child," her aunt fairly screeched, "were you raised by heathens? A woman is never without stays ever, for she never knows when she may find herself in a position of entertaining unexpected guests. A *true* lady is prepared, continually, for any eventuality. Do you understand?"

"Yes, Aunt Magdalene," Iliamna whispered, feeling ugly and uncouth. Surely, she hadn't heard her aunt call her mother a heathen. After all, her mother had taught her manners, and how to be a lady from the day Iliamna could walk and talk. She simply thought in a different way about fashion, and, apparently, stayed atop the current trends, unlike her aunt. Perhaps had they lived in town, where unexpected guests were a likely occurrence, her mother might have viewed things differently.

Not that it mattered now, for she had done everything possible to try to adjust to the confining undergarment and failed wretchedly. She simply could not take a breath deep enough to fill the cramped space of her lungs and wondered why she did not simply cease in her attempts. She tried one more time and then finally resigned herself to quit—again—settling for the short, raspy breaths she had become accustomed to of late. She resolved then and there that she would save some of her money and visit the boutique in town; see if they had a girdle she could wear instead or maybe even a brassiere.

The night was humid, and she dabbed at the perspiration that popped out ceaselessly on her face and neck. Still, out here, despite the heat, she felt a moment's reprieve from the suffocating air that the mass of bodies generated in the ballroom.

She looked up at the stars and blocked out the music drifting from one floor down. A light shot across the sky and Iliamna closed her eyes and made a wish. It was not the same, she was sure, as making a wish on the first star that appeared with the setting sun, but she was bordering on desperation. She ached for her renewed freedom; wished and prayed for it every chance given. "Please, please, please. I just want to find my own way; to live a life with love and kindness, not this life I've been forced to live filled with hostility and...I'm sorry," she whispered, her wish turning into a prayer, "I don't mean to sound ungrateful."

In truth, she really wasn't ungrateful to her Aunt Magdalene and Uncle Christopher for taking her in after her parents' deaths, but she was simply ill suited for the life that her father's brother lived, nor did she know how to handle the constant barrage of negative comments aimed in her direction.

More than anything was her confusion over this ball, thrown in her honor. She didn't know what to make of it all. Especially when all her aunt had done since her arrival was to grumble about having another mouth to feed and whine about the funds her parents *did not* leave her when they died. Such lavishness in light of all of the complaints simply did not make any sense. Still, she supposed it was worth it in her aunt's mind, if it meant relieving them of their burden and responsibility by finding a husband to care for her. Between the comments related to her manners, about her lack of wealth, and finding her a husband, Iliamna's head pounded continually.

If she were a weaker woman, she would break apart beneath the unrelenting onslaught of sometimes hidden, but often blatant, derogatory comments directed at her from sunup to sundown, but what made it even more difficult to comprehend was how her aunt's complaints often followed an offer by her to assist with the household expenses. She had, after all, managed to find gainful employment shortly after her arrival, but her aunt had treated her offer as an outright insult while continuing to grouse about the financial strain. "Your mother and father, God rest their souls, left your care into our hands, and we would be failing miserably if we allowed you to pay your own way," her aunt said, her tone strangely accusatory.

Iliamna sighed again. If she could only find room and board as well, she would leave her uncle's home immediately. Preferably, before her aunt found her a husband from the pretentious frauds gathering in the ballroom this evening. She'd befriended a parent at the end of her first teaching day, who said that there was a boarding house that should have an opening at the end of the month. Iliamna planned to go inspect the facility tomorrow and hopefully make a suitable impression upon the proprietor so that she'd be offered the available room.

"Here you are, Cousin!"

Iliamna recoiled at the shrill voice that intruded on her peaceful moment; however, she refused to allow her discomfort to show. She may not be her aunt's ideal of a lady, but her mother had taught her that a lady never showed disdain toward someone different than herself. At least a true lady didn't. She pasted on an artificial smile— something she affected more often these days—and turned around to face her cousin. "You found me," she said cheerily, trying to hide her frustration at being disturbed.

"What are you doing out here? Momma is going to be dreadfully put out with you." Alana lifted her fan and popped it open with a practiced flick of her wrist. "It's alarmingly hot and humid tonight. You know it's going to upset Mother, Iliamna, if you remain outside and wilt."

"I'll wilt faster inside. Hot and humid or no, I am having a more difficult time breathing in there than out here. Could you simply be a dear and explain to your mother that I wasn't feeling well and needed to retire early?"

"Absolutely not!"

"Why ever not? It is not a lie. I *am* feeling rather light-headed. It must be the excess heat this evening. It's taking its toll on me," she said, dabbing at another round of perspiration.

"The only thing taking its toll on you, Cousin, is attempting to find a husband among the many eligible men that, need I remind you, my mother went to a lot of time and trouble to invite to the party, from all over the state. All for you!"

Iliamna did not miss the resentfulness that slipped into Alana's tone, nor did she need to guess what caused it. Alana had only just reached marriageable age, but since there was an elder, unwed female in the home now, her mother felt obligated to see the eldest wed first. This, of course, would deplete the funds needed to find Alana a husband, even if only by a year.

Still, it was not as if she'd asked her aunt to spend money needlessly on her behalf. She had even expressed her opinion about it to her aunt; had stated that she'd happily remain unwed and allow Alana to wed first, but her aunt wouldn't hear of it. After all, to remain unwed would mean remaining in the Dearborn home longer than any of the female occupants cared for—admittedly, even she abhorred the idea.

She didn't need to own a crystal ball to comprehend that this was the other area from where the not-so-subtle hostility stemmed. Both wanted her gone, but neither was pleased at having to expend the time, money, or energy needed to find her a husband, in which to see to her departure; however, finding her a husband, in their opinion, was the only possible way that she could ever leave. After all, that was the only way *most* women escaped their homes, but Iliamna was different; she preferred to make her own way first. She'd voiced that point so many times, she thought she'd grow weary of receiving derision and mockery from her relatives, in reply. Her only reasoning as to why she persisted, was that she was as stubborn as they.

"I can't help but wonder, Cousin, why my absence below stairs would have you so distraught," Iliamna said with a sigh.

"It's not your absence, but your total disregard for my mother's efforts. The least you could do is pretend to enjoy the affair and show an interest in some of the men she has invited. Maybe if it's so suffocating indoors, as you suggest, you could allow one the men to escort you about the gardens."

"Actually, I don't have to do anything of the sort," Iliamna said, raising her chin a notch. "I never asked for any of this, and, in all honesty, I find it offensive that this soiree was planned without my consent only three months after my parents' demise. It shows a complete lack of etiquette. In fact, it has disturbed me so much, that I was thinking that it would be best if I left your household all together and struck out on my own. I'm certain that I could find a place with a friend until a room opens up at the boarding. . ."

"You ungrateful wench!" Alana snapped. "My mother has done nothing but try to make you feel welcome since you showed up unannounced on our doorstep, and now you have the audacity to throw her good intentions back in our faces!"

Iliamna sighed for the millionth time that evening, "You're right—to a point," she conceded. "Aunt Magdalene didn't have to take me in, and I'm grateful that she did, but what I cannot fathom or agree upon is this husband-finding party. The timing of which is ill-conceived, as I am still in mourning, and not mentally fit to locate a husband. Once an acceptable time of mourning has passed, then perhaps I will start looking for someone, but someone of my own choosing; not someone of someone else's choosing, invited to a party for me to be paraded in front of."

"Your own choosing," Alana scoffed. "You'd probably find the least suitable male on the planet, if you thought you loved him."

"And what's wrong with love...oh, never mind. I will continue on with my teaching and locate a place to live in town. Perhaps never marry."

"Well-bred ladies don't work," Alana said, then sneered. "Oh, that's right—you're just a country bumpkin dressed up to look like a lady."

Iliamna decided to overlook the insult. She had become used to them by now, "In my opinion, well-bred ladies should know what's happening in the world, and do their best to help make the place in which they live a better place. Keep their ears open to what's happening, so as to be better prepared to help, if needed."

"What a bunch of banana talk," Alana huffed.

"Yes, well, be that as it may, did you know that our men are talking about going to war? I overheard your father talking about how a German submarine sunk some fancy ship..."[4]

---

[4] May 7, 1915, a German submarine sunk the British passenger liner, Lusitania, killing 128 Americans.

"It's not ladylike to eavesdrop, and there's no way our men would abandon us for some other countries' war! That's just dumb, and certainly not conversation for women folk."

Iliamna sighed. She was wasting her breath anyway, "You know, I'd think you'd be happy about my plans to leave. It's obvious that you've been unhappy since I came to reside here, so I'd expect you to be in my room helping me pack instead of arguing over trivialities. Come to think of it, you're marriageable age, so why don't you go back in there and attempt to locate your own future spouse, and leave me be? The last thing I'd expect is for you to be distraught that I'm not interested in the men in attendance tonight."

Alana was suddenly thoughtful. Why was Iliamna's desire to find her own way aggravating her so? Iliamna was right about everything. She had despised her from the moment of her arrival, so she should be thrilled that she wanted to leave; she should be in the ballroom attempting to snare her own husband...she should be, but she couldn't, and she remembered why. Iliamna's plans were a threat to her own plans; plans that she had labored over, with loving care and intimate detail, for the past three months; plans that she'd set in motion only recently. Iliamna would douse the flame of power she thrived on if she left, and that thought angered her. More than angered her, it drove her to the brink of lunacy.

She also realized that she shouldn't be trying to push Iliamna back into the ballroom, because her well-laid plans depended upon her being outside of the ballroom. Admittedly, she thought her plans depended upon convincing Iliamna to take a stroll alone in the garden, but...

This location would work just as well, she quickly decided when a movement along the railing caught her eye. She was going to have her moment of glory very soon, and Iliamna would be gone—not in a way of Iliamna's choosing, where she could live a life of pleasure and happiness; but according to her own plans, where there would be no joy.

Iliamna looked at her cousin and actually felt a twinge of pity for the young girl standing before her. Alana was not a beauty. Her hair was a drab mix that was not quite brown or blonde. Her face was pot-marked and pasty and her speech held a high-pitched nasal quality that grated on nerves. She suspected that Alana would never attract a man willing to wake up next to her on a daily basis, unless, of course, he was as unattractive as she and willing to overlook her shortcomings; or perhaps if he was deaf and blind.

Iliamna wanted to feel bad about the negative thoughts that paraded through her mind about her cousin, because she sincerely attempted to think positively about people; however, in this case, she couldn't control the negativity since Alana had whined about her and at her incessantly since she arrived, and Iliamna was fed up with it all.

"You are right," Alana said suddenly, snapping Iliamna from her own musings. "Good riddance to you, then. I'll be happy to see you go."

"See now," Iliamna sighed, thankful the unpleasantness had passed, "it is possible for us to get on well if we put our minds to it. Now all I need to do is decide where I want to go and when I will leave, and, of course, we will need to find a way to break the news to Aunt Magdalene. What do you find so humorous?" Iliamna asked, flinching at the sound that issued from her cousin. She assumed the snorting sound was laughter, since mirth lined her cousin's amber eyes.

"I said I agreed that you should leave, but I didn't say how you would be going," Alana said in a tone that made shivers race along Iliamna's spine.

"I beg your pardon?"

"I don't believe begging will do you any good, Cousin."

Before Iliamna could reply, a large hand slipped around her waist, clamped onto her abdomen and yanked, pulling her tightly against a distinctively male body. A hand, holding a vicious-looking blade, shot around the side of her face, which stopped just shy of slicing through her carotid artery.

# CHAPTER FOUR

Iliamna stiffened. She wanted to scream, but the pressure around her abdomen signaled a warning, as if her attacker could sense her need to yell for help.

"Make one sound, *mi querida pequeña*, and I slice your head off your neck." The words spoken in such a sexy accent and sultry tone decreased the threat of the words, but the blade pressing into her soft flesh affirmed that this man was serious and her circumstances precarious. "She is no really so little, is she, *mi compañera?*" He asked Alana, a grin on his face. "Perhaps I call her *mi querida estatura* instead, hmm?"

"I do not particularly care what you call her and what took you so long?" Alana said, popping her fan back open. She waved the fan rapidly in front of her face trying to dispel the thick layer of perspiration that had formed on it in the short time since she had last closed it. "It's so dadblasted hot, and you've kept me standing in this pool of humidity far too long."

If nothing else, Iliamna could empathize with her cousin on that point. She felt a trickle of sweat pool between her breasts and roll toward her belly, only to have its journey halted as the material of her corset absorbed the droplet, but it did not matter—very quickly, hundreds of droplets formed, traversing the path between her breasts, and between her shoulder blades. However, she could not blame the humidity alone for the profusion of perspiration, for her current predicament was just as much to blame.

"It is no so easy to climb up *un* trellis," the voice replied conversationally, although Iliamna felt his body tense every time Alana spoke. It was one thing she could empathize with, which she found absurd, considering he was holding her captive. "I thought you say you bring her to the garden, and instead I look up and see you talking with her here, up high."

"I was trying to convince her to take a stroll, but I lost my temper."

"So how you think that I get her down from here without breaking *mi cuello*—or *hers*, hmm?"

"What in Hell is a *cuello?*"

"Neck."

"Oh, well her *neck* I don't much care about, but she is part of your payment so you'll just have to figure a way to get her down *and* keep her alive, unless you know a place that will pay you for a corpse."

Iliamna's eyes widened further at the enmity in the words Alana spoke. She knew the young ninny disliked her, but she had not realized just how deep that hatred ran—until now. She had to think. What was she going to do? If she yelled, she would be minus a head.

"I find a way," he said and released his grasp on Iliamna's midriff long enough to shove his hand in Alana's direction, palm up, "*Ahora*, the rest of my payment, *por favor.*"

Alana reached into her reticule and pulled out a small purse. Its bulging appearance told Iliamna that her cousin had scraped together quite a sum to dispose of her. Even in her current predicament, Iliamna wondered where she had managed to procure the funds. After all, she knew her aunt to be a very stingy woman who never gave Alana extra money for anything. Well, no matter now—Alana had obviously found the money somewhere, and she was using it to get rid of her. She had to do something.

"I like that purse, so pull the bills out and return it to me," Alana said offhandedly.

Gitano rolled his eyes at the request, especially as it would be difficult to keep Iliamna restrained and follow through with her request. He'd do it when he was able. She could wait.

"Please," Iliamna whispered, speaking finally, yet fearful that anything above a whisper would startle her captor into slicing her throat. "I'm not sure what I've done to warrant such drastic measures on your part," she said, her gaze pleading with Alana, "but as I've said, I'm already willing to leave here on my own accord, so this really isn't necessary. Isn't there some grand gown you'd rather spend that money on? Or perhaps it would suit as an enticing dowry to a potential mate."

Alana snorted again and she felt her captor stiffen even more. She felt pleased that he suffered at least a small measure of discomfort because of what he was doing to her.

"Don't you see, Cousin," Alana said, a wide smile on her lips, "that I control your destiny—not you? And the money I'm using for your disposal is a mere trifle. If I need new clothes or a handsome dowry, I can always acquire more; perhaps I will even help myself to that small stash you have hidden away in your room from teaching. But I haven't need for more at present, because I saved just enough to see my plans executed." She laughed at her chosen word, "Executed! Oh, that's so apropos, don't you think?"

"You no pay me for to execute," Gitano said quickly.

"Oh, pooh. Well, since I have been planning this moment for quite some time, I'll not argue over trivialities, nor will I allow you to ruin it," she spat at Iliamna, "with plans of your own. Ah, believe me when I say that the look on your face at present will bring me pleasure for the remainder of my years."

"What have I ever done to you to make you hate me so much?" Iliamna whispered, trying desperately to forestall the inevitable.

"Nothing and everything, figure that one out."

Iliamna was not even going to try. She needed to save her energy for getting herself out of this situation—not that it seemed likely with each passing second. That thought sent a shiver racing along her spine, but it also caused her temper to flare uncharacteristically. How could this little fifteen-year-old nuisance create such havoc in her life, and where had she developed such a malicious character?

"You say you're planning on stealing my money, and that you could easily get more from wherever it is you got the money to pay this thug?"

"I have more money coming in even as we speak, Cousin."

"Perhaps you should have waited a little longer, and collected enough to pay this hooligan to kill me, Cousin," Iliamna whispered, "because it's a mistake to let me live."

"Perhaps I don't want you dead," Alana huffed, but the hair on her arms stood erect and a chill shot down her spine. She snapped the fan closed, suddenly feeling cold. She'd never heard her cousin utter words filled with fury before; didn't even think her capable of anger, so to have her threaten her was more daunting than she cared to experience. It made her mad to feel that her cousin had this much bravery in the face of danger.

"Huff all you want to," Iliamna said softly, "but heed me, Alana, no matter how far your cohort takes me, I will come back and you will rue the day when I do. Then you'll need every penny you can find to try to get far away from *me*."

"Ooh hoo!" Gitano laughed. "This one, she has much spunk."

"Oh, do shut up," Alana snapped at Gitano, her anger elevating at his confirmation; at making her feel intimidated. Her resentment toward her cousin intensified in so short a span that it began to affect her mental balance. "Perhaps I *will* pay him to kill you, after all," she hissed.

"That will be five hundred dollars more," Gitano interjected, without batting an eye.

"Five hundred dollars! I've already paid you half that just to get her out of here. I will make it an even five hundred—total. Take her away *and* kill her for an additional two-hundred fifty. I am sure that my cousin has that much stashed away. Imagine the irony—my paying a hired killer with *your* money, Iliamna."

"Five hundred," Gitano interrupted, "more. You already pay me far less than I normally take."

"You were willing to take less before, so why not now?"

"Because now—I will have to draw blood."

Alana grinned at the thought, but Iliamna grimaced, unable to fathom the conversation that was taking place. When she lost her temper and challenged her cousin, she never imagined the little twit would dare consider it, much less believe that she could stand there negotiating with the hired hand over what a fair sum would be to kill her.

"You don't happen to have five hundred dollars hidden away do you, Iliamna?"

"You must be joking!"

"It was your idea."

"Why, you..." Iliamna snapped. "You'll pay..."

"Oh, do shut up! And you, get her out of my sight," Alana said, looking at Gitano.

Retaliation was the last coherent thought that Iliamna had, as her captor spun her around sharply and slammed his fist into her jaw, sending her into the arms of oblivion.

# CHAPTER FIVE

"Do get her feet out of my face!" Alana slapped at Iliamna's legs and skirts as Gitano caught her limp body and hoisted her over his shoulder.

"Women wear *muchas* clothes," he groaned, as the muscles in his wiry five-foot-six frame struggled to lift Iliamna's five-foot-eight body.

"So, what are you going to do with her?" The gleam in Alana's eyes sent a shiver down Gitano's spine.

*Such treachery in someone so young,* he thought. "Well," he said, finally managing to straighten, his reply issuing in a groan, "I think about some things, but now I see her and how *muy linda* she is, and I think of a few things that give me more money than the other things I think of."

"Ooh, what are they?"

Gitano was taken aback. He'd run across his share of miscreants, had done things of his own in his thirty-five years of living that would make a nun cross herself and cry over his fate, but this one...she made *him* feel like a saint. He could not believe that she was standing there rubbing her hands together like a child waiting for a birthday present, and simultaneously licking her lips like a cat anticipating a bowl of heavy cream, all because of what he had said. He had not even mentioned harming the woman, or taking her anywhere where she would be harmed...another shiver raced down his spine. *Whatever this Iliamna did, she did to the wrong girl*, he thought.

"Is *muy difícil* to stand here to talk. She heavy *mucho*."

"I want to know!"

Gitano sighed. Sometimes the people that hired him were so tiresome. "There is a chieftain up north. He like white woman much, but he may no pay with nothing but furs and trinkets, and this things I do not need. Still, I might sell for money. I do not know. No very much money there, and I prefer money."

"It doesn't matter what you need," Alana protested. "I've already paid you a lot, and she would suffer a good deal in the hands of a savage."

"Why you care if she suffer?" Gitano asked, suddenly curious, a trait he normally abhorred. The thought of involving himself in his clients' business was a thought he would not normally entertain. Why he chose to do so now, he couldn't fathom. Still, for the first time since turning gun-for-hire, his curiosity was piqued, but piqued was all it would be, he realized, when she responded to his question.

"That's none of your concern," Alana said. "Just make certain you take her where she won't be known, can't escape to return here, and her future is guaranteed full of misery."

"Well, what you pay me is no very much for me," Gitano argued, "and I no care to have no more money. Besides, you pay me to take her away, now she is mine to decide with what to do. Not yours. Now I go. I no wish my back to break." He moved closer to the railing, and looked over, wincing at the feat before him.

"Where, then?" Alana demanded, ignoring his discomfort. "If not to savages, where can you take her that will ensure you get paid more? I want her far away, do you understand that at least? And since I obviously can't accommodate your need for more funds, I'll have to *rely* on you to take her far away."

"Well, there is a whorehouse in Texas that I know would pay *mucho dinero*. Is she untouched, do you know? *Una virgen?*" Gitano carefully lifted his leg and placed it over the railing. He suddenly felt very foolish for climbing up to take care of this job. He should have waited until the woman was walking in the garden, as he was told she would be. He steadied himself, trying not to listen to Alana's incessant droning and complaining. He only wished he could escape her voice quicker. No matter what he said, she was determined to tell him what to do; something he refused to allow.

"Doubt it," Alana snorted, "but don't take her to Texas. I may find myself living there one of these days and I wouldn't want to run into her," Alana said, thinking back to the last letter she had received from Shreve. If he had gone to the trouble of building her a grand manor, then she might just decide it was time to stop corresponding and pay him a visit. She recalled the letter she had sent him a few days ago. It was different from the others. This time virginal shyness was giving her reservations. She smiled as she remembered his return letter that arrived only that morning, expressing his understanding. He assured her that he would not shower affections upon her without her consent. Sucker.

"Texas is *muy grande*," Gitano groaned, slowly lifting his other foot over the railing. By the time he'd managed to situate himself on the trellis, he was sweating profusely.

"Not Texas," Alana persisted adamantly.

"As I say," Gitano sighed—both in exasperation and in relief that he hadn't yet slipped and broken his neck—"is no your decision. Still, I can always go to Barbados," he continued conversationally, as he slowly stepped down to the next rung. He determined quickly that talking kept his mind off falling, and he needed that distraction or he'd just drop his prize and climb down after. A stupid move that would be. "The plantation owners pay *mucho dinero para un* slave girl, but I don't know that I wish too much time with her and it cost much money to pay for boat. Of course, the money I get from her sale may be worth it."

"Where is this Barbados? Is it far?"

"Far to the south. Many days from here, there is a vast body of water called the *Golfo de México*. Here, many boats come and go to islands far out to sea. At the very tip of these islands, there is a place with many plantations. This is the place called Barbados. I have traveled there much times to sell slaves, but that is when I have much money more than what you pay me. Perhaps I sell her to a captain and he take her there, if he wish to do so."

"Mmm, sounds delicious. Barbados it is," she said, ignoring his repeated statements that Iliamna's fate was not her concern. "That's so far away that, even with vengeance on her mind, she'll never be able to afford passage back here."

"Well, she is *muy bonita*. She may buy passage with her face or her body, no? And then I no worry if she *un virgen*, hmm?"

"Rape her yourself for all I care," Alana snapped, and Gitano laughed, but his mirth ceased quickly when the trellis shook. He took a steadying breath, and moved further down the trellis.

"Well, where I take her is no matter, there is always chance she get free and come back. Why not you pay me more money like she say, and I slit her throat for you, hmm? Then I no have to bother to sell her somewhere. Pay me now, and I drop her and break her neck here. Save me the climb down."

"You could slit her throat for free, if you weren't so bloody greedy. Still, if I had more money, I'd concur," she said without batting an eye over his suggestion, "but since I don't have your asking price, you'll just have to sell her and get what you can. If you take her to Barbados, at least there will be less chance of her returning, isn't that right? So, no more discussion. I'm paying you to haul her off, and I say to take her to Barbados."

Gitano bristled at that. He did not particularly care for a mere child dictating orders to him, especially one whose cruelty toward her cousin he perceived was mere spitefulness. If he did not love money more, then he would return his payment, dump the body back over the railing at her feet, and leave. Still, no matter what control she felt she had over his decision, once he left, where he took her was ultimately his decision to make. She was so beautiful, he may just retire from being a mercenary and marry her himself. But, unfortunately for this beauty, he loved money more.

"Well, *mi compañera*, since our business is done, I bid you *adios* and be on my way, but I am just wish to know how you explain that your cousin leave *su casa*?" Gitano called, as his head descended below the balcony.

"I don't have to, Iliamna will." Alana giggled at her plan and the confusion in Gitano's eyes when he looked up at her. "I have already placed a note on Iliamna's pillow for the maids to find later on this evening. It explains how Iliamna decided to leave our company and strike out on her own."

"What of her clothes? Will not they think why she no take them?"

"Those aren't her clothes!" Alana snapped childishly. "She had nothing but rags on when she came to live here. The clothes hanging in her armoire are courtesy of my mother. I should snatch the dress off her back that she is wearing and let her leave here naked. Those new clothes should have been mine!"

"I do not usually care about what I am pay money for to do, but

30

I cannot leave without I say to you something," Gitano said softly. "Something about what you do is wrong. This thing I feel."

"You are not paid to *feel* anything!"

"Yes, this is so," Gitano sighed, "I give my conscious away freely for money, still this thing you do for because you no like this woman...one day, I think you may pay much for this night, so I will give you one chance to tell me to give her and your money back to you...," Gitano laughed harshly. "I cannot believe I even say this thing."

"Well, I do not particularly care that you have said it, because it does not change a thing," Alana huffed. "Now, take her away!"

"Well, I will no see you again, *mi compañera*, so I will say *adios, otra ves.*"

"Wait! What if I need you again for something?" Alana complained leaning over the railing.

Gitano kept moving downward, not bothering to stop and look up when he replied again, "Do you have another beautiful woman you need me to take away?"

"No, thank goodness," Alana said and shuddered.

"Then I see no need for me to see you once more. Now *adios, finalmente.*"

"But if I do," Alana persisted.

Gitano stopped and sighed heavily. His muscles ached and were quivering continually. On top of that, his brain hurt from listening to this woman talk too much. He looked up in frustration, suddenly wishing that she would lean over too far and topple over the railing. After a moment glaring at her, he replied, "The Silver Palace, as before."

Alana nodded and watched as Gitano dropped to the ground. With a loud groan, he lowered Iliamna's inert body to the grass. His shoulders slumped and he lowered himself to the ground beside her.

"Don't just sit there," Iliamna hissed loudly. "Someone may come outside and see you."

Gitano's jaw clenched angrily, but she was right. He couldn't risk being seen; nor did he have the strength left to lift her dead weight. He stood up on quivering legs, leaned down, and grabbed hold of

Iliamna's arms, pulling her along the grass toward where he'd left his horse.

Alana waited until Gitano disappeared through the tree line before turning back to the ballroom and all those waiting suitors. Perhaps some of their attention would shift toward her when Iliamna did not reappear.

She thought of how upset her mother would be over the loss of so much money when she found Iliamna missing, but that was her mother's own fault. She should not have spent so much money on the little no-good moocher to begin with. Of course, if she found herself a suitor, then the damage would be mitigated.

She was just glad that her mother's attempts to locate Iliamna a suitor hadn't interfered with her own plans to rid herself of her cousin, or she may have had to deal unpleasantly with her mother and Iliamna's new beau also.

After all, she would never have allowed anything to interrupt her own plans which were made farther in advance than her mother's little husband-finding soiree. Fortunately, it had not. She had planned and timed everything perfectly, and now felt a thrill of victory race down her spine. She had won. Her cousin was gone forever. Not happily wed as her mother had hoped, but gone, to a life not of her choosing.

"Goodbye, Cousin", she murmured with an evil grin. "May your life be full of misery, wherever you find yourself. Now, I need to see about a telegram and maybe about finding myself a husband. I wonder what Texas is like?"

# CHAPTER SIX

"Ah, *mi diosa*, I do believe I see an eye peering at me from beneath those beautiful, long lashes," Gitano said, smiling gently at Iliamna. Iliamna opened her eyes and glared at her captor. "And I would say I am sorry for the pain that I cause you, but it was *necessario*, so I cannot."

Iliamna opened her eyes fully then and took in her surroundings. They were in a forest; that much was obvious by the density of the trees. If not for the small shafts of sunlight struggling to pierce the canopy overhead, she would be unable to determine whether it was day or night.

"Where are we and where are you taking me?" Iliamna demanded, struggling to sit up. "And are these really necessary?" She asked, motioning to the ropes that bound her wrists and her feet.

"*Si, lo esencial*," Gitano said softly. "I do wish you to know that I do not want harm you, okay? If you listen good, then I no have harm come to you. "So," he said standing, and bowing formally, "*mi nombre es Gitano Garcia de la Rivera y es un* honor to meet you."

"This is a joke, right?" Iliamna said eyes wide with incredulity. "You punch me in the jaw and abduct me for money, after threatening to kill me, all because my cousin doesn't happen to like me; and then you sit there and introduce yourself as if we are at a social function and think that I will possibly forgive you for what you have done and are planning to do to me? On top of all that, you expect me to believe that you don't wish me harm?"

"For your angry, I am sorry, *pero* I no can do nothing for this, so we try to stay nice with each other, *si*? As it is, you may find happy again when I tell you that I no take you to Barbados where your cousin tell me to take you, okay?"

"Ooh, if I wasn't a lady, I'd tell you just what you could do with your overtures," Iliamna huffed, and then struggled to a standing position, "as it is, I am in need of...well, that is to say...you wouldn't happen to know how I may...?"

"Ah! Say no more, *mi querida*," Gitano said, raising a hand to silence her embarrassing attempts. "I will unbound you and you may go there to the bushes, but *por favor*, do not do something stupid or I will...well, it will no be good. *Sí?*"

"You offered to kill me for money, so what could you possibly do that would be worse than that?"

"Make you wish for death," Gitano said, his tone soft and menacing, but oddly sympathetic.

"I see. So much for not wishing to harm me. Very well then," Iliamna said and disappeared into the woods as soon as Gitano freed her feet from their binding. She was tempted to run away, despite her promise not to try, but she did not have the foggiest notion as to where she might be and she was ill equipped to handle whatever dangers might be lurking about.

Iliamna settled by the fire again shortly after her trek in the woods, and breathed a sigh of relief when Gitano didn't immediately reach for the rope to re-bind her hands and feet. She certainly wasn't going to remind him. She decided that if she distracted him enough with conversation, he'd forget altogether. "So, where are you taking me, if not to Barbados where Alana wants you to take me? And how in the name of all that is holy did Alana know where to hire you?"

"Someone send her to the Silver Palace," Gitano replied, stoking the fire. "This is where I am most nights, when I no working. As for you—there is a place I know that will take much care of you and pay me *mucho dinero* for someone with your beauty. You no care to tell me if you are untouched?" He grinned at her look of horror, as he settled back onto a nearby log.

"No, I no care to tell you if I am untouched!"

Gitano laughed and then shrugged his shoulders, "I thought you no care to. Oh, well."

"Are you aware that you answered my question without really answering my question?" Iliamna said, taking a deep, calming breath.

"*Sí*, I did this thing."

"In other words, you are not going to tell me," Iliamna interpreted.

"*Sí*, this is so," Gitano laughed.

"Can you at least tell me how long it will take to get to this place that's going to take such great care of me and at the same time, pay you a great deal of money?" Iliamna asked. "That way I'll know just how long I have to suffer your company."

"Now that you are woke, we get there *mucho rapido*—maybe three days more. It would be faster if I take you on train or maybe use auto, but I can no risk someone to see me and you, so we go on horses, along back trails."

Iliamna ran a hand in frustration over her face and winced when it encountered her bruised jaw. "Are you going to punch me again?"

"*Si, posiblemente, pero* no right now," Gitano said matter-of-factly. "I need you to be woke, or we no move fast. But I tell you when, if you like me to do so?"

"You are *so* kind," Iliamna said, her tone sarcastic.

Gitano laughed, "You sleep now. We have much travel to do *mañana.*"

"I'm not tired," Iliamna snapped.

"Maybe not, you stay without waking for days so maybe you do not need sleep now. That is good."

"Why would you say that?" Iliamna asked, suspicious.

"Well, I no have many women that I have time to talk with," Gitano said, reaching down to stoke the fire again. "Most times the talking is done without words...,"

"You disgust me," Iliamna snapped.

Gitano laughed. "I no say nothing which could disgust, I only think that since you no wish to sleep, perhaps we can talk of things – or maybe we can do this talk without words? With our body? Hmm?"

"I think I'm more tired than I thought," Iliamna said, lying down quickly. She turned over on her side, presenting Gitano with her backside.

"The view is lovely no matter where I look," he said.

"Oooh! You pig!" Iliamna rolled over and glared at her captor. "I don't know what you're thinking about trying, but I'll hurt you if you come near me," she said, pulling herself back into a sitting position.

"You may try, but you will no succeed," Gitano said without a trace of a smile. "I will no touch you if you answer me a question."

"You were planning on touching me?" Iliamna asked, warily.

"You are *muy linda*. I would not be whole man if I not want to take you to my bed. Hmm?"

"What's the question?" Iliamna asked quickly, her breathing frantic, fear engulfing her. She did not know what was going to happen to her, but for some reason she had hoped that this man raping her was not to be one of those things.

"Are you *una virgen?* Um, a virgin? Untouched?"

"You asked me that before and I hardly think...,"

"It would be good to tell me—truthfully," Gitano interrupted.

Iliamna released a fearful sigh. If she said no, would he feel free to rape her? If she said yes, would he feel it an honor to be her first? She was suddenly scared that no matter the answer, she would end beneath him.

"Well?" He asked softly.

"Why do you need to know?" Iliamna whispered.

Gitano grinned, a lopsided thing that made him look very attractive. If not for the fact that he was evil, she might find him a very handsome man. Iliamna squeezed her eyes tightly closed against those thoughts and drew her knees to her chest.

"Why do you want to know?" She asked again, keeping her eyes closed. She did not want to see desire in his eyes, did not care to see him grin in anticipation of her deflowering, did not expect him to touch her....

Her eyes flew open and she slid away, her retreat hindered by a large oak.

Gitano laughed. Closing the gap, he squatted in front of her and reached a hand up to stroke her cheek again, only to have her turn away violently. "If you do not wish to answer me," he whispered, clasping her chin in his hand and turning her head back to meet his gaze, "then I will discover the answer for myself. Is this what you wish me to do?"

"I'm untouched," Iliamna said quickly, frenetic.

"I thought this is so," Gitano sighed. He looked at her gorgeous face clasped in his hand and leaned down, placing a kiss on her lips. She gasped and tried to pull from his grip, but his hand held tight.

"You are *muy linda*," he whispered against her mouth. "To take you to my bed would be..." he stopped on a sigh. "Perhaps you consider being my woman," he said impulsively. "Then I have no need to sell you for money."

"If I didn't think you'd hurt me, I'd spit in your face," Iliamna whispered in hostility.

Gitano's mouth twisted into that sexy grin he'd displayed earlier, and Iliamna's eyes widened. *How could someone so attractive be so evil,* she thought.

"You have much passion. I think you would enjoy sex with me."

"I'm untouched," Iliamna said again and her gaze widened further in alarm. "Remember?"

He knelt looking down at her for a moment more, and then stood and headed to the far side of the fire. "I remember. Go to sleep," he reiterated. He lay down and fashioned a pillow with his hands. Within minutes, Iliamna could hear his rhythmic snoring.

Iliamna placed her head on her arms, resting across her drawn knees and started to cry—the combination of stress, fear, and relief nearly too much for her to bear. So relieved at not having been raped, she did not even realize that her attempts to distract Gitano into forgetting her restraints had worked. Either that or he knew that she was incapable of making her way back to civilization alone, so didn't feel the need to bind her any longer.

She sighed, suddenly more tired than she realized. Still, despite the overwhelming fatigue clinging to her body and mind, she was afraid to sleep, afraid that if she closed her eyes something dreadful would happen.

She stared across the fire to where Gitano lie, his snoring keeping steady rhythm with the sounds of the night. It was not until many hours later, when she had assured herself that he was not likely to awaken until the morning, that she allowed herself to close her eyes and rest.

# CHAPTER SEVEN

"Come, you take bath and put on new clothes that I give to you," Gitano said, pulling his horse to a halt. It took a moment for the sound of rushing water to penetrate Iliamna's fatigued mind, but when it did, she perked up—body and spirit. She had not bathed since the day that Gitano abducted her from her aunt's home in Louisiana, and the results were devastating on her mental and physical state. She reeked—embarrassingly so.

"Why are you allowing me to bathe now when we've passed streams and rivers and you haven't let me so much as dip a toe in them?" Iliamna asked, taking the clean set of clothes from Gitano's outstretched hands. She held them by her fingertips, afraid of soiling the pristine garments with her filth.

"You smell like *una cerda*—a pig," Gitano laughed.

Iliamna's face flamed, because she knew he was right, but it was also inflamed as a result of the anger welling within her. By her estimation there'd been no reason to smell so wretched, "It's no wonder," she snapped, "when you haven't allowed me even the smallest of amenities, so who's the pig, huh?"

Gitano snorted, "I do this thing for your *protección*."

"My protection! Ha!"

"Laugh if you will, *pero* you are *muy linda*—beautiful, no? And I am no gentleman of honor. So, I keep you to smell like *una cerda* so I no come to your bed at night. If you are *un virgen*, as you say that you are, then I get much money if I no touch you. Hmm?"

Iliamna's eyes widened at that, but she grudgingly admitted that he had kept his distance, "If you weren't a gentleman to some degree, you wouldn't care what I smelled like or you would have let me bathe and taken advantage of me, I'm sure. Thank you for that small measure of courtesy," she whispered.

Gitano snorted, "Is no *para ti, mi querida*, but for me that I do this thing. As I say, if I take you to my bed then I no get *mucho dinero* for you because you now used goods. *¿Comprende?* Understand?"

"Oh! I understand, all right," Iliamna said, shaking her head in disbelief. "So what's to prevent you from taking advantage once I've bathed?"

"I tell you, I no want lose money, so I no touch. If you no guess, I love money almost as much as I love woman. We will be at the place I tell you very soon, so you need look nice now. I think is easy for me control my urge for little time, knowing the money I get will be much."

Iliamna stiffened visibly. Today her fate would be determined and Gitano still refused to enlighten her on what was to become of her. She felt a tremor of dread race down her spine and shuddered.

"You are strong woman, *mi querida*," Gitano said softly, noticing the worry etched on her face. "Do not become afraid now. You will need your strength, so keep it and go take bath. I have a nice smell of lavender soap, okay?" He reached into his saddlebag and handed her a bar of soap.

"Where did you get these things?"

"I carry much things with me. What I do, I have much need for many different things. When your cousin hire me to take you away, I watch you for short time to see what things I need for you. I go buy them and then I take you away."

"That's fair planning for a kidnapper."

"I very good at what I do. Go now. Bathe. I will wait here."

Iliamna did as he bade, simply for lack of a better option. When she reached the sight of the rushing water, she sighed deeply. It was such a beautiful place, but her heart was too heavy to enjoy it.

Slowly, dejectedly, she shed her clothing and carried the soap into the water. For the longest time, she remained standing beneath the falls, allowing the water to wash away her anguish, but it could not totally erase her worries. What was to become of her? Where was she bound and why couldn't Gitano tell her what was in store for her? Was it so awful that not even he could speak of it without feeling some small pity for her? After a while, she heard Gitano yelling for her; only then did she snap out of her doldrums.

"Do not make me to come over there to get you, *mi querida*," he yelled from a distance, "but if I do not see your *cara linda* soon, then you force me to do this thing that I do not wish to do. ¿*Comprende?*"

"I'm coming," Iliamna said and quickly ran the soap over her body and hair. It was another fifteen minutes before she stepped into the clearing in her new clothes.

"These are very beautiful. Where did you get these clothes?" She asked, fingering the Aztec-patterned skirt between her fingers. She took in a deep breath and then another, thankful that he had not thought to bring along a corset, or perhaps this particular type of clothing did not need a corset. The soft, cottony fabric of the blouse caressed her skin, billowing in the breeze where it fitted loosely. It clung to her waist and wrists seductively with an elastic band, as did her skirt cling to her waist by way of the same type of band.

"From a Mexican woman I know. *Tu es muy linda. Un diosa,*" Gitano said, his features registering awe.

"You called me *una diosa* once before. What does that mean anyway?" Iliamna asked in an attempt to divert the desire she saw in his gaze.

"It means you are a goddess," Gitano said softly, his gaze roving over her greedily. Iliamna saw the change in his demeanor and was suddenly thankful that he had prevented her from bathing until now.

"So," Iliamna started, clearing her throat, "what's next?"

Gitano snapped out of his daze and smiled sadly, "Now, I need hit you again," he said and started in her direction. Iliamna backed up rapidly, putting the fire between them. "Come now, *querida*, it is best that you know, *si?* That way you prepare in your mind."

"I don't particularly want to be hit at all," Iliamna said argumentatively. "Why must I be knocked unconscious? Can't you just take me to this place lucid?"

"No, *Señorita,*" Gitano said, sounding genuinely sad for her plight, "This place, they make the girls to come to them out cold."

"Why can't I just act like I'm unconscious?" Iliamna offered in a rising panic.

"*Por favor, querida,*" Gitano pleaded, "I no wish harm you, only punch you, but if I have to...," he threatened, pulling his knife from its scabbard.

40

"Won't you lose money if you use that?" Iliamna asked.

"*Si*, this is so," Gitano said, "but there is many place that I can aim that no show too bad. Of course, you could choose stay with me?"

Iliamna shook her head and moved around the fire to stand in front of him. Her heart was racing, but she lifted her chin bravely. "I can't stay with you," she whispered. "I don't know where you're planning to take me, but it has to be preferable than living with a criminal."

"Ah! Always stay brave, *mi querida, y* strong, hmm?"

"Are you going to hit me or not?" Iliamna snapped.

"*Si. Lo siento, mucho*," he said softly.

Her eyes closed instinctively when she saw his fist draw back, and then blackness enveloped her once more.

## CHAPTER EIGHT

Shreve Red Fox's horse moved along at a gait, traveling beneath the sign welcoming him to the small town of...he did not even know. The name on the sign had long ago faded, and he never bothered to learn the name of the small, inconsequential place. He only patroned one of the establishments—one of the few which remained in business, the primary establishment in this three-building town—a popular stop for people traveling between Dawson Creek and Twin Rivers; and of the local men who lived nearby. As he looked down the street, his gaze fell on the freshly whitewashed exterior, and he sighed for the hundredth time. He had no trouble reading the name on that particular building.

He spurred his horse into a canter, but his spirits did not lift to match the increased pace. He had never felt as low as he did today. He had finally finished the house he had been building, but Iliamna kept stalling with one excuse or another. Finally, he had to face the fact that she had been playing with him, for whatever reason and possibly never intended to join him in the new home. Never intended to marry him, as she said she would. Was her mother really sick? Did she even have a mother?

He dismounted in front of the Watering Hole Saloon and sighed heavily before dragging himself through the swinging doors. He stood for a moment squinting against the sudden gloominess, attempting to penetrate the veil of smoke lingering in the air. He probably could have walked in and straight over to the bar without hesitation only a month-and-a-half ago, but it had been that long since he'd stepped foot in this place, and his body had already become repulsed by the atmosphere, not as eager to enter. He started to turn and leave, but the full-bosomed scantily clad proprietor came tearing across the room at the sight of him standing in her doorway, halting his departure.

"Well, well, well. Lookee at what the cat done dragged in." She wrapped her soft, heavy arms around his neck and planted a none-too-shy kiss on his immobile lips.

"Hi, Red," he murmured, when allowed to come up for air.

"We missed you around here, Shreve," she sighed, rubbing her full breasts against his dusty leather vest. "I knew no proper-bred white female could hold your interest for long. Want to take a visit up stairs?"

"How about a drink, Red? That's really all I'm interested in."

"Don't tell me that my hot-blooded half-breed's done turned into a one woman man?"

"Nothing like that. Just need a drink, okay?"

Red gazed into defeated eyes that used to sparkle with mischief and life. She knew that she was not his type of woman, since his preference lay with full-figured blondes, not heavy-set redheads like her; but surely he would not be here if his new wife was all to him that a woman should be; unless she had hen-pecked him into lifelessness so soon.

"Sure, Shreve, whatever you say. Just mosey on over to the bar and I'll come and serve you personal-like."

"Thanks, Red."

"Don't mention it, sweetie pie. That's what I'm here for." Red moved behind the bar and pulled out a bottle of her finest whiskey. "Same poison, Shreve?"

"Yeah, and make it a double, will you, Red?" Shreve leaned his arms on the bar and watched with detached interest as Red poured a double shot of the amber liquid into a glass that was nearly the same color. This was another thing that he never thought he would do again—drown his sorrow in a glass of whiskey. The moment he'd determined to become a respectable rancher—an enterprise that he'd worked long and hard at doing—he determined to put drinking behind him, since imbibing whiskey tended to muck about with his ability to reason coherently. Now, thanks to the rejection of one female, he was sitting at a bar again, contemplating taking a drink. Thanks to that one woman, everything he worked toward threatened to crash down around his ears. Of course, he knew it would take no more than determination to prevent it all, but that was something in short supply at the moment, drowning beneath self-pity and loathing. He sighed. He could not believe he had let one woman get under his skin so easily. He pulled the drawing from his pocket and stared at it for a long while.

It was only a drawing, but though the color was lead gray, and there were lines creased throughout the page from his folding it repeatedly, he could tell she was a beauty. It still mystified him why such a woman would answer an ad for a wife to a stranger—a half-breed stranger at that; but merely clung to his reasoning that he must be blessed. A feeling of blessedness that held because the letters written to him appeared genuine; and she did not have the look of a tease, he reasoned, staring at her likeness. Her smile was bright and genuine, but perhaps he had read her all wrong. Perhaps she got her thrills leading strange men on a merry chase, or perhaps she had found out about his mixed blood and decided that living with the shame of it would be too much to bear. Perhaps the smile in the drawing was a ruse; or she really did have a sick mother and that's why she'd postponed her trip time and again, or perhaps she was overly shy as her latest letter inferred.

He folded the drawing with a sigh and tucked it back in his pants pocket, and then picked up his whiskey.

"Why not tell old Red what's troubling you, Shreve? Maybe I can help." Red watched worriedly as Shreve twirled his shot glass between his hands, drops of her precious whiskey sloshing over the sides. "Surely your marriage ain't all that bad?" Red probed, trying to get Shreve to open up to her as he had done in the past.

She would never forget that day over a month ago when he'd come bounding into her saloon and announced that he'd found himself a satisfactory mail-order bride from back East, and that he'd just come by to celebrate and say good-bye. He was leaving to build a fine home for his new wife, and she would be joining him just as soon as he had finished with the building.

"There wasn't no marriage, Red," Shreve murmured so low that Red almost missed what he'd said.

"What happened, Shreve? I thought it was a done deal?" Red queried, her heart breaking for the man staring dejectedly into his shot glass.

"So did I. Just didn't turn out to be so done after all."

"I take it that she called it off?" Red probed gently, as she had learned to do after so many years of tending to peoples' needs.

"Something like that," Shreve answered vaguely. "I really don't

44

want to talk about it right now, Red."

"Sure thing, Shreve, but if you change your mind, Red's here."

"I'll keep that in mind. Thanks, Red."

Red stood staring at the handsome half-breed for a minute more, and then turned the bartending duties back over to her partner, and went to seek out her bouncer. She saw him standing in his usual corner by the stairs, hands crossed over his barrel chest and that ever-present scowl on his rugged face, watching the patrons for any signs of trouble. Every so often, his gaze would stray up the stairs to the doors lining the second floor and he would tilt his head, listening.

Butcher was not only her bouncer, but he was in charge of the girls that provided her patrons with special services. It was his job to make sure that none of them got hurt too bad or it would be bad for business. When he saw his boss approaching, he lowered his arms, and pushed away from the wall.

"Trouble, boss?" He said in a voice that seemed to come from deep inside a cavern.

"Of a sorts, but not what you're thinking. I need to know if the new girl is up and about yet."

"I haven't gone to check. I've just been waiting for you to give me the word, so I can go on up. I have to tell ya, I'm eager to break that one in. Want I should go on up, then?"

"No. I'm sending up her first customer."

"Sending up...? Since when do we send up customers without a trial run first? She ain't been broke in yet."

Red cringed at the choice of words, no matter how accurate they were. Butcher had always taken first crack at the new girls, teaching them how to please a man and disciplining the ones who refused to learn. Eventually, the girls' spirits broke just enough to do anyone's bidding, which is exactly what Red wanted. She just preferred not to have to discuss, or listen to, the details of how they got that way. As long as there were no scars or bruises, she let Butcher handle the girls how he saw fit.

"No time for that now, Butcher. I got a special case," Red explained, but could tell by his expression that he was none-too-pleased, "and I want to give him a special girl."

"She's a looker, boss, and the doc says she's untouched too. That would be a mighty nice treat for me. And again, you know we never give over untrained females. It could cause trouble. She might even get herself hurt for fighting too much. What good will it do to have a newbie injured? Then there's medical bills and we'll lose money while she heals...,"

"I don't think we have to worry none about that," Red interrupted, a soft look forming on her face. She knew that no matter what savage blood ran in Shreve Red Fox's veins, he would never hurt a woman.

"Come on, Red," Butcher tried again. "You know I have a special way of breaking in a newbie." And this was one he had anticipated since her arrival last night; especially after the doctor examined her and informed them that she was a virgin. A trait becoming rarer in this century, he'd discovered. Too many women willing to bed a man prior to marriage, making sex less enjoyable for him. He liked the notion of being a woman's first...he sighed aloud at the contradiction. Here he was whining tacitly about the women he slept with being pre-bedded, when he was more than willing to be one of the men doing the deflowering. That led his thoughts back to the woman upstairs, and he felt his member get rigid again just thinking about bedding her; however now, Red was standing in front of him saying he couldn't have her. His member began to wilt.

"I'm sure you do, Butcher," Red responded in an authoritative voice that reminded him that she was in charge, "but I've already got plans for that one. I'm giving her to Shreve." Red nodded over towards where Shreve was still swirling his whiskey in a glass.

"A half-breed!" Butcher snarled. "You can't give that white angel upstairs to no half-breed Apache. Let him have one of the used ones."

"He's not Apache, he's Choctaw," Red answered instinctively, and then realized that Butcher was trying to dictate orders to her, "And since when do you decide what I can and cannot do? The last I looked, this is my business and those are *my* girls to do with as I choose, or have you suddenly forgotten that?"

"No, Red, I haven't forgotten," Butcher muttered, immediately wise to his mistake. "I was only trying to say that it ain't ever a good idea to give over a newbie without...,"

"Yes, I heard you the first time," Red said, "but Shreve's a bit low and I want to cheer him up...,"

"By giving him an angelic virgin?"

"You've said your piece, Butcher, but my mind's done made up. Now go see if she's awake," Red snapped, turning back toward the bar. "And, Butcher," she said, turning back briefly, "don't go in the room."

Butcher snarled, but knew that she was warranted in her mistrust of him. She knew him too good, knew that if he went in that room, he would force himself on the girl before allowing a half-breed a chance at her purity, but he also knew not to cross Red. He stomped heavily up the steps, murmuring vicious threats against half-breeds under his breath. When he reached the door, he leaned an ear against the chilly paneling and listened. He could not hear anything.

Against his better judgment, he reached for the doorknob, and then stopped. The last time he had gone against Red, some thugs paid a visit to his room and broke three of his fingers, promising to castrate him if he ever crossed Red again. He was a tough man, but his balls meant a hell of a lot more to him than getting off with some virgin whore. "Well, soon to be whore," he muttered, pulling his hand away from the knob.

He leaned his ear against the door again, pressing a hand against the other ear to try to block out the merriment drifting from below stairs. He focused his concentration on the interior of the room until he finally heard it—a loud sigh. She was awake.

He nodded at Red who stood by the bar expectantly. Red smiled and turned back to Shreve.

"So, Shreve, are you feeling any better?" Red asked gently, settling her heavy bulk on the stool next to him.

"What makes you think I'm ill, Red?"

"Well, for one, you haven't touched my best whiskey, just been sharing it with the bar top."

Shreve looked at the splotches of liquid staining the cherry wood and then at his emptying glass, "Sorry about that, Red."

"Think nothing of it, Sweetie. You know, Shreve, a man that

wastes whiskey like that...well, you may not be sick physically, but I can tell when a man is sick in the heart, and you're one sick man."

"Trying to cheer me up, Red?" Shreve said in attempted humor.

"Trying unsuccessfully to figure you out," Red replied. "Why don't you carry yourself upstairs and get some shut-eye? Maybe you'll feel better after a rest."

"Is that an invitation, Red?" Shreve asked, quirking an eyebrow in her direction.

"If I thought you'd take me up on it," Red laughed softly.

"Thanks, but I think sleep is really all I need tonight. It's been a really long day and I can't get back to the ranch tonight anyhow."

"Go on up. Third door on your right. I had Butcher prepare a room for you."

"Knew I'd be staying, did you, Red?"

"Figured you might be."

"You're a mind reader, Red," Shreve said, sliding from the stool.

"If I was, I wouldn't have served you my good whiskey," Red said, pretending to be distraught over the loss.

Shreve planted a light kiss on Red's permanently flushed cheek. "Well, if nothing else, you are a real friend. Thanks, Red."

"We'll see if you think so in just a few minutes," Red murmured to Shreve's back as he made his way upstairs, and then she turned on the stool and addressed her manager, "Give me a glass of the good sherry, Frank. I need it—bad."

Shreve hauled himself tiredly up the steps. Maybe Red was right. Maybe all he needed was a good sleep to lighten the burden that he carried around in his heart. It had been a long haul into Dawson Creek to pick up his fiancé, only to have a taunting telegram waiting for him instead.

He shoved his hand deep into his pocket and wrapped a tight fist around the paper that was still there, but did not dare pull it out and look at it again. His anger at reading it the first time was still too fresh.

He could still see the sneer on the man's face that took the message. *That is what you get for trying to marry a white woman,* his expression said, and Shreve felt the urge to wipe the look off the man's face—permanently.

Instead, he collected his horse almost as fast as he had stabled it, and rode hell-bent for home, but somehow, instead of heading north, he headed west—straight for the Watering Hole Saloon. A place he hadn't thought of twice since beginning his correspondence with Iliamna.

Now, he wished he'd headed north instead, but it was too late to start home now. When Shreve reached the door to his room, Butcher shifted slightly, but not enough to permit his entrance. Instead, he stood glaring, his gaze attempting to bore a hole in Shreve's head.

"Leave off, Butcher," Shreve said softly. "I ain't up to it tonight."

"Leave off, Butcher," Red called from downstairs, and Butcher stepped further to the side, a growl issuing from deep in his throat. Shreve knew the man didn't like him none, but there was something else eating at him tonight, something that made him want to tear Shreve's head off. Shreve could sense it. His only concern was that one day he would have to do something about Butcher and his obvious hatred. Not right now though, when he was barely lucid enough to put one foot in front of the other; which meant he'd be lucky to find his fists if a brawl were to start. "You gonna let me pass?" He asked, when Butcher continued to glare at him.

"I said leave off," Red yelled from below stairs, and Butcher finally shoved past, shouldering Shreve firmly against the wall. Shreve closed his eyes, and resisted the urge to toss him over the banister. Instead, he sighed heavily and reached for the doorknob.

# CHAPTER NINE

Shreve opened the door to his room so deep in thought that he did not readily notice the woman standing near the open window. When he finally did realize he was not alone, his anger flared anew, as he took in the long blonde hair, covering a bare back of an ivory hue. Only the sheet she had wrapped loosely around her was whiter.

Now Shreve knew what was eating at Butcher. Red was giving him a new girl. If this girl were used goods, Butcher would care less. It was the only explanation for Butcher's intensified hostility. Only thing was, he did not want her; any other time maybe, but not tonight when he was tired, frustrated, and irate. Maybe he should turn around and go get Butcher. Offer him the girl in exchange for an empty room.

*I really must be tired,* he thought, *if I'm willing to hand over a helpless female into Butcher's clutches.* He shook his head and stepped further into the room.

"What are you doing in here?" Shreve asked only to be rendered speechless as the woman spun around and he found himself staring into translucent sky blue eyes—and into a face disturbingly familiar. But where...?

The nagging sensation and the question flew from his mind as the woman gathered the sheet snugger around her naked form, not realizing that by doing so he could make out every curve. He cursed Red under his breath for putting him in this situation, as tired as he was.

"I'd like to know that also," Iliamna whispered lifting her chin, trying hard to maintain her last shred of dignity.

Shreve was awe struck. The gentle tone in which she spoke, despite the underlining desperation, said that this was a lady of breeding. *So how in hell did she end up here?* He wondered. "Do you have any idea of where you are?"

"I've only just regained consciousness. When I opened my eyes, I found myself in this room—like this." Her pale cheeks reddened to a delightful shade as she glanced down at her scant covering. She gasped, as she realized just how tightly she was clinging to the material, and just what her actions revealed to the man standing in the doorway. She loosened her hold slightly, the tint in her cheeks intensifying, "so, no, I haven't the vaguest idea where I am," she said, attempting to focus on conversation and not on her mode of undress. "All I know is that I'd very much like to have my clothing returned to me and leave here posthaste."

"Why don't you sit?" Shreve said. He gestured toward the bed and instantly regretted doing so when he saw her back stiffen.

"I'm not that kind of woman, sir," she said indignantly, drawing further away.

"What does telling you to sit, have to do with what kind of woman you are? Do ladies in distress have to remain standing where you're from?"

"It's just that you gestured toward the bed...." Iliamna started, her embarrassment heightening. "I meant that I wasn't going to...well, I'm simply not doing anything that involves a bed."

"I guess that means that sleeping is not an option for you tonight then, but it is for me. As for not doing anything that requires you to be on a bed, you are not going to have much choice after tomorrow. As for right now however, you are perfectly safe. Now sit, so we can talk, or I may just forget my manners. I'm in no mood to pander to a spoiled brat."

"I'll stand, thank you just the same," the woman murmured defiantly, "and I'm not a spoiled brat. I just happen to value morals too much to place myself in a compromising position with a man I don't know."

"You are already in a compromising position if you hadn't noticed, and what did you mean—with a man you don't know? In a habit of compromising yourself with men you *do* know?"

"Don't be deliberately obtuse, if you please, or twist what I say," Iliamna said, lifting her chin a notch higher. "My head aches something fierce, I'm unclothed, in a strange place, and in the company of a strange man on top of it all, so I do believe that I'm entitled to be a little tiresome without you calling me a brat."

Shreve shrugged. "Are you gonna sit? I promise not to attack you."

"I think it's best if I stand," Iliamna said, "but thank you for the offer. And I'm not being difficult, I'm simply uncomfortable with...well, with...I'm just uncomfortable, okay?"

"Suit yourself." Shreve slammed the door and moved toward the bed, flopping heavily onto the lumpy mattress. With an audible sigh, he pulled first one boot off and then the other, wriggling his cramped toes. "New boots," he said, when he saw her watching him.

"Ah!" Iliamna said, but could not care less if the boots he wore were a thousand years old. She was simply trying to will him, silently, to leave the remainder of his clothing on. When it seemed the boots were the only things he planned to remove, she relaxed a bit.

"What did you mean by what you said?" She asked quietly, trying to ignore the fact that this man was in her room, making himself comfortable on her bed. "About my not having a choice after tomorrow? Where am I exactly?"

"You're not going to like the answer, so you might want to take me up on my offer and sit."

"Thank you, but..."

"I know, you'll stand. I still think you should sit, but since you insist on standing—you're in a house of ill repute, if you must know," Shreve stated matter-of-factly, standing to remove his gun belt and vest.

"I'm *where*? This is a *what*?" Iliamna gasped. Now she realized why Gitano refused to tell her where he was taking her. He knew full well that she would have done everything in her power to escape had she known, threats or no. She was not certain where she thought he *intended* to take her, but his attempt at kindness and his assurance that where she was going would be a place that would care for her, was deceiving at best. Why she thought he would take her somewhere she would be safe from the clutches of Alana, and anyone else, she did not know, but she did and her naïveté annoyed her.

"I told you that you needed to sit," Shreve said, interrupting her thoughts. He waved a hand toward the bed. "Preferably before you fall down. And don't worry, I said I wasn't going to touch you, and I'm not."

"Why not? What's wrong with me?" Iliamna asked impulsively. It was not conceit that piqued her curiosity rather worry that something dreadful may have happened to her while she was unconscious. She knew that a week worth of grime no longer covered her, and that grime was why Gitano had not wanted to touch her, but what reason did this stranger have for not wanting her? Had Gitano damaged her face more than she assumed? Had the people that now held her captive harmed her...her tacit inspection came to a sudden halt when her gaze met the stranger's gaze.

It was easy to see that disbelief warred with desire in the dark green eyes. He shook his head and his gaze narrowed. *Angry, now,* she thought, *and frustrated.*

"Geez, lady! Now is not the time to question my honorable intentions with obvious invitations. I'm too tired to mess with spoiled brats *or* virgins; although the proprietor of this establishment sent me up here for that very purpose."

What little color in her cheeks quickly drained as she stumbled toward the bed. Perhaps he was right, she did need to sit. Her system was receiving too many shocks for her body to assimilate standing up. "Oh, my!" She whispered, lowering herself onto the very edge. Her shock vanished at his nearness. "You *do* give your word as a gentleman, not to touch me. You said so. Despite where we are and why you were sent up here?" She asked quietly, tugging the sheet more securely around her.

"You have my solemn oath," Shreve muttered, "which I don't give lightly. Not that you'd really have any choice in the matter if I decided I *did* want to do something." He removed his hat and tossed it on a nearby chair, and then plopped backwards onto the bed. Iliamna jumped up and edged back toward the window. "Since I gave you my word however, and since I'm too tired for anything more than sleeping," he said, stifling a yawn, "you don't have to worry about me. Just be lucky that I was the one that Red sent up here and not some Randy Rooster, or worse, Butcher. You gonna sit back down, or don't you believe me?"

"I believe you, I think."

Shreve snorted, then closed his eyes, "I'm going to get some shuteye now, or I won't be able to sit in the saddle long enough to get home."

"Where's home?" Iliamna asked, shyly settling back onto the edge of the bed. She yanked the sheet up around her shoulders, but still felt naked, so she needed some form of conversation to distract her from her current predicament.

"What?" Shreve murmured, already feeling sleep coming to claim his mind.

"Where do you live?" She asked again, relieved to know that he really had no intentions of forcing himself upon her, at least not at the present time.

"Three days ride north of here. Just above Lake of the Pines."

"Where's here?"

Shreve opened his eyes and glared at the woman sitting stiffly on the bed beside him. His irritation fled as the feeling of familiarity he had earlier struck him again, staring into her innocent, big blue eyes. "You don't know me, do you? I mean, we've never met, right?" He asked suddenly.

"I've never met you, no." Iliamna answered cautiously.

"Then why do I get the feeling that I've seen you somewhere before. Where are you from?"

"I think it only reasonable that you answer me first, as I asked first."

Shreve snorted and shook his head.

"Well, ma'am, you are in Texas now. A small, no-name town about an hour west of Dawson Creek."

"Texas!" The woman shook her head, fighting back tears that threatened to fall.

"Damn you, Red," Shreve murmured in angry astonishment. He opened his eyes, rubbed as much sleep out of them as he could, and then sat up, propping himself against the scratched and aging headboard. "So," Shreve started, sighing, "since I'm not able to sleep at the moment, maybe you can tell me how a well-bred lady like you managed to end up in a Texas whorehouse."

"My cousin hired a Spaniard to kidnap and dispose of me," Iliamna said in a rush, running a hand down her jaw. It still felt sore. It also drew Shreve's attention. "I spent a grueling five days in that man's company before he belted me across the jaw, for a second time and, obviously, dumped me here."

That startled Shreve. Why would someone do something like that to someone so obviously undeserving? He didn't know this woman, despite the familiar feeling that refused to quiet, but she had a gentle, quiet-spoken manner that made him want to shield her from harm, not bring it down upon her head—or across her jaw. "Why would your cousin want to get rid of you?" Shreve asked, but already sensed the reason.

"Because my aunt was throwing a ball in my honor trying to find me a husband; and since I only just lost both of my parents and didn't feel it was right for me to marry so soon after, my cousin thought that I might be staying around a lot longer than she wanted. That, of course, would have been detrimental to her own marriage possibilities; or so that's what I gathered by our final conversation before Gitano punched me in the jaw, for the first time."

Shreve listened intently. He did not want to get involved with this woman's problems, but it angered him that someone would try to hurt someone else simply because they were jealous of them, and he had not a doubt that this woman's cousin had every reason to be jealous. The woman sitting beside him, bruised chin or not, was one of the most beautiful women he'd ever seen. It was a pity really, since after a few weeks in Red's place, that beauty would diminish dramatically. Oh well, she was not his problem.

"I'm sorry for you, Miss," he said softly. He had appeased his curiosity about her, and despite the lingering feeling of past acquaintance, decided that he did not know her and was not planning to get to know her, so he could sleep now and rest. He closed his eyes against the sadness he saw lingering in her gaze. He was not going to get involved.

"I can see that," Iliamna replied quietly.

"Sometimes life hands us horse dung instead of gold," Shreve said, ignoring the sarcasm he heard in her tone. "If we adapt, we win despite. Of course, I don't envy the load of dung dumped on you. It's one of the worst smelling I've encountered in quite some time."

"Can't you help me in some way, perhaps?" Iliamna asked, her tone hopeful, desperate.

"You're in a bad way, lady, to be sure, but it ain't my life to get involved in. Sorry."

"So, that's it?" Iliamna said, trying to keep the frustration in her tone to a minimum. "You're sorry? Despite everything that I've told you; despite knowing what will happen to me if I stay here, all you are is sorry?"

"And sleepy," Shreve said, stifling a yawn, closing his eyes so he wouldn't have to see the deep sorrow in her gaze.

"So you aren't going to do a blasted thing?"

"Like I said. . . ,"

"I know, it's my dung heap of a life," Iliamna snapped.

Shreve sighed heavily and opened his eyes, "What would you do if you did leave here? I mean, let's face reality. At least here, your circumstances are better than a man in the middle of an ocean without a boat. You have food and a roof over your head. What would you do if you left here? You can't provide for yourself. . . ,"

"Yes, I can. I'm a teacher," Iliamna declared.

"And at what school are you planning to teach? They are few and far between out here."

"Perhaps, but not nonexistent, and if you could just see your way into helping me get out of here. . . ,"

"Sorry, lady," Shreve said, interrupting her, "but we wouldn't get past Butcher or Red."

"Well, how do you know unless we try?"

"Stubborn female, aren't you?"

"A bit, yes," Iliamna said, undeterred. "A lot, when it comes to my personal well-being."

"I'll tell you what. Let me sleep on it," he said, closing his eyes again.

"Well, would it be possible at least, to get some clothing beforehand, sir?" When she did not receive a response, she looked at him and leaned a little closer, "Sir?"

The faint sound of snoring reached her ears and she sighed heavily, "Well, isn't that just grand!"

# CHAPTER TEN

There was a definite likeness.

Shreve crumpled the drawing in his hand and closed his eyes tightly to try to ward off the attack of negativity swirling around in his mind about the woman that lay sleeping on the floor. Why the pretense? Why lie? Wouldn't she know he had her drawing? He'd sent a likeness of himself to her also, only recently, so she should have at least sensed something familiar about him also, yet she was adamant about not knowing him.

On top of that, she had deflected his questions about where she lived. Maybe she knew that if she revealed where she lived, he would immediately know who she was; but if she had been on her way to meet him and been waylaid by a nefarious man who'd brought her here, wouldn't she want his assistance by explaining the truth? That she was kidnapped on her way to meet her affianced—him? Why make up a story about a jealous cousin? The thought must have crossed her mind that he'd have been more amiable to assist her if she were his fiancé, would actually be legally able to help; more so than were she a stranger.

There were too many unanswered questions, and a likeness that was too coincidental to be ignored.

"Maybe the likeness is just that—coincidental," he murmured.

She squirmed a bit in her sleep. Her face scrunched as if dreaming of something unpleasant. She moaned and squirmed again, and the bruise lining her cheek came into his line of sight. She said a cousin had hired someone who had punched her. The bruise lent some support to her story, but why lie to him then; why not immediately say that she was there for him? His anger flared again— both at her apparent deceit and at the person who would dare cause her injury. The feeling of familiarity struck him again, and he closed his eyes, drawing in deep calming breaths.

There was no denying that she looked a lot like his drawing, which he could clearly discern now that he had rested a bit. Why he couldn't make the connection last night, he could only blame on his feelings of sadness and weariness. Perhaps that was why she hadn't recognized him. Because her circumstances had made her too distraught and mind clouded.

He unclenched his fist and unwadded the drawing. He stared at the face, now more lined and wrinkled throughout as the result of his anger. Still the charcoal image was clear enough, the detail astonishing. An artist had rendered this likeness; a very good artist.

Another moan brought his attention back to the woman on the floor. She was writhing about now, the sheet sliding scandalously to one side, revealing an entire leg, one hip, and part of her waist.

Another moan issued, but this time it came from him. If he did not waken her soon, she would be lying completely uncovered, and then maintaining his promise not to touch her would be nearly impossible. He leaned down on his haunches and cleared his throat loudly. Her eyebrows knitted, but her eyes remained stubbornly shut.

"Um, Miss?" He said loudly, and cleared his throat again.

Iliamna's eyes flew open and she gasped, instinctively drawing away. She squealed when the sheet slid down her body, revealing her nakedness to the man kneeling over her. She snatched at the sheet, tears stinging her eyes.

Shreve quickly averted his gaze. "I didn't mean to frighten you, but I need you to wake up. We need to talk."

Iliamna glanced toward the curtain, still drawn. "It's dark out. What time is it?"

"A little after two in the morning," Shreve answered after a quick glance at his pocket watch.

"Two in the morning! And I thought I was an early riser." Iliamna shifted to a sitting position, carefully drawing the sheet back around her shoulders. She was so tired of being naked that she would welcome even a corset at this point. After the sheet was secure, she stood and made her way to the bed.

Shreve smiled and stood too, making his way to the only available chair in the room. "I usually wait a few more hours before rising myself, but something has been disturbing me since I met you, and I just realized what it was."

"So you needed to discuss it with me—now?"

Shreve wadded up the picture and tossed it in Iliamna's direction. It landed on the mattress next to her, but she did not pick it up. A warning bell went off in her mind that there was something seriously wrong with that piece of paper, and if she picked it up her world would shatter.

Shreve watched her reaction carefully but again, no recognition lit her face, only curiosity and, was that wariness he sensed in her? "Aren't you the least bit curious?" He asked.

"What is it?" Iliamna asked, but still made no move to pick up the paper.

"I think perhaps you should look at it," Shreve said but offered no clue, which only added to her trepidation. If his tone were less taunting, perhaps she would not feel so uneasy. Still, whatever it was, it obviously had him waking at an ungodly hour to deal with, so deal with it she must; especially as it obviously concerned her in some way.

She reached down and slowly uncrumpled the paper. She stared at the drawing, her eyes widening in disbelief. "I don't understand," she whispered, her gaze remaining on the likeness staring back at her. "This is me."

# CHAPTER ELEVEN

"So you don't deny it," Shreve said, leaning forward.

"Why would I?" Iliamna asked. "Unless I have a twin out there that I'm unaware of," she whispered, "there's not a doubt that this is a likeness of me, but what I don't understand," she continued, finally looking up and meeting Shreve's gaze, "is what you are doing with this and where you got it from."

Shreve reached into his pant pocket and retrieved another crumpled piece of paper, tossing it in her direction.

"Are you going to keep hurling things in my direction?" Iliamna asked sardonically, as the paper landed in her lap.

"The only thing left is this chair I'm sitting on," Shreve answered, but Iliamna couldn't tell by his tone if he meant to throw it at her next or not. She hoped not. He was definitely agitated. His body was tense, despite his calm speech.

She picked up the telegram.

*My Dearest Shreve. Stop. Your kindness means so much. Stop. Can't wait to meet. Stop. Picture handsome. Mother taken ill. Stop. Join soon. Stop. Love, Iliamna.*

"Iliamna!" Iliamna screeched. "That's *my* name!"

"Precisely. Wait! You *are* Iliamna?" Shreve asked, suddenly unnerved. He half expected her to say that her name was Martha, or Mary, or something else, but to admit to being his Iliamna, and with the drawing to back it up...he suddenly didn't know how to react. If she were trying to deceive him, why be truthful about the likeness and her name?

Iliamna shook her head, but the jumbled pieces refused to fall into place. "I think we need to sort through this mess."

"Damn straight, and how can you still sit there and say you don't recognize me after I mailed you a photo?" Shreve snapped, suddenly angry over her calm.

"Please, do try to calm yourself. I can only assure you I have never seen you nor any likeness of you," Iliamna said, taking a deep breath. "You are not, apparently, the only one whose life is being manipulated. And I can only think of one person with the mean-spirited nature to do this."

"Manipulated, you say?"

Iliamna sighed. "Yes, and I have a feeling that the person manipulating you is the same who is trying to manipulate my life. Alana, my cousin. She is also an artist. Oh dear Lord in Heaven!"

"What?"

"It makes sense now. It all makes sense," Iliamna whispered, staring down at the telegram.

"What? What makes sense?" Shreve snapped, moving from his chair to sit next to her on the bed. "Nothing you are saying at present, for certain."

"Did you send money to Alana?"

"I sent money to you, for your train fare, yes, and well you know it," Shreve answered, stubbornly refusing to accept her explanations as fact.

"I'm telling you, that I am not responsible for this—for this telegram or for this likeness. For God's sake, I cannot even draw a straight line, much less a person!"

"How about I reserve judgment pending further evidence?"

"Wow, and I thought I was stubborn," Iliamna huffed. "You sound like an attorney."

"I was."

"Really?"

"You were saying?"

"Oh. Well, I couldn't figure where Alana would get the money, two hundred fifty dollars to be exact, needed to pay Gitano to abduct me."

*Despite the evidence, you're sticking to your story, are you?* He thought, but decided to go along; see how long she could maintain the ruse, "So you're saying that this Alana is the cousin that wanted you gone from her home?"

"That's right, but you'd have had to send more than just train fare, because she had a large amount of cash, and I know for a fact that she didn't get it from my aunt." Iliamna shuddered, remembering, "Had she had five hundred more, Gitano would have killed me."

"Excuse me?"

"The two were haggling over how much Gitano would accept to kill me," Iliamna said with a sigh. "Alana wanted to pay only two hundred fifty dollars more, but Gitano refused. Had she had the extra money, I would be dead right now. Of course, she did say that she wanted me to suffer; for my life to be filled with misery, so it wouldn't be if I were dead. Oh, no!"

"Another revelation?" Shreve said, unable to keep the sarcasm from his tone. While she seemed quite convinced in her facts, what she said seemed too outlandish for him to accept outright.

"She said that she could easily get her hands on more money, which means you couldn't possibly be the only...,

"Man that she's duped. Is that what you were going to say?"

Iliamna nodded, "It would also explain why she told Gitano to ship me off to Barbados and keep me away from Texas. There is a good possibility that she really intends to join you out here at some point. Maybe after she's convinced that you are too enthralled with her on paper that you won't mind...," Iliamna paused.

"Another problem?"

"It's just...well, if she really intended on joining you, why send a drawing that she knew she could never pass for? Why send a picture of me?"

"Perhaps you sent the letter and the likeness, but changed your mind about me once you found out that I was a half-breed," Shreve offered, trying—but not quite succeeding—to keep the derision from his tone.

"I would never," Iliamna said quietly. "I could never. Can't you see that? That I am just as surprised at seeing these things as you are at seeing me? And Alana's statement to Gitano makes me think that she has more than just you dangling on a line. It is also possible that she sent everyone a picture of me."

"Why the deception? Why not just be honest? Send a picture of herself and her real name? Have a theory on that also?"

Iliamna was pensive for several minutes, but when she finally looked at Shreve there was a confidence in her gaze and her tone, "I can think of two very good reasons."

"Let's have them then."

"Firstly, Alana is not exactly someone's dream girl, not to be snippy about it; if she were, she wouldn't have been threatened by me. Second, if her deceit was to be discovered, then who would be the one to take the fall?"

"You?"

"Oh dear. That's right. She really was determined to get rid of me one way or another."

"Well, lady, I must admit it all sounds very logical. You certainly seem to be certain of your facts; still, in the end, there is only one way to clear up any confusion," Shreve concluded.

"Nice to know that my word isn't good enough," Iliamna sighed, "So then, Mr. Attorney, how do you plan to clear this mess up?"

"I'm going to Louisiana."

"What?"

"I'm going to Louisiana," Shreve repeated. "Look, while I think your story sounds a little crazy, you do seem to be sticking to it; which means that you are either the cleverest liar in the world, or you are genuinely a victim. Neither of which concern me as much as the obvious fact that someone has perpetrated a fraud—upon my person, and possibly others. That person is either you, which unfortunately the evidence points to; or, it's this cousin of yours. If so, then not only will she be arrested and tried for fraud, but also kidnapping. It's my duty to see justice served."

"For an attorney, you aren't very intelligent."

"Excuse me?"

"Apparently, you are allowing your anger to dictate your actions, which isn't helpful. Think rationally, will you? While I agree that justice should be served, how will going to Louisiana prove my innocence? Do you expect Alana to simply confess to what she's done? That is about as unlikely as your horse starting a conversation with you."

"True, but perhaps there is a way to get her to confess."

Iliamna sighed and shook her head, "She was able to arrange and carry out a very intricate plan to get rid of me; was capable of locating a man...oh, that's it?"

Shreve had to admit, he loved this woman's ability to reason under stress, but while he appreciated her apparent brilliance, the evidence that it was she who perpetrated the fraud was overwhelming, "Another revelation?"

"The Golden...oh, shoot...what was the name of that place again? No, not gold, silver...The Silver Palace," Iliamna said, suddenly, snapping her fingers.

"What of it?"

"Your evidence. If you have any chance to prove I am telling the truth, that is where you'll find it," Iliamna sighed. "I really can't say if you'll have success getting my abductor to talk, anymore than Alana, but that is where she found him—at the Silver Palace. If you offer him money—he seems to respond well to that—he may be willing to turn against Alana."

"Hmm, I'll keep that in mind," Shreve said, moving back to the chair. He reached for his boots and started pulling them on, "I should be back before too long."

"But what about me? You can't possibly leave me here!"

Shreve stood and stretched, and then looked at his pocket watch. "Oh," he murmured, and then headed back to bed, "It's too early in the morning, and we both need some sleep," he said, stretching back on the bed.

"Sleep? But you just put your boots back on."

"I know. I wasn't thinking. And now I'm too tired to remove them again. We'll discuss what to do with you after the sun comes up. At least I know that I can close my eyes and you'll still be here in the morning," He quipped. "You aren't a killer are you?" Iliamna could tell that he was deliberately provoking her, so chose not to answer. Shreve grinned, placed an arm over his face and fell silent.

"I guess this means our discussion is over," Iliamna retorted, but received no reply. She leaned over the bed and tried to see his eyes beneath his arms, but could only hear a soft resonant snore. *The man*

Barbara Woster

*can drop off like a hat in a strong wind. Unbelievable.*

# CHAPTER TWELVE

"The man has a lot of nerve," Iliamna huffed quietly. "First, he intrudes into my room, and then he wakes me up and drops a bolt from the blue in my lap, accuses me of being deceitful, threatens to leave me in a whorehouse, and then proceeds to fall asleep!"

Iliamna moved to stand next to the window, the only thing standing between her and freedom were the bars firmly implanted in the cement on both sides. She may as well be in the jail that Shreve was threatening to put her in.

She would like to go back to Louisiana to get her hands on her cousin, for if not for Alana, her future may be undecided, but it would be far from uncertain. She looked over at Shreve again, sleeping soundly now, and wondered what he had planned for her. He was hesitant to believe that she was not the woman who'd been conversing with him. Of course, with that blasted picture as evidence contrasting her story as well as her name written on that telegram, she would be hesitant to believe it also if she was in his position. At least he was willing to check her story out, even if it meant making a trip all the way to Louisiana and leaving her here in a whorehouse; even if his intent was to prove her guilty, not necessarily determine her innocence.

She groaned. She could not stay here. This man may have been a gentleman and sensitive to her plight, but once he left, others would come, and to think they would listen and leave her untouched was naïve at best.

Maybe if she really tried hard, she could convince Shreve to allow her to accompany him back to Louisiana. She would certainly love to see her cousin's face when she came strolling back into the house; would love to be there when the sheriff hauled her away and threw her in jail.

Still, whatever was going to happen was not going to happen the remainder of this evening. He had satisfied himself regarding the picture, so now he was able to sleep soundly. Never mind that her mind raged restlessly.

Restless mind or not, she was tired. She stifled a yawn and stretched languidly. Her mind was protesting against remaining awake, and her body ached from sleeping on the hard floor. Her irritation returned. He had her bed. Some gentleman that was. He should have offered to take the floor, but no....

She looked over at him once more to make certain that he was asleep, and then moved silently to the bed. She needed sleep if she was going to be cogent enough to talk him into taking her with him come daylight, but he took up most of the bed and there wasn't another place in the room that was conducive to a good night's rest.

Perhaps if she slid beneath the covers...she carefully lifted the edge of the blanket and, as gently as she could manage, sat down on the edge of the mattress, wincing as it squeaked loudly in protest. Shreve muttered something in his sleep and rolled onto his side. Iliamna took advantage of the movement to slide quickly beneath the musty blankets. She crinkled her nose and slid the covering a little lower, and then pressed her index finger firmly on her upper lip to try to contain the sneeze that threatened. After a moment, the urge to sneeze passed and she relaxed.

She lay on her back for another hour, listening to the sound of his breathing before allowing sleep to claim her enervated mind.

# CHAPTER THIRTEEN

"Good morning, sleepyhead."

Iliamna jerked at the sound of the strange voice so close to her ear and tumbled in a heap of blankets to the hard wood floor.

"Did I scare you?" Shreve asked a huge grin on his face.

Iliamna huffed and jerked the blanket down over her head, sneezing as the dust balls assaulted her nostrils. With angry movements, she yanked at the material clinging persistently to her legs, kicking and tugging until she was finally free from the cottony clutches.

She bounded to her feet and glared at Shreve, her hands on her hips. "Don't ever startle me like that again," she snapped. "What in the devil's name are you gawking at?"

When Shreve did not answer immediately, Iliamna instinctively followed his gaze and gasped, "Oh my Lord in heaven!" With lightning speed, she grabbed hold of the blankets and wrapped them around her naked body. "You could have said something, you know!" She scolded.

"Ma'am, I couldn't have uttered a word even if I wanted to," Shreve grinned, coming back to his senses, which he definitely lost at the sight of her standing there in all her glory. "And, if you don't mind my saying so—whew!"

"My word," Iliamna whispered. She quickly moved toward the window, wishing that she could open the lock and allow some fresh morning air to enter and cool her heated flesh.

"So," Shreve said with a laugh, springing from the mattress, "I suppose I ought to tell Red that we had a hell of a night, otherwise old Butcher is going to think he needs to break you in."

Iliamna spun on her heels and her eyes widened when she noticed him attaching his gun belt. He was preparing to leave her, she realized in a rush of panic. He really intended to do so!

"Wait a minute! What about me?" Iliamna asked, trying to keep her voice calm. "You said we'd discuss it this morning, and you...No! You can't really think to leave me here! You said so yourself, that I wouldn't remain untouched if I stayed here any longer. The next man that walks up those stairs isn't going to be a gentleman like you...,"

"I wasn't being gentlemanly, lady," Shreve said. "I was just too tired to take advantage, but I'm awake now, and the bed's still warm," He intimated with a grin.

That jolted Iliamna and her legs gave way.

"Whoa! Are you okay?" Shreve asked, rushing to her side. "I didn't think it was possible for you to get any paler. Look, if it'll make you feel better, I was just kidding. I'm not going to assault your virtue, okay? And I said I'd clear up this mess and I will."

Tears stung Iliamna's eyes, and when she finally looked up at Shreve, his face was a blur. "Please. I know you don't believe that I haven't deceived you. That, because of the picture and the telegram, you think I'm somehow beholden to you, and probably think I deserve to remain here and anything that happens to me will be justifiable, but if you do, you'd be making a terrible mistake." Iliamna clutched Shreve's sleeve in desperation. "I'm not the person that wrote those telegrams. Yes, my name is Iliamna Dearborn, but I'm not a liar," Iliamna said. "Please, you can't leave me here, you just can't."

"Calm down, okay," Shreve said kneeling beside her, "and for heaven's sake, please don't start blubbering."

"I'm not blubbering," Iliamna sniffled loudly.

"If we can just be reasonable here," Shreve said, lifting her from the floor by the elbows, and leading her to the bed, "even if I did agree to take you out of here—crazy at it is—how do you propose I get you past Butcher and Red, considering your current state of undress and the lack of clothing with which to remedy that? Huh?"

"I don't know, but you're an educated man. Think of something."

"I need to know you are somewhere I can find you again," Shreve said. "And if I leave you here, I know you won't be going anywhere."

"Because you still don't believe me, and if you don't find

evidence that I am who I say I am, you are going to come back and throw me in jail, right? I understand," Iliamna sighed, "but there's a solution to that."

"You don't say."

Iliamna nodded frantic, "All you need to do is take me back to Louisiana with you. I can prove I am who I say I am, see justice done, and...well, I'll think about where to go after that."

"That's right. You said your parents died, and if you turn on your cousin, then your aunt isn't going to feel obliged to shelter you any longer. Does that about sum it up?"

Iliamna nodded, "Yes, but I can find employment as a teacher again...oh, I'll think of something, but anything is better than staying here to be repeatedly...,"

"Don't say it," Shreve interrupted. "Just don't say it. But even though I sympathize, I'm not taking you to Louisiana. Your reputation would be in tatters if we were in each other's company alone for that long, and if you are telling the truth, then you'll want to marry someday."

"I just spent five days in the company of a Spaniard," she said, her tone incredulous, "and am alone in a room, naked, with a stranger. I think that whatever reputation I may have had is pretty much ruined, wouldn't you agree?"

"Actually, no," Shreve countered. At her continued look of disbelief, he elaborated. "Think carefully. Use that logical intellect that you've been hammering away at me with since early this morning—no one saw you abducted. There was no one who saw you with the Spaniard, and the only people who know you are in this room are Red, Butcher, and me. We ride into your hometown, everyone sees. Relax, Iliamna," Shreve said softly, moving to stand beside her. "I'll pay Red well to keep other patrons away. Tell her that I've decided to make you my personal...well, just want to keep you for myself."

Iliamna didn't really hear his offer. His words from earlier in his sentence still ringing in her ears, "No one knows about the abduction," Iliamna said softly. "I can't prove it ever happened, other than a bruised jaw; and unless this Red person tells you that I was brought here unconscious, or unless you find Gitano so that he'll admit he abducted me, or force Alana to confess...oh, but not one of those people will help me or confess to anything because it will make them look bad; worse, they could end imprisoned. So, we're back to you leaving to prove what I say is true."

"I said that I would pay Red to keep you for me alone—or did you miss that part? You'll be safe enough until I get back."

"You're only hoping that the money you pay this Red is enough to keep people away from me. Aren't you crediting the woman with a bit much? After all, she paid my abductor a goodly sum to acquire me, which means she isn't exactly flush with scruples."

Shreve rubbed his jaw, sighed, and then ran his fingers through his hair and sighed again. It was obvious he was having as difficult a time deciding how to resolve her dilemma as she was. At least it was something. Better than pure callousness.

She glanced down and a thought struck her.

"You're wearing two pistols on your hips," Iliamna said suddenly, "so why don't you pretend *you're* abducting me and I'll worry about my reputation later?"

Shreve smiled, but then eyed her blanket skeptically, "Let's just pretend that's an option, you can't go traipsing around in a sheet or a blanket," he sighed heavily, "so I'll see if I can't locate something that you can put on. Everyone should be abed at this hour of the morning. We'll see if we can't sneak out and then I'll take you to my home to stay while I'm gone. I've got people that can watch over you until I return."

"Don't you mean, people that can keep an eye on me?" Iliamna said. She was not happy that this stranger did not believe her story, but she was thrilled at not having to stay in a house of ill repute. If it meant leaving this place, she would leave here naked and allow him to tie her up in a cave.

"Both. Now stay put. I'll be back in a flash."

In fact, it was faster than a flash. He returned within a few minutes of his departure—empty-handed.

"Couldn't find anything?"

"I peered in a couple of other rooms on my way to the office, but Red doesn't seem to keep clothes in her girls' rooms. Guess she wants to prevent this same thing from happening on a regular basis. Can't run a business if the clients run off with the supply. Anyway, the door to the office is locked, which is likely where she keeps the girls' clothes. The only way to get in is to crash through, and then everyone would wake up and we wouldn't be able to leave without guns blazing."

"Guns blazing? Being a little melodramatic, aren't you?"

Shreve shook his head, his lips pursed in thought. He rubbed at his nose and then responded to Iliamna's question, "Actually, I'm not, no. The last man who purportedly fell in love with one of Red's girls and attempted to abscond with her was found dead behind an alley—shot through the head. No one steals from Red and lives to face charges."

"Oh my."

"Yeah, but I have an idea," he said suddenly with a wide grin, looking at her sheet. "Come here."

# CHAPTER FOURTEEN

"No matter what, stay right behind me and keep very quiet," Shreve said, moving closer to the edge of the stairway.

"Don't worry about that," Iliamna whispered. "I wouldn't want to be anywhere else if this makeshift dress that you concocted decides to fall off."

Shreve laughed softly and then moved closer to the rail, peering over the side. He hadn't ever had to be this hyper-vigilant that he could recall, and he thanked his lucky stars that he was good with a gun, or they'd be in serious trouble if Red discovered what they were up to. As he took one more glance below stairs, he questioned the reasons for his actions. He couldn't figure why he was attempting to rescue this female. She denied knowing him, so it would be nothing for him to wash his hands of the whole affair and just leave her there. If she didn't know him, then she was certainly not his to be rescuing. He'd used the law as an excuse, but did he really care to see her put in jail if she had duped him? Would that be a better alternative to the whorehouse? *Perhaps that's my motivation*, he thought, as he skirted toward the staircase, *perhaps she'd be better off in jail than being raped for the rest of her life.*

He stopped at the head of the stairs, and let his gaze move about the bar downstairs. This third scan revealed that all were still abed, as he'd hoped. Good! It was simply too early in the day for patrons, or for Red and Butcher to be up and about. He only hoped his luck held; that their luck held.

He motioned for Iliamna to follow, and then stole down the stairs, stopping and listening when he hit the bottom landing. The hairs on the back of his neck jumped upright and he crouched lower, his gaze fighting to penetrate the shadows in the room. They weren't alone anymore; he could feel it. They hadn't made it out, and now that gunfight was more a likelihood. He began cursing beneath his breath, his inability to spot whoever was nearby. Whoever it was kept well hidden.

Iliamna saw Shreve tense and crouched behind him, "What is it? What's wrong?" She whispered, and then let out a strangled cry as a hand closed over her mouth and yanked her backwards up the staircase.

Shreve spun on his heel, drawing his gun, "Let her go, Butcher," he said softly.

"He can't do that, Shreve," Red said, stepping out of the shadows on the upper landing. She was wearing only her dressing robe, which meant that something had alerted her to an unusual movement in her place.

Shreve forced his breathing to remain calm, but it was difficult. He was angry—at himself, at Butcher, and at Red. If he allowed his anger to overwhelm him, he knew he'd never be able to shoot with accuracy, and those hairs standing erect on his neck told him that he would be engaging in gunfire before much longer.

"I treat you like family," Red was saying in a tone that told Shreve that she was furious also, "and give you my prized possession for a night of passion, and this is how you repay me? By trying to make off with my newly acquired asset? Or were you merely planning on buying her an early drink—with your gun drawn? Because I'd rather believe that than believe you'd stab your friend in the back over a whore."

"Tell Butcher to let her go," Shreve said. "It's only out of respect for you that I haven't put a bullet between his eyes yet, but I will if he keeps heading up the stairs, and we both know she isn't a whore, Red. You want to talk about friendship? You send me upstairs to break in a virgin for you, someone that is here against her will, that you paid money to own? Why would you do that to me, Red?"

Red shrugged, "I thought you needed a little diversion, and I'd rather you introduce her to her new job than...," Red stopped when she realized she had almost insulted her bodyguard.

"Well, she's got a new job title now—my wife. She's my woman, Red, so let her go."

"I don't recall seeing no minister step foot in here last night," Red retorted sardonically.

"She's my mail order bride," Shreve said suddenly, his face devoid of deception. "That's why she didn't meet me at the station, because she was abducted and sold to you."

"Now, Shreve," Red sighed, "first you insult me by trying to steal my new girl and then you try to insult my intelligence with an obvious lie. I know you are upset that your mail order bride failed to uphold her end, but that don't mean that you are entitled to my girls. If every guy that came in here took a liking and tried to run off with my whores, I'd be out of business."

"I'm telling you, she's the woman I was supposed to meet at the train station. When she didn't meet me, I just assumed she got cold feet." Shreve conveniently left out the part about the telegram, but he was convinced he had enough evidence on him to substantiate his story—if he ended up needing it. He hoped that Red liked him enough to believe him. She didn't.

"I think you'd better head on out and leave the girl to me," Red said softly, danger in her tone.

"I can't do that, Red. I can't leave her here, knowing she belongs to me; knowing that other men are going to have a go at her. I'm walking out of here with her and that's all there is to it," Shreve said, keeping his gun trained on Butcher, "and if you ever cared one whit about me Red, you'll let me."

Red sighed again, "You know I love you, Shreve, but you're behaving like a madman, right now. Heartbroken doesn't mean possession. It doesn't matter if I love you or hate you, I can't let you replace your missing woman with one of my girls."

"I'm going to count to ten, and if Iliamna and I are still standing inside this saloon, then...ah, hell, Red, don't make me do it. You know I will."

Red sighed heavily, when Shreve aimed the gun straight at Butcher's head. "Only because I do love you, Shreve, I'll give you one chance to prove to me that she's your mail-order intended. Do that, and you've got a bargain. You and she walks. Butcher, stay put. You can haul her away in a minute, but I don't want Shreve getting any more itchy on that trigger right now."

"Sure thing, Red," Butcher said smugly, "and I want your word too that you'll give her to me now, since it's obvious...,"

"That'll do, Butcher," Red interrupted, watching the thunderclouds descend on Shreve's face. He may be an educated

75

half-breed, but there was still a savage beneath that disciplined veneer. To Shreve she said, "He won't touch her unless you can't prove she's yours."

"I have your word, Red?"

"Yes, Shreve," Red said, "and I've never broken my word; which is more than you deserve at the moment, but I want your word that you'll leave peaceably and never step foot in my place again, and leave the girl to me—if you can't prove it."

"Very well," Shreve said. Without taking his gaze or his gun off of Butcher, he reached into his pocket and retrieved the drawing. "I've had this picture for over a month. My fiancé sent it to me to let me know what she looked like, so that I could recognize her when she stepped off the train." Shreve tossed the paper up on the landing. Red knelt down and picked it up. "I didn't touch her last night, because she's a virgin and, when I realized who she was, I wanted to wait to make love until we got married. We spent the night talking, and planning."

"Yeah, and then, instead of waiting to bring the matter to me, you decided to sneak out."

"Because I knew you wouldn't let her go."

"Maybe I would, maybe I wouldn't, but you've upset me a good deal by taking the decision out of my hands." She held the drawing up to the light and scrutinized it, longer than need be in Shreve's opinion.

"Well, Red? You gave me your word, so tell Butcher to leave off."

Red remained silent for a moment more, still intent on studying the drawing. He glanced over and saw her nostrils flaring and her jaw clenching. He saw the knowledge light in her eyes. She knew he was right, but when she spoke, Shreve wanted to put the bullet in *her* forehead. "It's a mighty fine likeness, I'll give you that, but there ain't nothing here, Shreve, that says she belongs to you. For all I know, you two fashioned this drawing during the night, as a way to deceive me." She sighed heavily again, "I let you take her away, and I'll lose the hundred seventy-five dollars that I paid for her and all the money that a beauty like her will bring. You can see my dilemma, certainly."

"I'll be happy to pay you your hundred back."

"I'd make ten times that on her in a month. A hundred times that over several months. Hell, by the time she's too old, I'd have garnered more, because of her beauty, than from any of my other girls combined. You willing to pay a hundred thousand for her?"

It was time from Shreve's nostrils to flare and jaw to clench, "If I had it in cash right now, I'd throw it at your feet. But you know I ain't got it right now. You know she belongs to me and are simply using money as an excuse not to let her go."

"All I see is attorney trying to prove a case on nothing but flimsy evidence," Red snapped and then sighed. "My advice to you, Shreve, is to keep your word. Go back to that big house you've built and forget this girl, and if you don't want to do that, you can always keep the picture," Red said, tossing the paper in his direction. "The girl stays."

"My gun says otherwise," Shreve said.

"Then you leave me no choice," Red said, waving her hand. Iliamna screeched behind Butcher's hand, and Shreve spun on his heels and fired.

# CHAPTER FIFTEEN

The man that snuck up behind Shreve, dropped his rifle, clutched his chest, and toppled over. Two more men, emerging from the shadows met the same fate, each letting out a pained yell as the gun slipped from each man's hand and life slipped from each man's body.

"Leave off, Red!" Shreve yelled, taking out two more men that came running at him from behind the bar.

"You left me no choice, Shreve!" Red yelled, and then Shreve heard a door slam.

He stayed hidden beside the staircase, his gaze rapidly scanning the main salon. When the smoke cleared, all he could see were dead bodies littering the floor. He shot a glance up the staircase and his heart lurched. Red was gone. So were Butcher and Iliamna.

"Red!" He yelled, hesitant to move from his hiding spot, knowing that if he didn't move quickly, Iliamna would become Butcher's latest broken female. A thought struck him then; that Butcher wouldn't go easy on her, for the sheer fact that Shreve had laid claim to her. That thought had him throwing caution to the wind. He quickly stood and ran up the staircase. He barely had time to aim and fire, as another of Red's men emerged down at the other end of the landing. Shreve's pace didn't slow, as he fired his last bullet, striking the man in the chest. Dramatically, Red's henchman clutched at his shirt, and then toppled over the railing, crashing heavily onto a table below.

Shreve holstered his now-empty gun and pulled his other. When he reached the end of the hallway, he stopped, listening.

"Iliamna!" He yelled, but heard no reply. "You can't have her, Red!" He yelled again, pushing into the room where he and Iliamna had passed the night. A quick scan of the room showed that it was empty.

He moved room to room, until only one room remained. Locked. "Red, open the door, damn you!" Shreve yelled. "If Butcher harms one hair on her head…," his threat was cut short by the sound of a muffled whimper coming from the room.

"Leave off, Shreve," Red called through the heavy oak. "By the time you get in here, Butcher will have finished breaking her in and then what? You take home used goods? You kill us both? What, Shreve? Go home. End this!"

Another muffled cry tore at Shreve's heart. He took a step back, lifted a booted foot, and drove the heel into the wood beside the knob. The door shook violently, but did not budge. He stumbled backward and nearly toppled over the railing as had the man he shot, but he shifted his weight and quickly righted, moving rapidly back to the door, pounding on it angrily.

"This is a special room, Shreve," Red called, her voice taunting. "Solid oak door. Makes it mighty difficult for the law, or an angry patron, to get at me. So, go ahead and kick away, it ain't going to do you no good," she continued to taunt. "Get on with it, Butcher." Shreve heard her say, and a louder cry rent the air.

Shreve took another step back, aimed, and fired a bullet directly into the lock. Someone on the other side screeched loudly, but Shreve was beyond caring. He lifted his foot again, slammed it into the door, and nearly fell when it gave way. He could see from his periphery that Red was down, but his main concern was the activity on the bed. Iliamna was naked, her wrists tied to the bedpost. Butcher, also naked, was on top of her, attempting to pry her legs apart with his knees.

He shot a wicked grin over his shoulder, put all his might into the effort, and yanked Iliamna's legs apart. With a triumphant look, he positioned his hips and prepared to thrust. Shreve fired his gun.

# CHAPTER SIXTEEN

"Are you all right?" Shreve asked, frantically untying her hands. When she was free of her bonds, he sat down on the bed and pulled her into his embrace. Iliamna lay still, too shaken to answer or to care that she was still unclothed. She nodded, and shuddered. Another shudder passed through her when her gaze fell on the body lying at the side of the bed. She glanced at the hole in the man's neck and the blood splattered across the carpet, and felt a quiver of revulsion race along her spine. She turned her face into Shreve's chest and began to cry, the shock of nearly being raped replaced with the fact that a man had been shot while laying atop her. With a gasp, she pulled away from Shreve and glanced down at her body, curious as to why she wasn't coated in blood. There was so much blood. She shuddered again, thankful that she was wearing no more than Butcher's sweat, but even that left her feeling disgustingly dirty.

A groan on the other side of the room drew her attention, which she was grateful for. She needed a distraction, even if it was Red doing the distracting. Red moaned again, and Iliamna realized that she'd been shot. From where the blood oozed, the bullet hit her in the side, but it wasn't serious enough to render her unconscious. Nor did she appear to be in shock, since her gaze was boring a hole in Shreve.

"You've got what you want, Shreve," she whispered, pain evident in her voice. "Now, get out of my place."

"I ought to kill you, Red," Shreve whispered harshly, pulling Iliamna tighter to his side.

"Yeah, well, it would have been my desire to see you dead too, so...just get out, before I have you arrested for murder."

"I think you know it wouldn't stick. You're lucky I don't send the sheriff to arrest you for attempted murder and assault. All you had to do was give her to me, Red, and all of this bloodshed could've been avoided." Shreve shook his head, feeling suddenly de-energized. One thing's for certain, you'll never see me again, *friend*," Shreve said, and then stood, lifting Iliamna into his arms. "Where are her clothes?" He asked, stopping beside Red. Red nodded toward a corner armoire.

"Can you manage?" He asked Iliamna, moving in that direction.

"I'm a bit shaken, but I think I can dress myself."

He lowered her to the floor and smiled, a pained attempt to lower the tension smothering the atmosphere, "Good girl, because I'm having a hard enough time keeping my eyes off of you. If I had to dress you, I'd be totally lost," he quipped and Iliamna's face turned a bright shade of red. She moved away from him quickly and retrieved her clothing, dressing as quickly as her shaking hands allowed.

"I'm ready," she said a few minutes later, grateful she had little clothing to put on—no corset, or other undergarments. Just the attire Gitano had given her.

"I'll send a doctor," Shreve offered offhanded, addressing Red as he moved toward the door, pulling Iliamna along behind him.

"Don't bother. Just get out of my place," she snapped, closing her eyes against the pain.

"Glad you said that, because that's one less thing holding me here," He snapped, continuing toward the door.

"This isn't over, Shreve," Red screamed. "There's a bullet with your name on it now."

Shreve bristled at the threat, and he wanted to turn around and put a bullet in her head, but he had a difficult time with the idea of cold-blooded murder. He pulled Iliamna along behind him instead, alert for any additional signs of attack. He didn't really expect anyone else to hinder his departure, since he'd shot all of Red's men; however, that didn't mean company of another sort couldn't arrive in response to the sound of gunfire.

"We'll go out the back way," he said, as they moved quickly along the upper landing. "This town may not waken this early in the day, but someone's bound to come and check out what all the shooting's about. Of course, they could simply be used to it, which is what I suspect."

"Can she really have you arrested for murder?" Iliamna asked, staying close behind Shreve.

"She could try, but it wouldn't be convictable. Still, they may just find me guilty because I have Indian blood. Either way, I'd rather not stay around and provide proof that I was here."

"You lied to Red about my being your mail order bride, about our being man and wife, to save my hide, so I guess if I need to then I can lie about your whereabouts today."

"Thanks, but let's just hope Red doesn't pursue it further. Besides, I didn't exactly lie. As far as I know, you are my mail-order...well...bride-to-be, if not exactly bride," Shreve said, then stopped at the side of the building. "My horse is tied up out front. I'm going to try to get to it without drawing attention. You keep behind the buildings, heading this same direction. I'll meet you at the end of the street and we'll head out."

"Why can't I just stay with you?" Iliamna asked, suddenly frantic again.

Shreve turned, the words that he wanted to say sticking in his throat at the look of panic in her eyes. He lifted a hand and stroked her jaw, "I'm not leaving you," he whispered. "That would be a rather stupid thing to do after going to so much trouble to get you out of that place, don't you think?" He smiled softly, the pad of his thumb continuing to stroke her cheek softly, comfortingly. "I want you to go along behind the buildings so that we aren't seen together. Anyone coming to investigate knows that the only women in this town belong to Red. I try to ride out of here with one of the better ones, and some man might take a notion to help Red out and put a bullet in my back in the hopes that Red will repay his assistance with...well, you know.

"Me," Iliamna whispered.

Shreve nodded. "Do you think you can run along behind the buildings now and meet me at the end down there?" He asked, nodding his head in the direction he wanted her to go.

Iliamna nodded, smiled, and moved away. Shreve watched her go, and then peered around the corner of the building. If anyone heard the shots fired inside the saloon, no one was coming to investigate—yet. He ran around to the front, pulled the lead rope free from the hitching post, and mounted quickly. With a flick of the

Barbara Woster

reins, he bolted down Main Street. It was time to get the heck out of this no-name town.

He got to the end of Main and pulled on the reins, waiting for Iliamna to catch up. She came running around the corner a moment later. He reached out a hand, which she grasped without hesitation. With a mighty heave, he tugged her up, waiting to release her hand until she was settled behind him. "You good?" He asked. When she nodded, he kicked his horse's haunches and took off at a gallop. It was time to get to the safety of home.

## CHAPTER SEVENTEEN

"How long are we going to ride without stopping?" Iliamna said close to Shreve's ear.

"Pardon?" Shreve said, startled out of his musings.

"Well," Iliamna ventured, keeping her mouth close to his ear so that he could hear her over the roar of the passing wind, "it's only we've been on this horse for quite some time—without stopping. And, while I don't mean to gripe, or to appear ungrateful, especially after you risked your neck to get me out of that place—I am really, really hungry. And I really need to...well, that is to say...could we possibly stop for just a moment?"

"I'm sorry," Shreve said, slowing his mount. He turned best he could so he could look at Iliamna, and suddenly felt more than sorry, he felt dreadful. There was a fatigue encompassing her, evident in the dark circles beneath her eyes and the heavy slump in her shoulders. He sighed, "I guess I was so consumed with getting out of town and to the ranch, that I wasn't thinking about whether you were saddle broken. Normally, I wouldn't even continue riding past sunset, but stopping just didn't seem the best option." The horse finally stopped and Shreve dismounted. He reached up and pulled Iliamna into his arms, carrying her toward the trees.

"I do have two feet, you know," she whispered, discomfiture flooding her cheeks.

"Yes, I know," Shreve grinned, "and you have two legs too, but neither is going to hold you at the moment. I'm used to being mounted and *my* legs are like rubber. It's what happens when you ride for too long, which isn't something I'd wager you do on a regular basis."

"So, if I can't stand, then how am I supposed to...well, you know?"

Shreve laughed, and realized just how good it felt to laugh. He hadn't much cause to do anything other than worry or fret of late, but their successful escape from Red had given him an emotional boost, so much so that he wanted to kiss Iliamna senseless. He restrained himself, but it wasn't easy.

"Well, I'm going to deposit you behind a tree. As soon as you feel able, stand to work the kinks out of your muscles. Once you've done that, you can take care of your business. Meet me back by the horse. In the meantime, I'm going to attempt to snare some dinner." Shreve lowered Iliamna to the ground carefully, and then knelt beside her. Gently, he lifted her chin and turned her face to examine the bruise lining her jaw. He grimaced slightly and then placed a reassuring smile on his lips, "The bruise is really turning a lovely shade of black and blue now," He said softly, and then the smile faded, "I'm sorry you were hurt."

"Thank you, Shreve." Iliamna said softly, lowering her gaze. She found his nearness very unnerving, and his touch even more so. Add to the discomfort she felt at needing to relieve herself, and she was fairly squirming with awkwardness.

"You're very welcome, Iliamna."

Despite how she was feeling, she was still unable to feel her legs sufficiently to stand, so she decided his nearness was the best distraction from the other urgency. He was about to stand to leave, but Iliamna stopped him, "I really will never be able to thank you for saving me from that place. I shudder to think what would have happened had you left me there. Since you helped me, does that mean you're ready to believe me? That I was abducted..."

"I believe that Red paid good money for you, but the attorney in me needs answers that one person's word can't supply."

Iliamna closed her eyes and sighed. She started rubbing her legs to hasten the return of feeling, deciding that conversation hadn't been the best idea for a distraction after all. Shreve was simply too stubborn to converse with pleasantly. "I guess it's a good thing that we aren't really getting married," she whispered, wincing when the tingle in her legs turned into needle-sharp annoyance.

"Why's that?" Shreve asked, his brow knitting.

"Because if you can't trust the woman you're to marry, then...well, let's just say that the starting foundation is going to be set on some mighty unbalanced stones."

"Good point," Shreve said, moving to stand again. "I guess it *is* a good thing we aren't planning to marry; but just so you know—I do like you, Iliamna, despite everything, or I wouldn't be trying to prove your innocence."

"Is that how you describe what you're doing?"

Shreve laughed softly, "Go ahead and take care of what you need to take care of and I'll take care of our food."

Iliamna watched as Shreve walked away. He was an unusual man, all the way down to his name. He was educated as an attorney, yet his belief was guilty until proven innocent. He must have been a prosecutor, or a very suspicious defense attorney.

# CHAPTER EIGHTEEN

After that first stop, Shreve felt more relaxed that no one was chasing after them; relaxed enough to stop the next evening to hunt.

"No need for us to starve," he quipped, pulling a bow and arrow from his saddle.

"You really use that?" Iliamna grinned, thinking of how Indians were stereotyped back east—savages brandishing bow and arrows fatally; shrieking war cries as they went about butchering white folks. Of course, that stereotype had lessened as they'd entered the twentieth century since the final resistance to forced relocation, headed by Geronimo, had been some thirty years prior[5]. Still, seeing Shreve pulling out a bow and arrow to hunt for their dinner, brought to bear the realization that he was, indeed, half native.

Shreve looked at her intently for a moment, trying to decide whether to be offended, or whether to simply brush off her comment as stemming from a lack of knowledge. He took a deep breath, and decided to brush it off, "It's quieter than a gun, and a bullet can ruin the meat if my shot isn't accurate."

"Ah, well that makes sense."

Shreve laughed, certain that she was merely inquisitive, not harboring some ill will towards him or his heritage. He decided just to relax. After all, his father had told him, "you can only feel prejudiced against if you are prejudice yourself" and he was more than certain he held no prejudice against white people, and didn't perceive that Iliamna held prejudice against his people.

"I'll be back shortly," he said, and then turned to head into the woods.

"Can I come with you?" Iliamna asked, tagging along behind.

"You're perfectly safe near the horse," Shreve said. "And if you're worried about wild animals, then consider starting a fire. Wild animals tend to avoid fires."

"I'm not scared," Iliamna said, "I just want to see how you use

---

[5]http://www.spartacus.schoolnet.co.uk/WWinreservations.htm

that thing, and I've never been hunting before."

Shreve stopped walking and turned to face her, "Been a lifelong dream of yours to see something killed?"

Iliamna stopped, her brow knitted, "Of course not," she said, uncertain if he were joking with her—much as when he'd mentioned the only chair in the room during their uncomfortable discussion a couple of days prior.

"Just making sure you didn't have a morbid streak," Shreve winked, and then turned to head into the woods. Iliamna shook her head to dispel the discombobulating feelings he elicited in her, and then jogged after him.

"Has anyone ever mentioned that you have a strange sense of humor?" She asked, falling into step beside him.

He grinned, "Not really, no. Admittedly though, the only people I have conversed with of late are my staff, and I'm not certain they'd mention it. Shhh, I see something."

Iliamna fell silent as he requested, squinting through the brush to see if she could spot what he did. When he saw her expression, he pointed to where he was looking. "Ah," she whispered, locating the two jackrabbits in the distance.

"Stay put," he whispered next to her ear, and her nerves fired at the heat of his breath. She let loose a whoosh of breath, nodded, and lowered her gaze, hoping he wouldn't see her reaction. He had, and smiled, but he couldn't stop to converse over it if they were going to eat.

He ducked low and moved carefully amid the brush, until he felt certain he could hit one of his prey. Carefully, he drew his bow and an arrow from the quiver on his back, steadied his breathing, sighted down the arrow, and let it fly.

"I must admit," Iliamna said when they were seated by the fire, watching the jackrabbit roasting on a spit, "that your skill is very impressive."

Shreve grinned, "I've had lots of practice."

"Well that certainly is obvious. I could never do that."

"You may learn the skill, but you would never be able to use it."

"Because I'm a woman?"

"Women do not have the strength in their arms to pull back on a bow. The string requires strong muscles."

"Well, I can't argue that. You're very good with a gun too."

Shreve nodded, "That skill takes a lot more continual practice."

"I don't doubt it; so how long will it take to cook, do you think," Iliamna asked as a growl let loose in her belly. "Sorry."

Shreve laughed, "It should be done." He reached over, and pulled the spit from over the fire and then jabbed the sharp end into the ground. "I can't offer a civilized manner for eating this, but I can offer to cut a few pieces at a time for you."

"Thank you," Iliamna replied graciously, "that's much appreciated."

Shreve reached over and pulled off the legs, "Let's consume these first. They are easier to manage, but be careful," he said, passing one leg to her, "they are still a bit hot."

Iliamna accepted the leg with care and took a tiny bite, "It's perfect," she sighed, thankful that the meat had cooled rapidly. She finished off the leg quickly, and requested another piece. Shreve shook his head in wonder. Most women would be put off by the thought of hunting, could never watch an animal skinned and spit, would never consider eating without a plate and utensils…but Iliamna showed no qualms over any of it, yet he knew her to be a lady of breeding. "You're very remarkable," he said. "You grew up in the city but behave as if you grew up…"

"…in the country, actually," Iliamna interjected. "My family owned some very beautiful farm land in the Virginia countryside. I used to help Sammy—he was our cook—chase down chickens to make for dinner. It was very entertaining to participate. I had to get used to his breaking their necks though. That took a while, but he helped me to understand why it had to be done. He said that God put the animals here for our consumption, but He didn't make it so they'd drop dead at our feet when we needed them to."

Shreve laughed, "Oh my, that's good. It would definitely be a lot easier if they'd simply jump into my pot when I was hungry, but as that isn't likely to ever happen…well, that's why I got good with a bow and arrow."

"You are indeed."

"What happened to them? Your parents?"

Iliamna sighed heavily, and couldn't stop the tears which formed in remembrance. She sniffled and then swiped at her nose and eyes, "I'm sorry. Sometimes I forget that it's been less than four months since I lost them, and I'm fine; but then..."

"Someone like me brings it up. I'm sorry, Iliamna."

"Don't be. Their deaths certainly weren't your fault. Um, anyway, a rancher bought the land adjacent to our property about six months ago. His first action as owner was to stop by to offer Dad money to sell out. Well, of course that seemed absurd to Dad. That property had been in Dad's family for generations. He turned the man down."

"I'm not certain I like where this is headed."

Tears welled in Iliamna's eyes again, and she shook her head, "A little over four months ago," she explained, her tone thick with emotion, "we started having difficulties with raiders. A bit odd, since we'd never had anyone attempt to steal our property before. The raiders grabbed at anything they could—chickens, pigs, cattle—even the corn in the field. The law didn't seem able to assist, so one day," Iliamna stumbled, swiping at the moisture dripping from her nose.

"You don't have to tell me," Shreve said softly, moving to wrap her into his embrace.

Iliamna cried for a time against Shreve's shoulder, but then sniffled loudly, dried her tears, and sat up, "One day," she continued, drawing in unsteady breaths between phrases, "my dad had enough and decided to put a stop to it. He had men keep watch over the crops and he intended to keep watch over the stock. Mom, being the woman she was, went with him. She used to tell me that a true woman stands shoulder-to-shoulder with her man. She said she wasn't going to allow Dad to face those heathens alone, when she was quite adept at handling a rifle. Not adept enough, as it turned out. Apparently, the men that came that night to raid the cattle were armed. There was a gun fight..." Iliamna laid her head down on Shreve's shoulder again as more tears started falling.

"Shh, I don't need to hear anymore," he whispered against her hair, holding her tight. "Don't tell me anymore."

"I'm sorry," Iliamna whispered, unable to stop the emotional breakdown.

"Oh, sweetheart, you've been through an awful lot, haven't you?" Shreve rocked her gently, and let her cry herself out.

When her tears dried, Iliamna sat up again, "Thank you," she whispered, again wiping the moisture from her nose and eyes, "I've had no one to talk to..." she stopped, leaned up, and placed a kiss on his cheek. "Thank you," she whispered again.

"You're welcome," Shreve smiled softly, wanting to kiss her back, but she was already pulling away from him.

*Definitely unusual,* he thought, as he watched her prepare for bed. He hoped and prayed that when he went to Louisiana, he'd prove her story true, because the thought of this woman being a swindler suddenly seemed highly improbable. Shreve sighed, settling next to the fire. "The problem with improbable," he whispered to himself, "is it isn't the same as impossible. There is always a likelihood with probabilities, no matter how slim."

# CHAPTER NINETEEN

Shreve knelt beside Iliamna the next morning, watching her sleep. He really needed to nudge her awake, but watching her sleep was pleasant. She was just as beautiful in repose, and a delight to observe, but then her brow knitted signifying a bad dream, and he suddenly couldn't bear knowing she was recalling the nightmare of the past month. He leaned over and placed a light kiss on her lips and the furrowed brow vanished, replaced by a soft sigh and a sweet smile. He smiled also.

"Iliamna," he said softly, placing a hand on her shoulder.

Iliamna jerked, eyes wide in horror. When the fog lifted and recognition dawned, she breathed a deep sigh and wiped the sleep from her eyes, yawning heavily, "You scared me," she whispered, stretching the kinks from her limbs.

He watched her squirm along the ground, stretching and twisting, and felt desire flare. *She is very desirable first thing in the morning,* he mused with a grin. Iliamna caught the look and stopped moving, sitting quickly. "So, why did you wake me? Is it time to go already?"

Shreve laughed, "Yes ma'am, and the sooner the better."

"Anything to eat before we leave?" Iliamna asked, rolling up the blanket he'd loaned her.

He took the blanket and strapped it to his saddle and then mounted, "Can you wait for a short bit? We're going to be at the homestead inside another couple of hours, and the food will be varied and aplenty."

"Sounds lovely." Iliamna clasped Shreve's proffered hand, and settled behind him, wrapping her arms around his waist, "Ready," she said after a moment.

Shreve shook his head and grinned, and then gently set his horse into a canter.

An hour later, they were moving across the plain, the grass slapping at their legs as the wind intensified; the clouds in the distance dark and ominous—foretelling a coming storm—when Shreve pulled his horse to a stop, "Can you hear me?" He called, turning slightly in the saddle.

"Barely, but well enough," Iliamna yelled back.

"We'll need to veer off and find shelter. There's a storm brewing that we don't need to get caught in."

"Okay," Iliamna said.

"Did you say something?" Shreve yelled, and Iliamna winced as the wind chose that particular moment to lessen its ferocity.

"Wow! You don't realize how deafening a wind can be until it isn't blowing."

"I'm just glad we can stop yelling, but there's a good chance we'll get soaked. I'm definitely going to have to find us shelter nearby until it blows over." Shreve tugged on Black Wind's reins, turning his mount in the direction of some nearby trees.

"But there doesn't appear to be anything 'blowing' at the moment. Doesn't that mean the threat of a storm has passed?"

"Ever hear the saying about being calm before a storm?"

"No."

"Well, the sudden drop in wind means that the storm is nearly upon us."

"Oh, well, I don't think I'll dissolve if I get wet."

"Never been in a Texas squall, have you?"

"Never even heard of one until that wind a moment ago."

Shreve grinned, "That was nothing. That was mild by comparison to what'll follow; which may not dissolve you, but it may pick you up and deposit you a few miles away from here."

"Oh, dear!"

"Yeah, precisely, now duck your head," Shreve said, jumping his horse over a rock and straight into a stand of trees. A few moments later, after climbing into some hills just opposite the stand of trees, Shreve dismounted. He led Black Wind along the loose rocks, searching. Just as he located the opening he was looking for, the sky opened up. He tugged at the reins and entered the blackness just as a crack of lightening and the roar of thunder rolled overhead. Within minutes, the level ground outside the cave was a deluge.

"Oh, my heavens!" Iliamna gasped, moving closer to the wall. "We're not in danger, are we?"

"That's Texas for you," Shreve said with a shrug. "A good downpour will flood everything in sight, but the minute the rain stops, it's as arid as any desert again, with a few patches of mud here and there. We're safe enough. There's a rock on the opposite side of the cave if you want to sit."

"No, thank you. I've sat enough in that saddle to last a good long while," Iliamna sighed and then sighed again when the downpour quickly turned into a drizzle. "It would appear that a good long while isn't going to happen. Is it over already?"

"Yep. It was just a small squall."

"I suppose you'll want to be on the way now?" Iliamna said, pushing away from the wall.

"Actually, yes," Shreve said, "but," he continued, reaching to latch onto her arm as she passed by, "I need to talk to you first."

Iliamna nodded and turned back to face him.

"We really should sit," he said, leading her further into the cave. "I know your fanny is tired, but I'd feel more comfortable having this conversation seated."

Iliamna winced as she settled onto the rock, but she didn't complain. She would suffer far more discomfort if need be, as it was a reminder that she was now safe and free, "I'm listening."

"When we get to the house, we'll need to tell them that we're married."

"What?" Iliamna exclaimed. "But, why?"

"The people that live in and around my ranch, and the people that work for me, have a very strong sense of moral values. I don't want to insult them by bringing a woman to live under my roof that's not my wife."

"But, don't you *own* the ranch?"

"Yes, but my people keep it running."

"Still, isn't it considered immoral to lie? Won't they be upset when they've learned we've deceived them?"

"We'll cross that trestle when we get to it," Shreve replied.

"If we don't get run over by a freight train first," Iliamna murmured.

"Good point."

"So, do all attorneys prevaricate when they find themselves in a sticky situation?"

"Are you calling me a liar, by chance?"

"Absolutely not! I don't know you well enough. I just noticed that you bend things about to suit the situation is all."

"That's a fancy way of saying I lie," Shreve said, "but don't worry—I take no offense. Actually, I've found myself being more dishonest the last few days than in my entire thirty-six years of living."

"Well, you can't exactly include your infancy."

"Don't be argumentative. You know what I mean."

"Yes, I do," Iliamna said. "You are saying that you have only begun to lie since you met me."

"Pretty much."

"Well, let's hope we part company soon or you may end up neck-deep in your own poppycock."

"And let's hope that you aren't prevaricating either, or you may find yourself spending your youth in a local cell." His tone was sharper than intended, and he sighed heavily, "I'm sorry."

"It's okay. Your point is very well taken, but must we lie about being married? I really don't know whether I'm good enough at lying to deceive a bunch of people like that. After all, how will we explain our lack of affection for each other?"

"Oh, I don't think I'll have any difficulty showing a beautiful woman like you affection," Shreve said, reaching out to stroke her cheek briefly. He laughed at the color that infused her cheeks.

"Well, I'm sorry, sir," she huffed indignantly, "but I don't care how attractive you are, I simply cannot fake an affinity for someone I don't know."

Shreve laughed again, "A little young to be a prude, aren't you? Well, I hardly think there will be a problem with faking anything, since I won't be there. And it's nice to know you find me handsome. Good for my ego."

"Don't dwell too hard on it. I guess I did forget that you'll be staying just long enough to dump me...,"

"I'm not dumping you. I'm just entrusting you into the care of my housekeeper, so I'll know where you are," Shreve said, standing abruptly. "Let's go." He reached a hand down to assist her from the rock and then helped her remount. "Keep your head down. I don't want you to get it lopped off by the branches."

"It won't. I'll have you in front of me."

"Well, if mine gets lopped off, then yours will be at risk, so keep low."

"Oh, I'm not worried," Iliamna retorted playfully as he walked his horse toward the cave opening. "If for any reason you lose your head, I'll simply duck behind your headless torso, and then you'll be dead, and I'll have a really nice mount to return to Louisiana on."

"Wishing me dead so soon, are you?" Shreve grinned, mounting in front her. "And seriously duck," he said, and then spurred Black Wind through the cave, tugging sharply on the reins as the horse slipped on a mud patch. Branches slapped at his torso. Iliamna kept her head buried between Shreve's shoulder blades, but winced as a few branches whacked at her sides. When the horse regained its footing and they'd returned to the prairie, Shreve pointed the stallion's nose toward home.

"Are you okay?" Shreve asked.

"A little scratched up, but nothing serious."

"So, still mad at me?"

"I am a little put out with you for not believing me," Iliamna resumed, "and for refusing to let me go home, but no, I don't think wishing you dead is justifiable. Besides, I know the results of harboring ill will against someone, so I'm not likely to do so ever in my life. That doesn't mean I'm happy with you though."

"So I gathered."

"Well, now that we've determined my current disposition, and are almost at your ranch, what are we going to do about this marriage nonsense?"

Barbara Woster

"I'll deposit you in the care of my housekeeper, Carmen, as I said, and leave immediately. Think you can act lovingly toward me for, oh, say an hour tops, while I pack some supplies?"

"Very well," Iliamna sighed, "but at precisely one minute past that hour, I turn into a shrew."

## CHAPTER TWENTY

Shreve pulled the horse to a stop before the archway leading to his ranch. The sign, welcoming visitors to his home, was new, just like the house nestled in the valley below. He had never thought of naming his parcel of land before he had started corresponding with Iliamna—or whomever wrote the letters.

Still, to honor her arrival, he had built this archway at the head of his drive. Now, he wanted her to see how much he had looked forward to bringing her here. Maybe if she saw all the care that had gone into welcoming her, she would see fit to level with him. Maybe even decide to marry him for real.

"This is home," he whispered. "I built it just for you."

Iliamna looked up at the archway and stifled a gasp. There were two hearts entwined atop, with the words 'Double Heart Ranch' below. The words had been painstakingly carved into the wood, painted a beautiful shade of red.

She looked down the lane and her heart missed a beat. A beautiful, two-story, ranch-style house with a porch that wrapped around the entire front, stood pristine in a valley of green. The cream-colored exterior, freshly painted with a burgundy trim was free of dirt and grime and gleamed in the afternoon sun; and in stark contrast against the aged buildings surrounding it. It was new, and it was built for her. No, not her. For Alana.

"It's the most beautiful sight I've ever seen, Shreve, but it wasn't built for me. If you built it for anyone, you did so for Alana."

"Are you so sure?" Shreve asked, but before she could reply, he spurred his mount down the drive.

"Ah, Mr. Shreve, welcome home," A medium-set elderly woman yelled as she pushed open the screen door, tucking a dishtowel in her apron pocket. "We weren't expecting you, and this," she smiled widely, noticing Iliamna, "must be your new wife. Welcome, mistress."

Iliamna cringed, but her smile did not falter. One hour, she reminded herself.

"I'm sorry I didn't wire to let you know when I'd be arriving, Carmen, but I was a little distracted." Iliamna huffed softly at his double meaning, and wanted to smack his head when he grinned at her mischievously over his shoulder. "Isn't that right, darling?"

"Oh, without a doubt, dear," Iliamna replied, squeezing his abdomen tight. She saw him cringe and her smile turned genuine. "I only wish that you didn't have to leave so soon after our arrival. I was soooo hoping to spend some quality time with my new *husband*," she cooed sweetly.

"Don't overdo it," Shreve whispered from the corner of his mouth.

Carmen eyed them strangely, "Where are you going, Mr. Shreve? Your wife is right, you know. You shouldn't just abandon her to the company of strangers when you've just gotten hitched to her. Besides, Betsy's getting ready to calve."

"Calve?" Shreve asked, dismounting in front of the house. He reached up and helped Iliamna alight, but his attention was not on her, for once. "What do you mean, calve? She's not due to deliver her calf for another couple of weeks."

"Premature," Carmen said, "Doc Harper's over in the barn with Jeb now."

"Can you get Iliamna settled, Carmen?" Shreve asked, grasping Iliamna by the hand and pulling her forward.

"I will, of course. And I must say, I find your name so very beautiful."

"Thank you."

"Do you think you can help me get dinner going for the menfolk? I'm a mite bit worn out," Carmen said dramatically, and then turned to Shreve, "Any word on someone to help out around here?"

"Not yet, Carmen. I'm sorry. Do you mind overly much helping Carmen out for a bit?" Shreve asked, turning to face her. "She's simply getting too old to do it all herself," Shreve teased.

"Now, you just listen here, young man," Carmen snapped, but

her bluster quickly faded when Shreve laughed and placed a kiss on her cheek.

"I'm just teasing, Carmen," Shreve smiled. "I'd be lost without you."

"Damned straight, boy."

Shreve laughed and turned to face Iliamna, "I know it's not the best homecoming, but Betsy's our prized possession, and I can't afford to lose her."

"Of course, Shreve," Iliamna whispered, "Go. I'll be fine."

"Thank you, Love," he whispered, and then instinctively grabbed her by the shoulders and pulled her in for a quick kiss. "Thank you," he said again, and then grinned at her bemused expression. He wanted to kiss her again, to see if he could change that bemusement into passion, but Carmen coughed and he pulled away.

"You have plenty of time for kissing and such later, Mr. Shreve. Now git on over to the barn. I'll have Kedric come take care of the horse."

"Thanks Carmen, I'll see you at dinner, Mrs. Red Fox," Shreve grinned, and then took off at a run across the yard.

"Looks like that boy took a mighty strong shine to you, Mrs. Iliamna," Carmen said, smiling. "In all honesty, I was a little worried when he told me that he was looking at a mail-order bride to take care of his home and a baby as well."

"Baby!" Iliamna said, snapping out of her daze.

# CHAPTER TWENTY-ONE

Carmen missed Iliamna's outburst, as she was already headed to the house, "Speaking of which," she called over her shoulder, making the assumption that Iliamna was following along behind, "the baby will be waking soon to be fed, so we really need to get dinner finished. I'm sorry I don't have time to show you around right now. Think we can wait for a formal introduction to everything later?" When she didn't receive a reply, Carmen stopped and turned around. "Is everything okay?"

"I...well..."

Carmen moved back to where Iliamna stood rooted in shock.

"Are you okay, Mrs. Iliamna?"

"I'm certain that I'll be fine, but what's this about a baby?"

"Oh my, Shreve didn't explain?"

"I guess we had so much happening, that he didn't get around to doing so."

"Where's your luggage, sweetie?"

"What?" Iliamna asked, confused by Carmen's sudden shift in conversation. "Oh, um, I haven't any. I'm afraid it was all lost. All I have is what I'm wearing," Iliamna answered reflexively, "but you were going to explain about this baby?"

"Oh, heavens me! How dreadful!" Carmen sighed, looking from her own frumpy body to Iliamna's tall, lithe one. "Well, you won't be borrowing my clothes. We'll just have to make sure that Shreve brings back some clothes for you when he gets back from wherever it is he's got to get off to. In the meantime, I think I have enough material put aside to make a dress or two. Please tell me you can sew, sweetie."

"Yes, of course, but what's this about a baby?" Iliamna asked again, trying to keep her growing frustration in check, as Carmen headed back to the house.

"Oh, that would be our darling little Brendan," Carmen said, pulling the screen door open and scurrying toward the kitchen. "It's Shreve's nephew, but I swear that he treats that child like he was born to his own wife, not his sister."

"Where is his sister, if it wouldn't be rude to inquire?"

"Well, that's a sad thing, to be sure," Carmen said, pulling the flour from the cupboard and literally tossing it on the counter. "Do you know how to make tortillas, by chance?"

"No, I can't say that I do," Iliamna said. "But you were saying about Shreve's sister?"

"Oh, yes, well, I'll do what I can to teach you how to make tortillas. They're easy to make and tacos and burritos are Shreve's favorite food. As for Shreve's sister," Carmen continued, pulling seasoning from nearby cabinets. She was such a whirlwind that it made Iliamna slightly dizzy. "Now you just watch what I do, okay? It's really not that hard. Can you fry up some ground beef, do you think?"

"I'm certain that I can."

"Great! The ground beef is in the icebox. Now, what was I saying?"

"About Shreve's sister?" Iliamna reminded, moving to the refrigerator. She pulled open the door, located the beef, and moved to the stove. "Skillet?"

"Under the cabinet. To your right, dear."

"Thanks."

"Now, what was I saying?"

"Oh, dear," Iliamna whispered with a sigh.

"Oh, yes," Carmen said before Iliamna could remind her yet again. "Dear wee little Dallas. The child birthing was simply too much for her and she bled out. She was such a sweet, dear thing too. We'll miss her something dreadful."

"Where's her husband?"

"Oh, there's a double tragedy. See, not soon after Dallas found out she was carrying Christian's baby, that was her husband, he was taken away from her. Stampeded by a herd of cattle. Really sad, it was," Carmen said, slowly stirring flour into a bowl full of seasoned water.

"Oh, heavens! That is awful!"

"Yes, well, wee little Dallas moved in with us shortly after, determined not to let her husband's death keep her from bearing a strong child. It worked too. When that baby was born, he weighed well over ten pounds and has a set of lungs on him that could wake the dead well over into the next county."

"Is that why Shreve wanted to find a wife then, to take care of the baby mainly?"

"That's when he started placing ads, yes, because no one around here would have him. Wasn't having too much success with the ads either, until you sent your reply."

"I don't understand why not," Iliamna asked. "He's handsome, he's educated, and he's been nothing but kind to me."

"The beans are in a pot on the stove. Can you mash them up? Make kind of a paste out of them? The beef ready?"

"Yes and yes." Iliamna placed the pan aside and reached for the pot.

"Thanks a bunch. Honestly, things have been very hectic around here with only me trying to take care of the cooking and cleaning, and now a baby. I'm simply too old to do it all anymore. Just don't tell Shreve I said so. Dallas used to help...," Carmen let her sentence hang. "Anyway, Shreve is trying to find another person to help out with the housekeeping, so if you could just help with the baby, I should be able to handle the cooking."

"I'll do what I can, but I haven't any experience."

"I know you will do just fine, sweetie," Carmen said, smiling. "You have a good heart in you. I can see it. And tending to a baby is instinctive." Iliamna blushed. "Anyway, if you haven't noticed, our Shreve is a half-breed. That's half Choctaw."

"And?"

"Well, you might say 'and', but most women say, 'no way'. And since Shreve decided to be up front and advertise that he was a half-breed, well, we haven't exactly had women beating down our door. We were kind of surprised, actually, when a beautiful, well-bred lady like yourself answered the ad and started corresponding with our boy."

"Why didn't he mention the baby, if he was trying to be so forthcoming?"

"Well...", Carmen's explanation was cut short by a loud wail. "Oh, dear, that's our Brendan. There's a bottle of formula already prepared. If you want to toss it over here, I'll warm it while you go and change the darling's diaper. Can you manage okay? There's some clean diapers in the drawer next to him, and some clean cloths to wipe him down."

"Like I said, I've never really had much experience with children, but," she continued with a sigh, "I've said I'll help how I can and I meant it, so which room."

"Just follow the screams, child. Just follow the screams."

# CHAPTER TWENTY-TWO

Iliamna left the kitchen in search of the "screams". It did not take long to locate the room. Carmen was right—the child had a set of lungs on him that could wake the dead. She moved quickly to the side of his bassinet and began cooing softly while desperately trying to figure out which drawer held the diapers and wipes.

"There, there, little one, it's okay," she whispered, pulling the blanket aside. "Well now, you are a wee little thing, aren't you? No more than a few months old." The baby stopped screaming long enough to inspect Iliamna, and then started up again, deafening her. "Now, now, little one, we'll see you fixed up right."

Iliamna crinkled her nose at the stench that arose when she unpinned the diaper and pulled the cloth aside. "Not too small to make a big mess though," she whispered. "I don't think that washcloths are going to serve us well at the moment, so what say you to a nice soothing wash before your bottle, okay?"

She re-pinned the diaper and quickly moved to the adjoining bathroom. She was pleased to see that Shreve had gone to the expense and consideration to add indoor plumbing. It was definitely a treat and, at this moment, a Godsend. She adjusted the water temperature, located a bath towel, and then quickly moved back to the nursery. The baby's face had turned a mottled red from screaming the house down, but the moment that Iliamna reached in and picked him up, he settled.

"Easily pleased, I see. That's good."

She held the baby at arm's length and moved back to the bathroom. When she knelt down and laid the little bundle on the floor, his lungs began its second workout, deafening her.

"Now, now, sweetie," she cooed loudly, "I can't very well clean you if you're still clothed." She crinkled her nose, quickly removed his nightshirt; and the wiped off as much of the mess from his tiny bottom-end as could be managed. She lifted him carefully and held his bottom beneath the running water.

Obviously, the water struck a sensitive spot, for the baby proceeded to gurgle happily. Iliamna's heart melted and she felt herself slipping closer to love. It would not be too much longer before the darling lad had her wrapped completely around his little fingers.

"There now all better," she continued in her soothing tone as she ran a washcloth over his bum. She double-checked to ensure he was thoroughly clean before pulling him from beneath the water; and then lay him carefully onto the towel. With one eye on Brendan, she reached over to turn off the water, "Now, why don't we see to that bottle as soon as we get you all dried off and dressed?"

Surprisingly, he did not protest when she laid him down in his crib to take care of redressing him. It was as if he understood that a bottle was on the way. Either that, or it simply felt good to have a clean nappy on.

"Smart, aren't you?"

"What do you expect? He's my nephew."

Iliamna spun around, and then shook her head with a smile. "It's not very nice to sneak up on folks, you know."

"I know," Shreve smiled. "Looking for this?"

"Ah, how did you know?" Iliamna lifted the baby into her arms and took the bottle from Shreve.

"Carmen waylaid me the moment I entered the kitchen, asked me to bring it to you."

"Thank you," Iliamna replied softly, settling into a rocking chair. As she started to feed the baby, she noticed that Shreve hadn't moved, "So, how old is this little darling?"

"He's nearing six months." Shreve moved to the only other chair in the room and smiled softly at the picture of domesticity they presented. "You're very good with children. I appreciate what you're doing, especially since you don't really have to."

"Yes, I do. Have to."

Shreve's brow knitted in confusion, "I've accused you of being a liar, I plan to go to Louisiana to find evidence that will either exonerate or convict you; I'm making you stay in my home under the guise of being my wife, you've been thrown into a chaotic situation before you've even had a chance to rest and breathe, tending to someone else's child. . . ,"

"And I understand the necessity of it all, truly. If I didn't, I would hardly be going along with it. Besides, I don't mind helping; since it gives me something with which to preoccupy myself," Iliamna interrupted, "and after all, I can't very well be selfish when Carmen is being run ragged and there's a child that needs someone looking out for him. That wouldn't be saying much for my character, now would it?"

Shreve merely smiled and nodded his appreciation.

"So, how is the calf? She and the mother going to be okay?"

Shreve nodded and smiled. "Fortunately, Jeb had the foresight to call the vet immediately."

"Jeb?"

"He's my foreman."

"A foreman that doesn't know how to deliver a calf? Isn't that unusual."

"Considering that we were both attorneys before starting this venture, no, it's not so unusual."

"That in itself is unusual. Two attorneys who resign their profession to start a new career completely alien to them? Very unusual. So why did you two decide to quit practicing law, if I may ask?"

"I was a prosecutor and Jeb was a defense attorney. We were best friends in college and many a time, we found ourselves pitted against the other in a courtroom."

"I don't know about your friend," Iliamna interjected, "but I have not the least bit misgiving that you were a very good prosecutor."

Shreve laughed softly. "I was. The best in Shreveport."

"Louisiana!"

"Yes, ma'am. Born and bred, believe it or not."

"Well, I'll be," Iliamna laughed. "Hey, Shreveport...Shreve...,"

"Fast on the draw, aren't you?"

"And you sister? Her name was Dallas."

"My mother was living in Shreveport when I was born and was in Dallas when my sister was born. Hence our names."

"Well, I guess there are worse ways to name a child than after the city of their birth," Iliamna laughed, "but if you were such a good prosecutor, why leave?"

"I'd been practicing law for nearly ten years, when someone discovered my roots."

"Which are?"

Shreve looked at her strangely. "I've already explained to you that I'm half-Indian, right? From the Choctaw nation."

"Good Lord! Such prejudice, and in this day and age?"

"Well, you need to remember that I'm nearly fifteen years your senior, so prejudice was still prevalent when I was attending college."

"Still, if your heritage was such a thorn in peoples' sides, how did you manage to attend school and practice law for so long without your roots being discovered before? No offense, Shreve, but it's rather difficult not to see your heritage—especially in your features."

"It is?"

Iliamna blushed. "So you were saying?"

"It's a rather complicated story," Shreve said.

Iliamna looked down at the baby, still munching on the bottle. "The baby has a few more ounces to go yet, so I have a bit of time. Unless you need to rush off."

"Not at all. Well, anyway it's not so much complicated as scandalous. You see, my mother was visiting friends near the Choctaw nation in Zwolle, Louisiana. She fell for one of the people and the next thing you know, she's pregnant with me. In about her fourth month, she took deathly ill and ended up housed at the local minister's home for a spell. The wife of the local preacher nursed her back to health; however, when she discovered that my mother was carrying a child, and that child was the spawn of a heathen—her words, not mine—the woman kicked her out of her house, so my mother made her way back to Shreveport. Soon after I was born, she met and married a wonderful man who owned this cattle ranch."

"This very one?"

"Except for the house, obviously."

"Of course, but how did she meet him if she was in Louisiana and he was here in Texas?"

"Well from what mother told me, she answered an ad for a bride. It didn't matter to mother that the man that placed the ad was half-Indian, hence my last name—Red Fox."

"Incredible."

"Anyway, when I got to be seventeen, he sent me east to receive a formal education. The law intrigued me, which is why I studied to become a lawyer."

"Well, apparently those at...which college did you attend?"

"The University of Maryland, why?"

"Well, you said you had difficulty when your heritage was discovered, but if your heritage is apparent, how did you get into University?"

Shreve smiled, "You're very bright." Iliamna blushed again, and Shreve laughed, "Well, one of the attorneys, the Honorable George Dobbin[6] read a paper I'd written as part of the interview process. He liked it so much, that he endorsed my enrollment. I guess that people respected his decision too much to question my heritage, or I hid it well, or I was just such a good student that it was overlooked. I'll never really know."

"I guess not. So then, if your father and mother lived *here*, how did your sister get her name?"

"Oh, that's no great mystery. Dallas was born three weeks prematurely. My father's mother was dying, so he and my mother traveled to Dallas to be with her. Mother delivered while there."

"Goodness."

"Yeah, imagine if she'd been born *here*."

Iliamna laughed, "That would have made for an interesting name, to be sure."

Shreve smiled. "Anyway, after Father passed, Mother moved back to Louisiana to be closer to her father, who was ill. Dallas and I joined her there. Several years ago, the same preacher's wife that

---

[6] Hon. George W. Dobbin, LL.D. was a member of the faculty of law at the University of Maryland, 1888.

nursed my mother was traveling through Shreveport and ran into us on the street. When she discovered who I was, or rather who my mother was, she took offense that a half-breed was succeeding in such a noble profession as the law, any profession, if the truth be told; so she ran to the newspapers to expose me as whatever kind of charlatan she perceived me to be." Shreve shook his head in renewed disbelief. "By the time the media was through with me, I was shut out of practicing law. My mother suffered a stroke and died shortly thereafter."

"Oh, Shreve, I'm so sorry."

"Well, to make a long story short," Shreve shrugged. "My mother never got around to selling this place, so I decided to move back here. Dallas, of course, came with me and soon met and wed a wonderful man, who you probably heard was killed in a stampede. Jeb, fed up with the legal system, asked if he could join me as well. The rest is...well as it is," Shreve said. "We're reading up on cattle ranching and farming, and kind of playing the rest by ear. We've been at it quite a few years now and haven't folded yet, so I guess we're doing something right."

Iliamna smiled. She looked down at the baby, now sleeping in her arms and her smile widened. She looked up at Shreve and placed a fingertip against her lips. Then she stood and carefully laid the sleeping babe into the crib.

She motioned to the door. They both slipped into the hall and Shreve closed the door quietly behind them.

"Unfortunately," Iliamna whispered, "there is a messy diaper in the bathroom that needs tending to, and I do believe I hear Carmen ringing the supper bell. What?"

"I have approximately," Shreve paused to look at his pocket watch, "ten minutes before the wonderful lady standing in front of me turns into a shrew."

Iliamna laughed, "Oh, dear. I guess you'd better pack and hightail it out of here quick."

Shreve smiled, but did not move. He looked at her, and then his gaze traveled to her lips. "Think maybe if I kiss you, I can hold off your transformation for a bit longer?"

Iliamna's eyes widened and she opened her mouth to reply, but nothing came out. Shreve took her face in his hands and moved closer, taking advantage of her stunned acquiescence.

Someone cleared his throat.

Shreve moaned and gave Iliamna a look of longsuffering before turning to face the intruder. "What is it, Jeb?"

"I'm sorry to interrupt, Shreve, ma'am, but there's a sheriff on the doorstep and he's looking for you—and you."

"Sheriff Barkley?"

"That's right."

"Okay, and Jeb," Shreve said, taking Iliamna's hand and leading her towards the front door, "there's a dirty diaper in the bathroom that needs cleaning up. Will you see to it, since we're going to be preoccupied?"

Shreve laughed at the look on Jeb's face, and then leaned over to whisper to Iliamna, "See, I'm a decent fellow. I managed to find someone else to clean up the dirty mess in the bathroom."

"Oh well, in that case, I'll be certain to nominate you for sainthood as soon as I become a Catholic."

# CHAPTER TWENTY-THREE

"Sheriff Barkley? What brings you 'round to my door?" Shreve asked, stepping onto the front porch. One look at the sheriff's demeanor and his own frisky demeanor vanished quickly.

"Hello, son," the sheriff greeted cordially, "Good to see you back, safe and sound." The sheriff dismounted and tossed the reins over the hitching post, and then moved up the steps. He took off his hat and slapped it against his jeans, and then extended a hand.

Shreve shook the older man's hand and motioned to the porch swing, "Have a seat?"

"Sure, why not," the sheriff said, moving around Shreve. He eyed Iliamna curiously. "Afternoon, ma'am."

"Sheriff. Would you like some refreshment?"

"Sounds mighty fine. I'm downright parched. Thank ye kindly."

"It's not a problem. Shreve?"

"No, thank you, Iliamna."

"I like the house. It's a nice improvement over the ramshackle mess that was left deteriorating for those years after your step-dad died."

"Thanks."

"So, is that her?" The sheriff asked abruptly.

"Depends on what you mean," Shreve asked, moving to lean against the railing.

"Well, a funny thing happened," the sheriff said, pulling a folded piece of paper from his shirt pocket. "About an hour ago, I get this here telegram telling me that one of my fine upstanding citizens has committed, not one heinous crime, but quite a few of them." The sheriff leaned forward and handed the telegram to Shreve. "Mind explaining what this is all about, son?"

Shreve quickly scanned the telegram and cursed under his breath. "Damn it, Red."

"Who's Red?" The sheriff asked.

"The person who signed the telegram. Her real name is Bridget Farlton, but her nickname is Red."

"So, am I here to place you under arrest, or what?" The sheriff grinned thinly, far from amused.

"I'd prefer to avoid prison, so I'll take the "or what"," Shreve said as Iliamna returned with lemonade.

"Here you are, Sheriff."

"Thank you, Miss," the sheriff said with a smile, "or is it Missus?"

Iliamna blushed, "Well, uh...."

"We're not married, Tom," Shreve interjected, "yet."

Iliamna's blush intensified, and she lowered her gaze.

"I see," the sheriff said softly. "Well, why don't you two sit and start from the beginning. Then I'll decide what to do about the charges this Bridget Farlton's accusing you of."

"Who's Bridget Farlton?" Iliamna asked, settling on a chair.

"Red," Shreve said, unable to prevent the hostility in his tone.

"Oh," Iliamna said, her hands wringing on her lap.

"Yeah. So, what happened is that I stopped in at Red's place— the Watering Hole saloon. Not too far from Twin Rivers," Shreve started.

"That's pretty far off the beaten path," the sheriff commented.

"Yeah, I know, but I was distracted and...well needed a distraction and the Watering Hole came to mind. I was actually on my way home from Dawson Creek. By the time I reached the saloon, it was too dark to finish the trip; so, like I said, I stopped in and Red offered a room. I knew that Red had a side business...,"

"Which is?" The sheriff asked.

"She runs a brothel."

"Ah, well, not with the consent of the law, she doesn't. The new governor of Texas outlawed that type of business[7], so there's one

---

[7] This is not an historically accurate fact. According to the Texas State Historical Association, prostitution flourished in Texas between the Civil War and WWI, and although communities passed ordinances outlawing the practice, those were widely overlooked, and rarely enforced. At the onset

plus in your favor. Am I to understand that you were a participant in those illicit activities, Miss?" The sheriff asked, addressing Iliamna.

Iliamna blushed again, choking slightly on her lemonade.

"No," Shreve answered in her stead. "Iliamna is my mail-order bride. She was on her way to meet me when an outlaw abducted her and sold her to Red. It's just coincidental that I happened to stop in that same night and found her there."

"Well, that *is* fortunate, isn't it?" The sheriff said with a slight disbelieving edge to his tone.

Shreve looked at Iliamna, "See now why I had a hard time believing you? Even the sheriff finds my part of the story a bit too coincidental. So just imagine then, how hard it was to fathom your side."

Iliamna nodded and lowered her head. Shreve was right, it all seemed too fantastical to be believed.

Shreve dug into his pant pocket and retrieved the drawing. He handed it over to the sheriff, and then pulled over a chair and sat down next to Iliamna, draping his arm along the back of her chair. "It's okay," he whispered in her ear.

"Well, this is a mighty fine drawing, and sure enough a good likeness of you, Missy."

"That's precisely what I thought when I was shown into a room where Iliamna was being held against her will. It's just fortunate that Red chose to give her "new girl" to me instead of to her bouncer, Butcher, first. When Iliamna and I discovered our connection, we decided to try to sneak out early in the morning, before anyone was up. I knew—or at least had heard rumors—that Red didn't hold to men taking off with her women and had killed a man for trying at one time."

"Well, that's another plus in your favor, if we're ever able to prove it."

Shreve nodded and then continued, "When Red caught us trying to leave she held Iliamna at gun point in an attempt to get me to

---

of WWI, the Federal Government cracked down on prostitutes services U.S. soldiers preparing to join the conflict in Europe be protected from prostitutes in order to prevent contraction of venereal disease. Although prostitution on a large scale was finally eradicated, whorehouses remained a staple of Texas communities well into the nineteenth century.

leave without her—which, of course, I wasn't going to do."

"I don't expect you'd want to, no. So then, I'll just add attempted kidnapping to that list in your favor."

Shreve nodded again, and then continued on with his explanation, "I told Red that Iliamna was mine, but she said that I'd have to prove it before she'd release one of her girls, so I showed Red that same drawing," Shreve said, drawing closer to Iliamna. "I could see that she knew—it was written all over her expression—but instead of allowing Iliamna to leave with me, what does she do?"

"You're going to tell me."

"Damn straight! Red has her hired guns attempt to kill me..."

"Attempted murder," the sheriff interjected, jotting another note into his notepad.

"And while I was getting shot at, Butcher and Red lock themselves in a room with Iliamna, with the express intent of raping my woman, because Red was convinced I'd leave if Iliamna were damaged goods! Now, you tell me Tom, what was I supposed to do?"

The sheriff nodded gravely, flipping a page in his notepad. "Seven dead and one wounded," he read. "You did that all by yourself?"

"Yeah. Protecting one's family makes a man a really good shot."

"Yeah, that was definitely some mighty fine shooting."

"I couldn't let them keep Iliamna there. I shudder to think what they would have done to her. And that shooting was purely self defense."

Iliamna had to force herself to remain quiet, not to argue the fact that Shreve had fully intended to leave her there—initially. She held her tongue because he hadn't left her; and while he may not be completely convinced of her innocence, he had finally come to the conclusion that she didn't belong in a whorehouse.

"So, you gonna take me in?"

"Not right now," the sheriff said. "What I'm going to do is fire off a telegram to this Red woman and see if we can head off further problems."

"How so?" Iliamna whispered, still trying to adjust to Shreve's possessive closeness.

"Well, now, I'm simply going to point out that she's engaged in illicit activities, and that fingers are pointing at her regarding some really nasty business, much as she's pointing fingers—and that knowing this, it might just be in her best interest to drop the charges against Shreve here, since it's obvious he was acting in self-defense."

"Sounds good."

"Now what about you two?"

"What do you mean?"

"Well, it isn't exactly proper for you to be living here in sin, now is it?"

"Oh, well," Shreve said, "we're planning to wed...,"

"Then might I suggest you get on with it?"

"Well, I have pressing business out of town, and I'm leaving first thing tomorrow morning. I brought Iliamna here to stay until I return because she has nowhere else to go."

"I see," the sheriff said softly. "First thing in the morning, you say?"

"That's right, Tom."

"And you give me your word, as a gentleman, that you'll treat this lady with the respect she deserves until that time?"

"You have my word, Tom."

"How long you planning on being away," the sheriff asked grinning, "just in case I need to be arresting your breed backside."

Shreve huffed. "A couple of weeks tops."

"Tops, huh?" Iliamna murmured softly. "You said you'd be leaving here in an hour tops, but that didn't happen."

"Shrew," Shreve whispered in her ear.

"Well, I guess I'll be leaving you two be for now," the sheriff said. Shreve stood and shook the sheriff's hand. "I hope I get an invitation to the wedding."

"Most certainly. Thanks for coming by to let me know what's happening, Tom. I appreciate it."

"Least I could do," the sheriff replied and jammed his hat on his head. He tipped his hat to Iliamna. "Ma'am, it was a pleasure to make your acquaintance."

"Likewise, Sheriff."

"You folks have a good evening, ya hear?"

"Will do."

Shreve sighed as the sheriff rode out of sight. He turned, plopping back on the chair next to Iliamna. "I'm glad that man likes me," he said, half in jest.

"That is a good thing," Iliamna said. "So, I guess we were wrong in our assumption about what Red would do."

"So it would seem. Looks as if she was more upset over losing you than even I figured she'd be. Just goes to prove how special you really are."

"Shreve?"

"Yes, Iliamna?" Shreve asked, placing his arm along the back of her chair again.

"Why did you tell the sheriff that we're planning to wed? More prevaricating?"

Shreve did not answer right away. He pulled his arm from behind her and leaned his elbows onto his thighs. "I don't rightly know. Does it bother you?"

"A little, yes."

"Why?"

"Because we're not, that's why?"

"I'm not so sure anymore, Iliamna," Shreve said softly. "I mean, you've made a good impression on me, and Carmen and Jeb, and, of course, our local lawman. You're good with Brendan too, and I'll admit I've grown rather fond of you."

"But you still don't believe me, or have you suddenly changed your mind about going to Louisiana?"

"No, I haven't changed my mind."

"Because the lawyer in you still has unanswered questions about me," Iliamna supplied, "despite the impression I've made."

Shreve merely nodded. "Don't you see that I couldn't marry you with doubts hanging over my head? I wish I didn't have such a suspicious nature, but I do. I don't trust very easily, I'm afraid."

"And I've already said that there cannot be a marriage without a foundation of trust."

"I could always hire you to work for me, until we work this crazy mess out," Shreve teased, but the look in Iliamna's eyes said that she was past teasing.

"Don't do that, Shreve. Not now."

"You're right. I'm sorry."

"So am I, believe it or not. We better go into dinner now. Carmen probably gave up on us long ago."

Iliamna made to stand, but Shreve reached up and pulled her back down beside him.

"Carmen is used to me showing up late for dinner. Besides, if I have to say goodbye to you, then I'd just as soon do it right now," he said, and captured her mouth with his.

Iliamna did not bother to struggle since she couldn't have prevented his kissing her even if she wanted to, which she didn't. If the memory of his kiss was all she returned to Louisiana with, then it would be worth it. She moved her hand up and placed it against his broad chest, leaning against him with a sigh.

Shreve smiled against her lips, "Does this mean I can kiss you?"

Iliamna's eyes fluttered open, "I thought you were".

"No, sweetheart," Shreve laughed softly, "that was just a prelude. Want the symphonic version?"

"Does it include bells, because I'm definitely hearing ringing in my ears," Iliamna grinned.

"Without a doubt."

"Hmm," Iliamna moaned just as Shreve covered her mouth once again. His tongue pressed against her closed lips, but her inexperience was working against her. She did not know what he expected her to do.

When she was about to say something about it, Shreve took advantage of her slightly parted lips and slipped his tongue inside. Iliamna didn't have a first clue about lovemaking, but she did like the feeling he evoked. She leaned closer, running her hand up and around to the back of his neck, entwining her fingers in his medium-length coal-black hair.

Shreve leaned over, slid one arm behind her back and the other beneath her legs and lifted her over the arms of the chairs and onto his lap, and then pulled her in tighter. His hand moved its way up her back, caressing each curve in her spine, and on up until his hand encountered the skin beneath her hairline. He stroked her warm flesh briefly, and then with deftness, pulled the pins from her hair until it tumbled free of its confines.

Just then, the baby started screaming and they reluctantly pulled apart.

"I'll get the little darling," Carmen called from the parlor. Shreve smiled mischievously and Iliamna blushed.

She drew back and sighed. "Thank you for that, Shreve."

"Oh, it was, without a doubt, equally pleasurable for me, ma'am. Of course, we don't have to stop, do we?"

"Yes, we do," Iliamna sighed. "I'd better go see to Brendan."

"Carmen has him, or didn't you hear her say so past the ringing in your ears."

"Oh, it's a full-blown symphony now," Iliamna smiled, but it did not reach the sadness in her eyes. "Be careful on your trip to Louisiana, Shreve. I'll stay put until you get back," Iliamna sighed, "but when you do, I'd appreciate it if you could put me on a train headed back east."

"After that kiss, you still think there's nothing between us? Nothing worth staying for?" Shreve asked as Iliamna pushed off his lap and headed for the house.

"Despite how you make me feel, no, there isn't anything; and there certainly isn't any reason for me to remain here in Texas. This isn't my home." Iliamna shot over her shoulder. "Did that kiss change anything for you? Did it make you suddenly see that I'm innocent? Did it change your mind about going to Louisiana?"

"No. I still plan to go. So, if you leave, what are you going to do back east?" Shreve asked in the hopes of bringing her back to sit with him.

Iliamna paused at the door and turned to look at the handsome half-breed, leaning forward in anticipation. Her heart ached to return to him, to sit next to him and let him wrap his arms around her, let him hold her close and kiss away her doubts and fears; but allowing him to do so would be condoning the lies and the mistrust. It would tell him that it was okay if he wanted to doubt who she was, but it was not okay. She was a good person, being manipulated by an evil witch, but instead of seeing her as the person she was, he was allowing doubt to blind him.

"I'm going to live a life free of lies and deceit, that's what," she said, her chin raising a notch.

"You have no one there to watch over you," Shreve argued, moving to stand next to her. "You're alone in the world, and if you think that it would be safe for you to travel to Louisiana alone and work and live there without problems, then you are deceiving yourself. You'll end up back in another whorehouse."

"Then maybe I'll answer my own mail-order advertisement, and find a husband to look after me. One who doesn't question my integrity," Iliamna retorted, and then opened the screen door and went inside. She made it only halfway across the foyer when a hand snaked out and yanked her around.

"I'll be damned if you are going to sit out there with me, kissing me the way you did and then turn around and give what belongs to me to another man," Shreve said softly, dangerously.

"What belongs to you?" Iliamna snapped. "Do you hear yourself, Shreve Red Fox? Do you? One kiss does not brand me your woman, but even if you believe that, really believe that, I would never belong to a man whose trust in me is more shallow than...well, like that little stream bordering your property! Never!"

Shreve sighed, his anger dying quickly. He ran his fingers through his hair and looked at the tile floor, "You're right. There's got to be a way to fix this crazy mess."

"There is," Iliamna said softly, placing a hand on his bronzed face, forcing him to look at her. "Forget Louisiana, and believe me."

Shreve reached up and pulled her hand away, holding it tightly, "Why can't you simply admit that you're the woman I corresponded with and drop the ruse. I'll work out a deal with the district attorney, something."

"Because that would definitely be a lie," she said with a sigh, "I guess there isn't any way to fix this after all." Iliamna pulled her hand away. "But let's just say that I admitted that I was that woman, what then Shreve? Will you call the sheriff back here and throw me in jail? How does that solve anything?"

Shreve ran a hand through his hair again, suddenly feeling very weary, "The deception I could probably forgive, but I can't allow you to get away with larceny."

"Oh Shreve, how many different ways do I have to tell you that I'm not..." Iliamna stopped, and lowered her head, shaking it slowly in frustration.

Shreve sighed heavily, "Go lie down and rest. We'll work this out when we're not so tired. I'll have Carmen put our dinner aside. We can eat it later."

"That's probably for the best," Iliamna said, turning and starting up the staircase. She turned when she was halfway and was startled to see that Shreve was still standing there, watching her.

"The master bedroom is the last door on the left," he said softly, indicating the location with a nod of his head.

Iliamna nodded, "Thank you, but I wasn't...do you think it would be possible to locate some clothes, just something to put on so that I could take a bath? I feel so dirty right now."

Shreve looked over her Mexican-made attire with admiration, having completely overlooked the fact that she had three days worth of dust and grime coating her hair and skin. Few women looked as good as she did—dressed or not, dirty or not. When his gaze traveled back to her face, he saw that his perusal was making her blush. He smiled and she lowered her gaze.

"I'll have Jeb drive you into town first thing in the morning to buy you some clothing. I'm just ashamed that your need didn't register," Shreve said, moving toward her. "In the meantime, you take a bath. I'll find something for you to wear."

"Thank you, Shreve," Iliamna said softly when he stopped in front of her. Her gaze remained pinned to the cherry-colored hardwood step.

Shreve brushed the back of his hand along her cheek, "I'm sorry that I am the way I am," he whispered. "I wish that I wasn't."

Iliamna nodded slightly, but could not find her voice.

"Maybe one of these days, you'll be able to forgive me?" He asked. When she did not respond, he moved his hand beneath her chin and forced her to look up. He was surprised to see her eyes closed tight and tears rolling slowly from the sides.

"Please don't cry, darling," he whispered, the pad of his thumb brushing at a runaway tear. "I promise we'll work this all out. Can you believe me?"

Iliamna sniffled softly and tried to nod, but Shreve's hand was still beneath her chin, "Why does this have to be so hard?"

"Life is hard, Iliamna, but you haven't been alive long enough to face too many of them, like I have. In fact, I'd wager you've faced more in the last few months than in your entire life," he whispered, brushing another tear away.

"I love it when you say my name," Iliamna whispered impulsively.

"Look at me, Iliamna," Shreve demanded softly, but Iliamna shook her head.

"I can't," she whispered, her tone agonized. "I can't, Shreve. If I do, I just know I'll be lost."

"I'm lost already," he said, moving his hand to her nape and pulling her mouth into contact with his. She did not need instruction this time. She clasped his sleeves to remain on an even keel and kissed him with all of her inexperienced might.

Shreve's hand moved from her nape to join the other in an exploration of her back, lovingly stroking each line and curve, from shoulder to hip, the curve of her side to the gentle curve of her breast. His hands roamed, missing nothing, while his tongue joined hers in desperate need.

His mind shouted at him to slow down, to savor and enjoy what time he had, for he didn't know whether he'd be able to hold her, love her after tomorrow. With difficulty, he obeyed the insistence of his mind.

Iliamna slid her hands from his broad shoulders around the back of his neck and entwined her fingers through his hair, a moan of

Barbara Woster

desire escaping when he slid his lips from hers to plant a kiss on the concave at the base of her throat. He pulled her tighter against him, leaning into her until her back arched, and then slowly traced his tongue along the top of her breasts.

Iliamna gasped and held on for dear life, her breath coming in short gasps.

Shreve wrapped an arm around her lower back to prevent her from falling, and then brought his free hand up to stroke the side of her breast through the thin cottony fabric of her blouse.

The sound of someone clearing her throat did not immediately register, but the tap on his shoulder startled Shreve sufficiently that he released Iliamna suddenly. She squealed and landed with a thud on the step.

Shreve turned, stepping in front of Iliamna to shield her. He could only imagine the horror and humiliation she was feeling at being caught groping each other on the stairwell.

"Carmen," Shreve said. He straightened his shirt and hair, trying to get his anger in check at being interrupted. "What are you doing going around sneaking up on folks?"

"Sorry, Shreve," Carmen said, a knowing grin on her face. "I did try to get your attention, but neither of you seemed able to hear."

"Well, what do you need?" He snapped.

Carmen responded in her typically blunt manner, "I *need* you to take yourselves to your room, since I don't *need* to be witnessing your *need* for each other, nor does anyone else who happens to wander into the house."

"Anything else?" Shreve said, just as Iliamna bolted upright and ran for the bedroom. "Great! Did you have to embarrass her like that?"

"Me?" Carmen asked, not the least bit offended. "I'm not the one who decided the stairwell was a good place to make his desire known."

Shreve sighed, "I know I was wrong, but you could have left us be, you know."

"For someone else to come in and interrupt you?" Carmen asked, laughing. "Or did you expect me to politely walk around and

123

lock all of the doors in the house."

"For heaven's sakes above, woman," Shreve nearly yelled, "we haven't even had our honeymoon yet, so a little courtesy and understanding might be nice."

"Oh, I understand what a powerful need is, but that doesn't give you the right to humiliate your new bride the way you did. Perhaps if you'd told me in advance, I could have sold tickets...,"

"Enough!" Shreve yelled. "Enough," he repeated on a sigh.

"Why don't you go upstairs and apologize," Carmen said softly.

"Apologize for what?" Shreve asked, running his fingers through his hair.

Carmen looked at him and shook her head, "Sometimes..." she huffed, and then stopped. "If you want a honeymoon, boy, you'd better apologize whether you think you need to or not," she concluded, starting back down the steps. "I'll see to it that you're not disturbed the rest of the evening—that is, if you can get her to let you in the room. And I'll put something aside for you two for whenever you get hungry for food."

Shreve watched his housekeeper leave, her head still shaking in bemusement, and then he turned his gaze toward the master bedroom door—firmly shut. Would she let him in the room? If she did, what would he do about it—continue where he left off? Would she let him near her again?

There was only one way to find out. He took the remaining stairs, two at a time. When he reached the bedroom door, he tried the knob. As he suspected, she'd locked him out. He popped the tension from his neck before lifting a hand and knocking softly.

"Go away, Shreve." The response was immediate.

"Let me in, Iliamna," Shreve replied, "we need to talk."

"I can't handle your form of conversing", Iliamna answered bluntly. "Not right now."

"I'm sorry about what happened," Shreve said, hoping that Carmen's suggestion would help her decide to unbolt the door, but he didn't hear anything on the other side to indicate her willingness to allow him entry.

"Go to Louisiana, Shreve," Iliamna said, and he could hear the tears in her voice. She was still crying. "Just go."

"Will you still be here when I get back?" He asked, damning himself to hell and back for making her feel so distraught and being unable to do anything to help her through it.

"I gave you my word," she whispered, her voice coming from just the other side of the panel. He closed his eyes and pictured her leaning against the door, her own eyes closed, tears falling freely down her cheeks. Another piece of his heart splintered.

"I'll be back in a few weeks," he said, placing his palm against the door, "will you be okay until I get back?"

"I'll be better once you leave," she answered. "I can't think when you're so close."

"That's supposed to be a good thing," he replied in an attempt at shifting her mood. She did not reply. Their conversation was over.

He turned and with leaden steps, made his way to the barn. He had planned to leave in the morning, but knew he could not stay in the same house with Iliamna any more than she could stay with him. He wanted her too much.

After quick instructions to Jeb, he mounted his other stallion, Star Runner, and galloped away, not bothering to pack—clothes or supplies; not bothering to look back. If he looked back, he knew he would return to the house and forget about Louisiana, but he could not forget. He had to satisfy himself that she was real, that she was not just playing him. He loved her, he could not deny that now, but if she was a fraud, he'd have to bury that love. He had to know.

# CHAPTER TWENTY-FOUR

Alana stretched the kinks from her legs and back, and then popped her neck before settling her bonnet on her head and tying the laces beneath her chin. She moved down the aisle toward the exit eager to escape the confines of her cabin. This was not a scheduled stop, so she would not have a good deal of time, but she wanted to see if there was a telegraph office nearby so that could wire Shreve and let him know she was on the way.

In hindsight, she wished she had sent the telegram before leaving, but was hesitant to let him know she was coming to join him until she was well on her way. She was not certain why she was cautious; after all, he'd sent the fare and knew she'd be joining him— soon. But for some odd reason, she had a terrible sense that if she wired him ahead of time, he'd reject her now. Maybe because she'd turned him away so many times; given too many excuses.

Now, however, the excuses were finished. She was finished. Now that Iliamna was gone, she was ready to make a life of her own; a life of her own choosing. And this Shreve fellow was just the one she was interested in making it with. After all, he had built her a home, which meant he was at least well off financially, and then there was always his heritage.

Being a half-breed, he was more likely to accept her shortcomings with grace—knowing what it feels like to be rejected, or simply because he would know that she would be one of the few women who would actually have him. He was a handsome man, if the picture he sent was a genuine likeness; but handsome or not, he wouldn't be advertising for a bride, if there was someone willing to marry him, which gave her hope that he'd overlook her flaws.

She stood at the head of the steps and raised a hand to shade her eyes against the noonday sun. Perhaps she should have chosen a hat instead of this bonnet, she mused. Or maybe she'd best return and retrieve her parasol before continuing. The sun was nearly unbearably bright and so very hot. A bonnet seemed ill suited. Still, she only intended to be off the train for a moment. She spotted the conductor moving along the track in her direction and waved him over, "Sir!" She called, and wondered why he covered his ears. She saw him glance in her direction and quickly pull his hands away from his ears before closing the distance.

"Sorry, Miss, did you call me?" He asked, and then had to fight the urge to cover his ears again when she answered him.

"Yes," Alana said. "I was wondering if there was a telegraph office nearby. I need to wire my fiancé and tell him that I'll be arriving soon."

"Fiancé?" The conductor said, and then cleared his throat. "Um, no, Miss, we've been stopped short, in between towns."

"When will get to Texas?" She asked, wiping the perspiration from her forehead.

"Why, we're already in Texas, Miss. You left from Shreveport, which is only about an hour from the Texas border," the conductor answered, wishing that she'd stop finding ways to keep conversing with him and delay his departure. "In point of fact, we were due to arrive in Dawson Creek this evening, but bandits have blown up the track up ahead, so we have to hold over here a few days and wait for repairs."

"Oh, my! We're not in any danger...,"

"Not at all, Miss," the conductor interrupted, not wishing to hear her speak any more than was necessary. "Um, if your fiancé was scheduled to meet you in Dawson Creek, I can assure you that anyone awaiting passengers will be notified of our delay."

"No, it's not that," Alana said, scanning the horizon distractedly, "it's...well, he doesn't exactly know that I'm arriving. It's kind of a surprise."

*Oh! you'll be a surprise alright! Poor man.* To Alana he said, "If you want to write out a note, I'll have one of the porters ride ahead to Dawson Creek and deliver it to the station master there. The station master may be able to send a delivery man on ahead to your fiancé to let him know of your pending arrival. I'm afraid that's the best I can do at this point."

"Oh! That's so very kind...,"

"Think nothing of it, Miss," the conductor interrupted. "The porter was going to leave shortly anyway, to inform the station master of the track damage. By the time we arrive in Dawson Creek, your man should know that we're on our way, now," he continued before she could utter another thanks, "I have to see to the other passengers. I'll send Gerald Davies over to collect your note. Good day to you, Miss," he said, tipped his hat, and walked away as quickly as he dared without actually running.

"Sweet man," Alana whispered, "if not a bit abrupt in his manner. I didn't even have the opportunity to let him know I hadn't any writing implements." She turned and made her way back to her cabin, entered and settled next to the window. She left the door open in anticipation of the porter's arrival, and then drifted off in thought.

She was not exactly certain what she was going to say in her letter and even less certain what she was going to say when Shreve discovered that she looked nothing like her cousin's likeness. Of course, she could always say that she simply took liberties with her appearance for fear he would reject her. Play on the sympathies of a gentleman to a lady. Of course, she was not precisely ladylike, but he needn't know that small detail about her personality.

Or perhaps, if he made mention of her looks, she could simply point out that he was no fine catch himself, being a near-elderly half-breed, if he'd inform her of his true age, and that both should be thankful to wed at all. A better alternative to being single, for certain.

What she did not want to happen, and the true fear she held, was that he would send her packing on the first train heading east, should he decide her deception was unacceptable. If that were to happen, she would have nowhere to go.

She had left her father's home in a huff with her mother yelling at her back, never to show her face in their house again. She had not truly considered herself the ungrateful child her mother accused her of, simply had not wished to wait the year or two more that her mother insisted was necessary before finances permitted finding her husband, and Alana had not missed her murmurings about not wanting to waste money on a lost cause. Her mother also readily pointed out that she'd had ample opportunity to locate a husband at the ball thrown for Iliamna, and that it wasn't anyone's fault but her own that she'd failed to do so, so couldn't fathom why she'd be expected to throw another ball at great expense that was just as likely to produce equal results.

The fight with her mother and her lack of husband prospects was another reason to hate Iliamna. Of course, if she was a rational person, she'd understand that her lack of prospects had nothing to do with Iliamna. That she would have had the fight with her mother and failed to find a husband, whether Iliamna had shown up at their home or not. It was just easier for Alana to assign blame rather than to accept that she simply was not attractive to the opposite sex; however, her mother wasn't shy about pointing out that fact, which made Alana want to kill her. Instead, she chose to leave; to marry Shreve; to prove that her mother was wrong; to prove she was capable of finding a husband on her own—now that Iliamna wasn't a distraction.

Fortunately, she had not the need to rely on her family's support, since she had acquired enough money to pay for her trip to Texas, but her mother had been incensed at the suggestion that she was planning to leave and wed a stranger, sight unseen. The fight had turned even uglier than when it started, but Alana was not to be deterred.

Perhaps destroying the path to her past had not been the wisest course; however, her mother simply was too put out with Iliamna's disappearance—and over her own complaints regarding the lack of resources with which to find her own husband—to listen to reason, so Alana had left without their blessing.

And now, should Shreve determine that she was not to be his wife...well, it was a risk she had taken the moment she began her correspondence with the man. A risk she took with each gentleman she sent a picture and letter to. Still, she might be able to persuade one of the other gentlemen of her worth should Shreve reject her outright. For now, however, she could only hold out hope that her money would sustain her until she found a husband among her many corresponding admirers. She simply couldn't think beyond that point. Not right now.

A knock brought her back from her musings, and she turned to find the porter standing in her doorway, wide-eyed.

"Is anything amiss, sir?" She asked. When he cringed, her brow knitted in confusion.

"Um, not at all, Miss, um," the porter stammered, "the, um, conductor said I needed to collect a missive from you...,"

"Yes, only I haven't any writing...,"

"If you'll follow me, Miss, I'll see to it that you get paper and pen straightaway," the porter said, and then turned and started down the corridor.

Alana, confused by the brusqueness of the entire train staff, leapt to her feet and quickly followed. She was not certain if the bandit's attack had left everyone feeling tense and hurried, but she planned on informing their employer at the first opportunity of their harried manner. It really made for a less enjoyable journey.

"In here, Miss," the porter said, opening the door to the dining area. "If you'll settle at one of the tables, I'll retrieve what you need and return them to you quickly, and if you could see fit to pen your note hurriedly it would be appreciated, as I need to be underway before dark. It's quite a long ride to Dawson Creek."

Without waiting for a reply, the porter turned and left the dining facility, leaving Alana standing in the doorway. She was glad the place was empty or she would have had to complain immediately for placing her in an embarrassing situation. After all, a gentleman simply did not abandon a female before seeing her settled. It just was not done.

She had just taken a seat when the porter placed a sheet of paper and a fountain pen before her. He turned to leave, but Alana halted his departure.

"Sir, I must protest your questionable behavior," she said, and saw his shoulders tense. "You have been extremely rude in your attentions to my needs and I feel that I may have to report you to your superiors."

The porter turned and pasted a smile on his face, "I do apologize, Miss," he said, trying to keep the strain of listening to her speak from creeping into his voice. "I guess we're all just a bit nervous at the moment with the train being stationary in a rather seedy part of the country. And since I need to be leaving as soon as possible in order to get to Dawson Creek before nightfall, I guess my urgency simply got the better of me. I do beg pardon and hope that you'll forgive my behavior."

Alana sighed, "Oh, very well, I'll forgive you if you'll fetch me a drink while I pen my note."

"As you wish, Miss," the porter said and turned toward the bar. Alana sighed because he'd not even requested what type of drink she wanted. Bandit or not, she would simply have to report his manner. First however, she needed to pen her note to Shreve. She placed the pen against her mouth in thought for a minute and then started to write.

*My Dearest Shreve,*

*I must beg pardon for not being on the earlier train, but my mother had a temporary relapse and only just recovered. I hope you will forgive my delay in joining you and know that I am eager to arrive and to finally meet you, my intended.*

*I had hoped to*

"Um, Miss," the porter said, halting her progress. "I hate to say this, but could you keep your letter very brief. I really must be on my way. Have to report the damage to the tracks and all. I'm sure you understand."

"Oh, dear, I forgot...oh, well."

The porter laid a glass of water in front of her, and then settled at the next table. Alana looked at the water and her brow knitted. Definitely needed to report him. He could have at least considered a lemonade or something tastier. She sighed, and placed the pen against her lips again, re-reading what she'd written thus far. With another sigh, she scratched out the last sentence she'd started, and then quickly finalized her letter.


*My Dearest Shreve,*

*I must beg pardon for not being on the earlier train, but my mother had a temporary relapse and only just recovered. I hope you will forgive my delay in joining you and know that I am eager to arrive and to finally meet you, my intended.*

*I had hoped to There has been damage done to the train tracks, so my arrival in Dawson Creek will be delayed several days. Hopefully, this note will reach you before I arrive and you can meet me upon my arrival.*

DESIRES OF A DECEIVER

*Sincerest regards,*

*Oh dear,* she thought, *do I continue to sign it Iliamna, or should I attempt to sign it Alana and just hope he doesn't notice the difference. They sound similar after all.* In the end, she decided not to sign her name at all. He would, after all, know from whom it originated without the name.

"Okay, ready," she said, folding the paper and handing it over to the porter. She turned to pull some change from her reticule, but when she turned to thank and tip him, he was gone.

# CHAPTER TWENTY-FIVE

"I can't believe that sheriff is siding with that no-account half-breed nobody," Red snapped, re-reading the telegram that she'd just collected. The telegraph officer snickered and she turned on him. "You got something to say, Frank, because if you do I can cut you off from my place...,"

"Not at all, Red," he said, and then fell silent when the door opened. "Help you, mister?"

"Yes," the porter said, pulling the note from his breast pocket. "I need to get this letter to a Mr. Shreve Red Fox, and inform the station master of some damage done to the tracks, but I can't seem to locate him—the station master, that is. Do you know where I can find him?"

The telegraph operator flicked open his pocket watch, "It's shortly after noonday, so he's probably at Marge's place eating lunch. Damage to the tracks you say? No one hurt, I hope?"

"No, but bandits tore the tracks up but good, and it's going to take some time to repair 'em. I'm to send repairmen out."

"If it's not too far out," Red offered, "you may be able to send out buggies to transport the passengers to and from..."

"No ma'am, it's a couple hours east. The passengers will just have to wait it out. If you'll excuse me now, I really need to see the station master, and then find lodging for the night."

"Um, excuse me," Red hedged, stalling the porter yet again.

The porter sighed heavily, but politely turned around, "Yes, ma'am?"

"You said you have a letter for Mr. Shreve Red Fox? May I inquire who the letter is from?" Red asked, batting her eyelashes seductively.

The porter blushed, "I'm sorry, Miss, but that's personal...,"

"You know, mister," Red purred, "I just happen to be the owner of the Watering Hole Saloon, a couple hours ride west of here. I know it doesn't seem like an appealing option, since you're already in Dawson Creek, but I can offer you something that can't be found here."

"Ma'am?"

"Let's just say that the *extras* that come with Miss Red's rooms ain't available here in Dawson Creek. Leastways, not anymore."

"You mean..."

"Precisely," Red purred. "And all you need to enjoy my special accommodations, on the house of course, is to let me have a peek at that letter that you're sending up to Shreve. He just happens to be a good friend of mine."

"Oh, well," the porter said, clearing his throat, "it's, um, from his fiancé. She's just letting him know that she'll be arriving in Dawson Creek a few days late, since, as I said, the train's delayed."

"His fiancé? But I thought he'd already collected her," Red said thoughtfully. "Does this fiancé have a name?"

"I'm sure she does," the porter said, opening the paper. "A rather young lady, by the looks of her, by the name of...um...well it appears that she didn't sign it."

"That's ok," Red said. "it's not really important. What is important," she murmured to herself, "is that if his fiancé is on that train, then the woman he stole from me couldn't possibly have been his. Could have been related somehow though," Red said, thoughtfully, "since there's no getting around the similarities in that drawing."

"You mean, there are *two* women what look like this one?" The porter said, dumbfounded. "Why would he want to steal *her*?"

Red laughed politely, uncertain as to the porter's tone of disgust. *Perhaps his preferences lean toward the male persuasion,* she thought. *Well, no matter,* "I certainly appreciate your letting me know. I'll let you get along. As soon as you finish your business with the station master, head over to the saloon. Due west out of town. Can't miss it. Just tell the man at the bar that Red sent you. He'll see to it you're well taken care of. If you ride hard, you should get there before dark."

"Thank you, ma'am."

"Think nothing of it," Red said, as they both stepped from the telegraph office.

The porter tipped his hat, and then mounted, spurring his horse down the street toward the only restaurant in town. Red flipped open her parasol, twirling it thoughtfully as she headed toward her buggy. "So", she started her one-sided conversation, "the woman Shreve took from me must have been the other woman's twin sister or some such. Fancy that. Wait until the sheriff hears that Shreve committed a crime after all. Still and all, if I stir up any more waters, I'm the one likely to get drowned; especially if that uppity sheriff takes a notion to investigate Shreve's allegations about my running a whorehouse. And I couldn't very well accuse him of kidnapping because the woman in question would simply deny it. And if I bring up the fact that he shot my men, I'd have to shut down a very lucrative business, even if temporarily, just to try to put his hide in jail. No, there's got to be a better way to repay Shreve for the damage he caused me. The no-good, half-breed, backstabbing ex-friend. Nobody crosses Red and escapes unscathed. Especially not when I treated him like family. Maybe I'll just stay a week longer here in Dawson Creek and inform the woman arriving on the train that her fiancé is busy preparing to start a life with another woman. If she truly cares, perhaps she'd be willing to join forces with me. Perhaps the two of us can devise a plan to make Mr. Red Fox suffer plenty." Red boarded her carriage and slapped the whip in the air, jarring the horses into a trot. "First, I'd better tell the porter to let Butcher know of my delay."

# CHAPTER TWENTY-SIX

Iliamna was falling. There was no other way to describe it. The sensations swirling around her daily that began to engulf her on day one, now, a week and half later, had nearly overtaken her. She had been walking steadily toward the cliffs, had reached the precipice, and was inches from falling head first over the edge. Falling irrevocably in love with little Brendan.

"Good morning, little darling," she whispered, unpinning the boy's diaper. "And how is my precious sweetie this fine day." She laughed when the baby gurgled and giggled. She tickled the little tummy and fell a little more when he cackled happily, not that she had much further *to* fall. Head over heels into an abyss was the only direction left.

She pinned a fresh diaper on his bottom, and then hefted him into her arms, "Ready for breakfast, my little darling?" She asked, heading for the kitchen. "Good morning, Carmen," she called as she entered the elder lady's domain.

"Good morning, my dear," Carmen said, without pausing in her breakfast preparations. "How are you and little Brendan this fine morning?"

"Hungry," Iliamna said, retrieving a prepped bottle from the icebox and popping it into a pre-heated pan of water to warm.

"Well, there's nothing new in that, now is there," Carmen laughed. "Honestly, girl, you'd think you never ate before coming here."

"Not for a couple of months, at least," Iliamna said, taking a deep, happy breath.

"Why ever not, girl?" Carmen asked. "Good morning, Karan," Carmen greeted the new housekeeper as she pushed through the door, stifling a huge yawn.

"Good morning to you all," Karan said, plopping onto a kitchen chair.

"Good morning, Karan," Iliamna said. She pulled the bottle from the hot water, tested it on her wrist, and then settled on her own chair to begin feeding Brendan.

"Good morning, Mistress," Karan said, suddenly alert. "What can I help with, Carmen?" she asked, eager to make a positive impression on the lady of the house.

"Just jump in where you see a need."

Karan stood up, stifled another yawn, and started a pot of coffee, before hauling some bacon out for frying.

"So, why haven't you eaten the past couple of months, Iliamna?" Carmen asked, resuming her earlier conversation with Iliamna.

"Haven't eaten!" Karan exclaimed. "Dear heavens, Mrs. Fox. How could you not have eaten and still be alive, not to mention looking so radiant."

"Well, she looks radiant because she's only recently married," Carmen said.

"Um, I didn't really starve," Iliamna explained quickly, "I merely had a hard time eating when I was wearing a corset, which in my aunt's home was very nearly twenty-four hours a day. Here, however, I feel free again as I did in my parents' country home. I never wore a corset there."

"Well, out here, you needn't worry about them," Carmen said. "Damned inconvenient contraptions considering the amount of work to be done here every day. Even if we did happen to entertain a neighbor, chances are they'd come straightaway from working in their own home and fields."

"Well, it's a blessed relief," Iliamna said. "Brendan's finished his meal, so I'll go and let the hands know that breakfast is nearly served. I'm sure they're eager to get in here and eat."

"Thanks, dear," Carmen said. "It'll be ready by the time they all haul their hardworking backsides in here."

Iliamna laughed, placed a cloth on her shoulder, and lifted Brendan up to burp, and then she headed outside. It was only half past six in the morning, but she knew that to collect all of the hands, she'd have to make a long walk around the property, as every man here was up a good hour prior, tending to the daily running of the ranch.

She did not mind the long walk as it afforded her time alone with Brendan, and a chance to breathe in the fresh morning air. It was, without a doubt, spectacular, and as with Brendan, she was steadily falling in love with this place, the people...

She sighed.

A week and half, and she was starting to think of this place as home, the people as family. That, alone, was playing havoc with her happiness.

How, she wondered, was she supposed to leave when Shreve returned? She didn't have one whit of worry that his journey would exonerate her, but she also knew that she could never stay and marry him, despite how she felt about him, despite how he made her feel.

Marriage between a man and a woman needed a strong foundation; a foundation of love as well as trust. It was the one thing her mother made certain she understood—that marriage should never solely be one of convenience, should never have a foundation of mutual attraction alone. Marriages built upon those foundations alone would topple with the first storm. Unfortunately, should she marry Shreve, their foundation would be missing half of the requirements for a stable beginning.

She sighed again.

"Good morning, Mrs. Red Fox," a cowhand shouted, as she rounded the barn.

"Good morning to you too, Steve, isn't it?" Iliamna said.

"Close, it's Stan," he said, his smile widening. "But don't worry about it, ma'am, you've only been here a short while. You'll sort us all out eventual-like."

"Thanks, Stan. Carmen has breakfast finishing up, if you want to go on ahead and wash up."

"Want I should go on up to the north pasture and fetch the rest of the men?"

"You ask that nearly every morning, Stan, and I always say no," Iliamna laughed.

"I know, ma'am, but I wouldn't be much of a gentleman if I didn't at least offer."

"Duly noted, and thank you, but as usual, I'll take care of it. I enjoy the walk. Of course, there may be a day when you'll need to do so, so I guess asking is a good thing."

"I expect there might, and I can certainly understand the joy of walking," Stan said, lowering his pitchfork. "I'll see ya at breakfast then."

"Let Carmen know we'll be along presently."

"Will do," Stan said, moving over to the wash barrel. "And you be careful where you're walking on your way up."

"That's another thing you always remind me of," Iliamna said, starting away.

"And I'll keep doing it," Stan called out as she turned up the hill, "you can bet your sweet potato pie on that one."

Iliamna laughed and, being careful to watch her footing, made her way over to the north pasture, singing softly to the baby.

She wondered where Shreve was at this moment. Was he already in Louisiana, checking out her story? Would he return soon?

She sighed.

She so wanted him to come back, but her reasons were mixed, confused. She wanted to see his handsome face again but at the same time, she needed to leave before she became so attached to everyone and everything around her. And she was quickly approaching that last threshold. The first hurdle, however...,

Shreve.

He was so handsome and sexy and strong and virile—and mistrustful.

He was everything she ever dreamed of in a mate—hard working, attentive, considerate, pleasing to the eye and senses, yet at the same time he was stubborn, prideful, suspicious...

"Well, you aren't exactly Miss Perfect, you know," she said aloud to herself.

"You speaking to someone specific, ma'am?" Judson asked, grinning, "Because if you want an opinion on that last statement, you're about as perfect as a woman can get without having wings. And Shreve is about the luckiest man 'round these parts."

Iliamna blushed, "That's very sweet of you to say...um...,"

"Judson, ma'am," he said, tipping his hat.

"Right. Judson."

Judson grinned, "I take it breakfast is ready?"

"That's right, Judson. Carmen sent me to fetch you boys."

"I'll collect the men. You take the baby on back to the house afore he catches himself a chill."

"It's hardly cold out here," Iliamna laughed.

"Maybe not, but it sure is damp," Judson said, seriously.

"Very well." Iliamna turned her back so he wouldn't think she was laughing over his concern, which she was. "I'll see you at the house."

"Yes, ma'am."

The men passed her en masse before she was even halfway back, each tipping their hats with a good morning greeting. She smiled widely at the sight of them rushing towards Carmen's hot home cooked meal.

"Oh, Shreve!" She whispered. "Hurry back. For everyone's sake, or I'll be so lost that I'll never be able to find my way back again."

# CHAPTER TWENTY-SEVEN

Shreve stepped off the train and collected his horse. He was about to mount, but with so many people and so many autos moving about...well, he knew Star Runner wasn't used to the hubbub, which made him wish he'd ridden Black Wind out instead.

"Let's take this slow, boy. I'll walk you through for now, okay?"

The horse whinnied, and Shreve tugged on the reins, leading the stallion around the nearest building. He marveled at the changes that the city had undergone since he had left just ten years earlier. So many more buildings, so many more people; so many more automobiles.

If he had stayed, if he hadn't let that old biddy run him out of town and out of practice, he'd probably be a richer man by now. Or not. The number of signs touting legal aid seemed to have sprouted in conjunction with the number of people.

Still, there were familiar landmarks, buildings that had not changed one iota since that time. Some he had visited regularly, others not so much, but it still struck a chord deep inside to see them again. He passed, what seemed like, hundreds of buggies going to and fro, along with the latest automobile to be marketed to the general public—Ford's Model T. He liked the look of the vehicle, but he didn't think his preference would ever shift from a horse to a contraption. With that, he knew he was getting old; he also realized just how inflexible he truly was. No wonder Iliamna was frustrated with him.

He shook his head, and moved down the main street. He nodded a few times at the people moving down the boardwalks, but soon ceased when he noticed that not one returned the gesture, each too busy bustling about their daily lives to pay attention to simple manners.

Instead, he turned his attention to the unfamiliar and the familiar signs of the shops and businesses lining the street until the one he was looking for came into view; one word, *marshal*, carved on both sides into a wooden plank, hung above the boardwalk.

That had not changed either, except maybe the paint on the sign was a bit more faded. He pulled his horse to a stop in front of the hitching post and dismounted just as his friend stepped from inside.

"Well, I'll be a possum on a dinner plate," the man exclaimed, spotting Shreve walking toward him.

"Yuk! I never did like that saying," Shreve said, extending his hand.

"What? I thought you Injuns could stomach anything," his friend grinned.

"Nope," Shreve rejoined, "Much prefer the taste of freshly scalped cowboys to possum any day of the week and twice on Tuesdays."

"Oooh, now who's being downright disgusting."

Shreve laughed, "How are you, Mitch?"

"Marshall Mitchell Crowell, at your service," Mitch said, taking a bow.

"Marshall, is it?" Shreve laughed. "And here I thought they was just letting your no account hide out of jail."

"Nope. This here is a bona fide Marshall's badge," Mitch said, moving his vest aside to display the shiny metal star. "Got appointed from a lowly deputy after the former Marshall decided to move on."

Shreve whistled appreciatively.

"Had to grow up sometime, I reckon. So, Shreve," Mitch said, "haven't seen you 'round these parts in quite a number of years. What you been up to?"

"Started my own ranch," Shreve said proudly.

"Sure shootin'? Well, I'll be damned. Why don't we mosey on over to the Country Griddle and you can tell me all about it over some breakfast?"

"Sounds like a plan," Shreve said, stepping from the boardwalk. "And since you're the marshal, I guess it's you I came in search of. I need your help with something."

Mitch grew sober at Shreve's tone, "Sure thing, Shreve. I'm pretty much certain that helping folks is in my job description."

Shreve followed Mitch to the restaurant, and then launched into the reason for his visit after placing their orders.

"I found me a mail order bride," Shreve started.

"Well I'll be," Mitch exclaimed. "That what brung you home, then?"

"In a way," Shreve said, and couldn't prevent the sigh that escaped.

"What's wrong? She find out you're a half-breed?"

"No, nothing like that," Shreve answered, far from offended. He had known Mitch nearly his entire life and knew him to be anything but bigoted. "She's just...well, I ain't all that certain I have the right woman."

Mitch rubbed his nose, hiding his grin, "You plannin' on making less sense?"

"Sorry, Mitch," Shreve said. "It's just that, the woman I was supposed to be engaged to, kept stalling her departure. Then, one day, I stopped by a friend's place a few days ride out from the ranch and there was this woman there, the exact likeness of my supposed fiancé. It was a...um...a...um...house of ill-repute."

"Good heavens!" Mitch laughed. "This is better'n than one of them dime-store novels."

"Well, I ain't laughing none. Anyway, she claimed that someone kidnapped her and took her there against her will. A scheme hatched by her cousin to get rid of her."

"And then claimed to be your fiancé so that you would take her away..."

"No, actually, when I told her who she was supposed to be, she said she had no idea what I was talking about."

"Think it might be because of your heritage?"

"No. One thing I did learn about her in the time we spent together, is that she doesn't hold that against me. No, she was genuinely surprised that I thought she was my affianced. Even when I showed her the drawing I had of her, she insisted that she was being manipulated by her cousin; that it was her cousin that had her kidnapped and sent to the whorehouse; and that it was her cousin that is my true fiancé."

"And her cousin would be?"

"Well, she says the cousin was named Alana, but, and this is where I get mighty confused. The telegrams and letters I got from my fiancé were signed by a woman named Iliamna, and that—just so happens—to be the name of the woman at the whorehouse. She claims her cousin paid a man to abduct her and get rid of her, because this Alana was extremely jealous of her."

"Did she mention the coincidence over the name?"

"Yeah, Iliamna said that it could have been Alana's way of pinning a crime on her, in case the fraud was discovered. In other words, Alana signed Iliamna's name to the telegrams and letters, so, if Iliamna escaped her captivity and returned to Shreveport, she would be arrested. Alana wins in either case."

"Well, I must say that Iliamna's reasons sound legit. Either that, or she is the fastest on-your-feet liar that I've ever heard tell of. I mean, she would have to be a mighty practiced deceiver to come up with those excuses off the top of her head."

"I know, and after talking to her, I'd have to say she isn't a liar or a con artist, but the prosecutor in me has to find out all of the facts before coming to a decision."

"You sure it's the prosecutor in you and not your distrust of people in general?"

"A little of both I guess." Shreve reached inside his breast pocket. "Do you think it possible for you to tell me who this is?" He said softly, unfolding the drawing.

"Well, I'll be a goose's egg, that's a mighty fine likeness of Miss Iliamna Dearborn," Mitch said. "When you told me her name, I didn't put the two together, although I guess I should have. It's not exactly a regular-like name. A prettier girl you ain't likely to find this side of the moon."

"So then, does she have a cousin named Alana?"

"Well, I've known Alana Dearborn her entire life," Mitch said, "and I have to say I can't recall a time that she's ever lied to me over something, but that isn't to say she ain't capable."

"Well, if Alana isn't a liar and a cheat, then that would mean Iliamna is the liar...or is she?"

"You said you found Miss Iliamna in a whorehouse? Where is she now?"

"At my ranch," Shreve said. "Awaiting my return."

"She's waiting for you to get back?" Mitch asked, incredulous.

"Yeah, why?"

"Damn boy, but you really are thick. Do you really think that if she wasn't who she said she was—and hadn't told you the truth— that she would hang around your ranch waiting for you to haul your backside down here to Louisiana and swear out a warrant for her arrest and then sit, pretty-as-you-please, waiting for the local sheriff to arrive and arrest her and throw her in some godforsaken hole-in-the-wall? Ain't no woman I know willing to do that, unless...,"

"They weren't guilty," Shreve finished, closing his eyes and shaking his head in self-loathing.

"Sounds to me like you're in a pretty pickle," Mitch said, "especially if you're as attached to Miss Iliamna as you sound like."

"I am," Shreve sighed again.

"And if we're concluding that Miss Iliamna isn't a liar and a deceiver, then that would mean that Miss Alana has done gone and gotten her own self in a pretty pickle, if she's guilty of what you and Miss Iliamna are accusing her of."

"Well, unless you think that Iliamna hauled *herself* all the way to Texas to join a whorehouse, then what other explanation could there be?" Shreve asked. "Which I should have thought of myself, and saying it out loud now makes me feel like an even bigger heel."

"Well, be that as it may, you're an attorney, and as an attorney, you know that a body ain't guilty unless proven guilty, so what say we finish up our eating and then go and pay Miss Alana a visit. See if we can't get to the bottom of this mess. Then afterwards, I'd suggest you haul yourself on over to the telegraph office and wire that beautiful woman staying at the ranch that you've discovered the truth—so far as we know—and then you might consider doing some forgiveness begging. Especially if you plan on keeping her in your life."

"Thanks a whole heap for that mouthful, Mitch," Shreve said sarcastically, "but I didn't need you to tell me all of that. I already knew what needed doing."

"Never hurts to have it reiterated though, by someone *not* lacking common sense."

"Ha ha. Think we can get out of here, without my having to listen to your smart mouth too much?" Shreve asked, slapping his four bits on the counter. "We've got some investigating to do and I've got some air-clearing to do."

# CHAPTER TWENTY-EIGHT

Alana laid her head against the rest, her gaze scanning the desolate horizon. She hoped that the ranch that Shreve owned had more trees about and less cactus and shrub grass. Still, at least she was not perspiring as much as she had back home. She was thirsty however, and leaned over to pull the bell chord.

A porter appeared at her door at the same moment as a heavyset redheaded woman.

"A lemonade, please," Alana said to the porter, eyeing the woman hovering in her doorway, a strained look on her face. Much the same as the porter wore when she requested lemonade.

"Make that two, will ya?" Red said to the Porter, after she managed to drag her gaze away from the young girl seated in the cabin. When the porter departed, Red straightened her shoulders and strengthened her resolve, then turned back to Alana, "Mind if I join you?"

"And who might you be?" Alana asked and watched shock flitter across the heavyset face again. It vanished quickly however, and the woman moved to settle on the bench across from her. Alana looked at her questioningly, awaiting a response.

"Name's Red. I'm a friend of Shreve's," Red said and then muttered 'sort of' beneath her breath.

Alana snorted, and the woman's eyes widened. "He build you a house too?"

"Pardon?"

Alana waved a hand in dismissal, "Oh nothing, just thinking on things."

That had Red thinking on things also -- this young girl's declaration being one of them. It was very telling and erased any doubt that this woman was indeed Shreve's true intended. Although she seemed less than confident in that fact. Still, if this was Shreve's intended, then why was he carrying around a picture of the woman he abducted, claiming that *she* was his intended? Probably drew the picture that night, as she suspected—the lowdown half-breed. Still, if Shreve had to have a choice between the two, she could readily see why he'd have chosen her whore over this…geez, words couldn't even describe the nightmare sitting in front of her.

"No, Shreve didn't build me a house," Red laughed. "He and I go way back, which is why I'm here. When the porter arrived in Dawson Creek with a letter to deliver to Shreve from you, I initially was going to sit it out there; wait for the train to come in. Then I decided not to. I figured we could talk—plan—while the track was fixed."

"I have no idea what you're talking about."

"I think Shreve is making himself a real huge mistake, and when I heard that a woman claiming to be his intended was headed out to Dawson Creek to meet up with him…well, I just felt it was my Christian duty to do something to help my dear friend."

"What sort of mistake are you talking about, and what do you mean by a woman *claiming* to be his fiancé. I happen to have his letters to me, proving I am who I say I am."

"Well, that certainly beats a single drawing," Red muttered.

"Pardon?"

Red shook her head slightly to clear the buzzing that the girl's speech was causing in her mind. If she were going to have to spend any amount of time in the company of Shreve's fiancé, then she was going to have to learn to overlook her voice or she might just end up pulling the girl's tongue from her head. "The fact of the matter is, when you didn't show up like you was supposed to, well Shreve showed up at my place completely out of his head. He stole one of my whores, claiming that she was his fiancé and now plans on marrying her instead of you."

"Just great," Alana snapped, "so it's feasible I wasted good money and time on this trip…"

"Not necessarily. After all, he doesn't yet know that his real fiancé is on her way, now does he? I mean, if he knew you were headed in his direction, he might just feel inclined to let me have my whore back, and you could wed as planned. So you see, we can very well benefit each other. I want my whore, and you want Shreve."

"Well, if Shreve already plans to marry someone else, what makes you think that he'll just toss her away should I arrive at his doorstep?"

"Now see, that's the thing," Red said, pretending to be thinking carefully over the situation, "the way I figure it is, Shreve was just upset that you didn't show when you said you would, but once he calms down, it will be only a matter of time before he sees reason. After all, what man would choose a whore over a young lady?"

"You'd be surprised," Alana muttered, and Red had to stop herself from agreeing.

"Why didn't you come sooner? Could have spared a lot of people a lot of aggravation if you'd done so."

"I had some things to take care of before I could," Alana replied cryptically.

Red waited, but Alana provided no more information. She shrugged, "Well, as I said, things definitely got derailed when you were delayed, but now that you're on your way…well, I know Shreve to be a man of his word. So, if he promised to wed you, then he should uphold his promise; also, I think there might be laws preventing a man from dumping a mail-order intended. Of course, I'll have to look into that; but to makes things a sight bit easier, we can always remove my whore from Shreve's home. Take her back to the whorehouse where she belongs. Out of sight, out of mind, wouldn't you say? Then you'll be there to work your…um…well…work your womanly wiles on him. You *do* have womanly wiles, don't you?"

Alana cocked her head and eyed the woman like a hawk for a minute before answering, "I may not have any right now, but I'm sure it isn't too difficult a task to master."

"Hmm." Red returned Alana's stare without faltering, which was an effort, considering that she felt as if she was staring into an emotionless chasm. She'd met some cold-hearted girls in her time— hell, she herself was about as cold-hearted as they came—but never had she met someone who could, no doubt, teach the devil lessons. Until now. Still, if Alana was going to win Shreve over, she was going to have to hide her coldness and learn how to be a woman, or….

"You got any objection to being taught on how to please a man? How to capture his attention, and keep it?"

Alana cocked her head in the other direction and stared at the heavy-set woman for a bit longer than last time before answering, "You going to cut the act and tell me what this is really all about?"

Red grinned, *So young to be so shrewd and shrewish,* she thought, but decided it best to level with this girl. She hadn't thought that she'd encounter such an evil-minded witch when she set out to exact vengeance, so figured a stance of kindness would be sufficient to get the girl's assistance, but kindness wasn't going to work with this one..."Vengeance, girl. Pure and simple. As much as I love Shreve, he had no right to steal my best girl. Killed a bunch of my men in the process. I want her back, and at the same time—well, Shreve and I really do go a long way back, so if I can teach you to pleasure him and get my girl back in the process, then I might just let bygones be bygones." *And if he gets stuck with you instead of that beauty he has now, that will be vengeance enough, that's for sure,* Red thought to herself. "Thing is—we have to find a way to get her away from Shreve in such a way that he thinks she up and left willingly, else wise he may just pay me a return visit."

Alana nodded her head, "Fair enough, and since I didn't make this trip for no reason, I'm inclined to help you. Do you have an idea on how to get this girl away from Shreve? If he stole her from you, he may not let her go easily."

"All I need to do is find a way to get Shreve away from his ranch. I do that, and it's just a matter of sending someone in to retrieve the girl."

Alana looked thoughtful for a moment and then grinned, "I know someone who is very good at snatching things away, quiet like, if you're willing to pay for him to make a trip out here."

"I have my own men that can do the job..."

"No one that I know, and if I don't know them, I ain't likely to be able to trust them," Alana interrupted. "The man I want to hire has done a job for me before, so I know he's competent; capable of doing this."

"Matter whether I trust him?"

Alana just sat staring at Red; her gaze revealing sufficiently her immobility on the matter—it was her way or no way.

Red sighed. She was beginning to see herself mirrored in those eyes. She too was inflexible over many issues and generally refused to budge when she was determined to have her own way. The only difference between her and this little twit, was that she still had a fragment of a soul. "Very well," she conceded. After all, her only concern was getting even with Shreve, and she could do that with her own men or a man of this girl's choosing.

"How long will it take for him to get here? We don't want Shreve walking down the aisle before we abscond with his current wife-to-be."

Alana grinned, "He's in Shreveport, so should be able to arrive within a day or two, unless some nut job blows up the tracks again. In the meantime, you can teach me all about being a proper wife to Shreve. Porter?" She called at a man passing in the corridor.

The man visibly cringed, and Red empathized. This Alana certainly was hard on the hearing. After a minute, the porter turned toward the door, "Yes, Miss?"

"Please bring paper and pen. I need to send a letter to Shreveport."

"You'll have to hire someone, ma'am, willing to travel back the way we came. Can you send a telegram instead? Dawson Creek is a few hours out."

"Yes, of course. Now fetch me my writing implements." Alana waved the man away with a flick of her wrist. "I'll go ahead and see to the telegram, so that my hired man can arrive sooner rather than later."

"Have the reply sent to Twin Rivers. It's closer to my place, and we should be back there in a couple of days."

Alana nodded, "So, you'll teach me how to be a proper woman and I'll help you get your whore back, yes?"

"Precisely," Red said, stretching her hand out. When Alana clasped it, something in Alana's gaze made Red feel as if she had struck a bargain with Lucifer himself; so cold and calculating was her gaze. It took a tremendous effort to contain the quiver that ran about inside her stomach at the thought.

# CHAPTER TWENTY-NINE

The marshal knocked on Alana Dearborn's door and waited patiently, but a glance over at his friend said that patience for him was in short supply. He wanted answers yesterday. He leaned over and whispered, "Try not to throttle anyone before we ask the questions, ok?"

Shreve grinned at that, "I'll just pretend I'm a prosecutor again. Behave real professional-like."

"If your tone wasn't so sarcastic, I might just believe...good afternoon, ma'am," Mitch said, when the door opened, "I'm Marshal Mitchell Crowell, and this is my associate, Shreve..."

"Pleasure ma'am," Shreve interrupted before Mitch could announce his surname. The last thing he needed was for the woman to slam the door in their faces should she turn out to be an Indian hater.

Mitch didn't react. He realized the mistake he'd almost made and adjusted quickly, "We have some questions for Alana Dearborn. Is she home at this time?"

The woman snorted, mumbling something unintelligible beneath her breath, "She's not here," she said finally.

"May we come in?" Mitch asked. Something in her mutterings and her tone relayed that she was carrying around a burden and needed to unload. Whether what she had to say proved useful was yet to be determined, but she may unwittingly impart something valuable to their investigation. Only time, and a conversation with her, would tell.

"Of course," she said, affecting a gracious air, "and may I ring for some refreshments?"

"That's very kind, but not necessary, as we've just come from our morning meal. If we could just speak with you about Alana..."

"Ungrateful child," she muttered, moving toward the solarium.

"Not to be nosy, but why do you refer to your daughter as ungrateful."

That was it. That one question opened the floodgates of emotion within a mother torn apart emotionally by a child. She spun about suddenly, her face turning red from a sudden rise in aggravation, and began pacing the length of the room, "I do declare that I'm not at all surprised to find the law at my door. I knew there was something wrong with that daughter of mine, the ungrateful wretch. Up and walked out without so much as a by your leave simply because I couldn't afford to fund another ball in which to locate a husband. After all, it took considerable funds to throw the ball for her cousin; and it certainly wasn't my fault that the girl disappeared in the middle of the ball and Alana couldn't find a husband at that time. And it certainly wasn't any fault of mine that that girl showed up on my doorstep after her parents' passed. It wasn't as if I could marry off my own girl, younger than her cousin, without first marrying off the elder, but did Alana see it that way? Of course not! And then to have Iliamna run off followed soon after by my own daughter, who swore that she'd met some beau through a newspaper advertisement and was off to marry him. My nerves are quite unable to handle all of the distress those girls have caused me." With a final swish of her skirts, the elder woman flopped onto a chair across from Mitch, her back straight as an arrow, hands wringing in agitation on her lap, her gaze glazed over as if she'd left the room and was wandering about in her own thoughts.

"Um ma'am," Mitch interrupted, his head swimming from everything she was spouting, most of it a jumbled mess. One look at Shreve's tense body revealed that *he'd* discerned enough of her ramblings to be extremely distraught over the revelations. He'd blundered big time by not believing Iliamna and now could lose her because of his suspicious nature. "I hate to interrupt, but...well...that's a lot of information that I need to sort through."

"Oh, I'm sorry. I quite understand. I just get so upset every time I think about what Alana and Iliamna put me through."

"May I ask a few questions?" Shreve asked.

"Of course, and I will certainly attempt to remain composed."

"Much appreciated. From what I gathered, you seemed to infer that Iliamna left without notifying you, the evening of the ball? Is that correct?" Shreve's composure was stiff and agitated; and he was relying solely on his expertise to get him through this interview.

*Pretend you're still a prosecutor*, he told himself.

"That's right. Just up and left..."

"Ma'am, I certainly am not questioning your recollection of events, but what happened the evening of the ball that made you aware that Iliamna just up and left. I assume that she didn't walk in and announce her departure?" If she had, then that would mean that Iliamna lied, and although he now felt more certain that she was being truthful and was the victim of a violent crime, the answers to his questions would seal his certainty.

"Most certainly didn't. She didn't even stay for the entirety of the ball; disappeared midway. If it weren't for the note that was found on her pillow, I probably wouldn't have discovered her absence until well after the noonday meal the next day," Mrs. Dearborn said, and then scratched at her head, "I did find it odd that she'd leave without taking a thing with her. Although I suppose that she felt guilty over walking out, after all I'd done for her, and decided to leave it all behind because I'd bought and paid for it..."

"Ma'am," Mitch interrupted again, rubbing a hand along his jaw line, with a sigh, "Do you happen to have her note still, or could you recall what it said?"

"Oh, yes, yes, of course. I kept the note," she exclaimed, standing abruptly and walking over to a desk in the corner of the room, "I don't know what possessed me to keep it." She opened the top drawer and pulled out a balled-up piece of paper. Apparently, she'd kept it, but only after she'd crumpled it up in anger first. She straightened it, laid it on the desktop, and flattened it best she could, and then returned to her seat, passing the note over to Mitch.

Mitch scanned it quickly and then handed it over to Shreve, who perused it far slower, absorbing the words.

*My Dearest Auntie,*

*I'm sorry to say that after all you've done for me, I don't want to stay with you and Uncle Charles any longer. I know that this makes me a selfish person, but I will gladly allow you to feel that way about me if it means leaving your house to never return.*

*Sincerely, your niece, Iliamna*

Mitch watched Shreve closely, waiting for his reaction; however, it was difficult to determine his opinion, for he kept his face neutral of all emotions. Mitch knew that wasn't a good sign, because it was a sign that an emotional upheaval could very well follow.

"May we keep this?" Shreve asked.

"Oh, well, yes, of course," Mrs. Dearborn said, a bit uncertain, "Anything to help. Of course, I'm not quite certain what it is that I'm assisting with?" She quirked her head in question, but neither man answered her query.

"One more question, ma'am, and then we'll leave you in peace," Mitch said.

"Oh...well, of course."

"You said that Alana left shortly after Iliamna; that..."

"Ungrateful wretch," Mrs. Dearborn spouted, "She did indeed. A couple of days later. Came down for breakfast and simply announced that, because we wouldn't be able to afford to find her a beau, she took matters into her own hands. Waved a letter in the air from a man out west who purportedly proposed marriage—sight unseen. Well, I'll tell you, that man is in for a surprise, isn't he? After all, Alana is...well, she's not exactly the belle of the ball..."

"Yes ma'am," Mitch sighed, feeling very rude for having to interrupt yet again. Still, he feared that if he didn't continually interrupt, this woman would go on and on and on..."We certainly appreciate your time. Your help was invaluable," Mitch said, placing his hat upon his head.

"You know, you never did mention why it was you are looking for Alana. Or your interest in her cousin, Iliamna," she said. "Are they okay? Are they in some kind of trouble?"

"Unfortunately ma'am, our investigation is ongoing, so we can't really say too much, but we can say that no harm has befallen your daughter, or your niece." Shreve tipped his hat, "Thank you again for your hospitality, ma'am." He turned and headed down the steps, his anger elevating with each step. It had taken a colossal effort to keep from exploding the more Alana's mother revealed; but the final straw that nearly pushed him over an emotional edge, was that note—obviously phony—which lent credence to Iliamna's assertions that she was being manipulated by Alana; and that made him feel even more wretched for not believing her initial claims, which made his anger elevate faster.

"Ma'am." Mitch tipped his own hat and then trotted after Shreve. "Keep a lid on the explosion," he murmured, as it was difficult to overlook the storm clouds that had settled over Shreve's features.

Shreve nodded curtly, "That letter was written by the same woman that has been corresponding with me," he hissed.

"How do you know?"

"Same handwriting." Shreve continued on toward his horse, his footfalls heavy with the fury brewing inside, "which means that either Iliamna is a fraud and a liar, or that her cousin is covering her bases fairly well, determined to point all fingers of guilt at Iliamna. That would mean that Iliamna is being manipulated by the whims of a mad woman. On top of that, I'm being manipulated also, and it's a feeling I don't like." When he reached his horse, he mounted in one fluid motion, kicked the horse in its haunches, and galloped back toward his friend's office. He skid to a halt soon after, leapt off its back before it had completely stopped and stormed into the marshal's office. Without breaking stride, he walked over to the nearest wall and slammed his fist into it. The pain jarred him enough to bring him to his senses. He exhaled in a loud whoosh and sank to his knees, cradling his injured knuckles in his other hand.

"You okay now?" Mitch asked, leaning against the doorjamb.

"I don't know. I feel so damned angry."

"I have a feeling that what I'm about to say is going to make you want to shoot something or someone—possibly yourself."

"What are you talking about?"

"Didn't you hear what the mom said?"

"I heard everything that she said."

"Obviously the part about Alana leaving to meet her suitor flew over your head. She said that Alana has been corresponding with a potential beau; and you just stated that the handwriting in that letter is the same as that of a woman..."

"Oh my God, I'm the biggest fool this side of the Texas border," Shreve whispered, "and I may have just cracked my knuckles to boot." He tried to prevent the wave of emotions welling inside from developing into an embarrassing display of tears, but he seriously wanted to cry like a newborn babe in need of momma's breast.

"Well, I'm not arguing that," Mitch quipped, removing his hat and moving to sit at his desk, "So, I don't think I'm jumping into a pit of stupidity if I say that *you* are that intended, which means we can probably conclude that Iliamna is innocent. Still, the evidence is overwhelmingly against her, so the question now becomes, how do we prove that Alana is a kidnapper and a perpetrator of fraud? By the expression on your face, you are more inclined to go off half-cocked, which we both know wouldn't accomplish anything. What we need right now is a strategy and evidence. Now simmer down and think."

"Evidence, right," Shreve said, closing his eyes and drawing in deep, calming breaths. "There isn't any evidence, except against Iliamna," he concluded quickly. "It's all assumption." It was then that he recollected what Iliamna told him, "Do you know a place called the Silver Palace?"

"Whew, do I ever! Most of my problems originate from that place. It's located in a real nasty part of town, near the docks, nestled along the Red River. Why do you ask?"

"Iliamna mentioned a man—her abductor. Said that she recalled him saying that that is where Alana found him, to hire him to kidnap her."

"And you think that he'll corroborate Iliamna's accounts? A criminal willing to provide testimony is a rare thing, as well you know. Nor do they make the best witness in a court of law."

"It's our best hope of pinning everything on Alana—the kidnapping and the fraud; or at least to start building a case. If he'll corroborate Iliamna's story, then it will be a start. We'll worry about credibility later."

"Well, we best get a move on then, because Alana is no doubt headed for Texas, and she'll likely run into Iliamna again if she gets to your place ahead of us—and if she's as shrewd and malevolent as her actions portray her to be, then Iliamna could be in more danger."

"Then why are we still standing here?" Shreve said, breathing heavily through his nostrils.

"Oh right. Sorry, let's go."

# CHAPTER THIRTY

Mitch and Shreve rode along the avenue toward the Silver Palace, warily eyeing those warily eyeing them. Not all of the men working in this part of town were criminal-minded, but they were hardened by hard labor and suspicious of the law. Those who *were* criminally minded and hardened by this life, were doubly suspicious of anyone wearing a badge.

They dismounted in front of the saloon, "How do you want to do this?" Shreve asked.

"We'll make a simple inquiry," Mitch said with a grin, and then grew serious, "Let me handle this, okay? I don't want you attempting to beat answers out of people."

Shreve laughed shortly, "How well you know me."

They stepped into the saloon, and immediately the raucous conversations ceased.

"You know if you didn't flaunt that badge, we could pass for dock workers," Shreve whispered.

"Yeah, I know," Mitch whispered back, "but I must confess to having a small bit of an ego."

Shreve laughed and slapped Mitch on the back, "Let's grab a drink."

They sauntered up to the bar, ignoring the stares of suspicion aimed their way. Every man in the place knew that the law was only there to get answers, and every man knew it could be about any one of them, since they'd all broken the law in one regard or another.

"Afternoon," Mitch said when the bartender walked up to serve them. The bartender didn't return the salutations.

"Two whiskeys," Shreve said.

The bartender nodded and then removed a bottle and two glasses from beneath the counter, "Four bits," he grumbled. When Mitch placed the coins on the bar, the bartender took them and then started to move away.

"We're looking for Gitano," Shreve said quickly, before the

bartender disappeared altogether.

The bartender stopped, but didn't turn. "Can't help you," he mumbled, and then started back toward his office behind the bar.

"Gitano is a gun for hire and he'll be mighty put out if he loses money because you mistook our reason for being here," Shreve called out.

"Indeed I would," a man said from a darkened corner of the room.

"Nice call," Mitch whispered as Shreve and he turned and slid from their stools, "How'd you know?" He asked softly as they made their way over to Gitano's table.

"I didn't," Shreve replied, equally quiet. "It was the way that Iliamna spoke of his lust of money that gave me the clue, but I didn't have a clue he'd be here. I'm just glad I listened to her accounting well enough to remember the name of this place and the name of her abductor, or our investigation would have been over real quick."

"Hey mister," a bar patron called, standing next to their whiskey, "you gonna finish this?"

"Help yourself," Mitch replied.

"So, what is it that the law wishes from me," Gitano said, as the two men sat down at the table. "I do not think I have break the law—at least not in this month," he grinned, and Shreve thought that, had he not been such an immoral man, he'd be quite remarkable looking. He also recognized that he was very much a man, so was rather surprised that Iliamna had escaped his company unscathed. At least Iliamna said she had. He shook his head before more doubt crept in. If she said she had, then by all that was holy, he'd believe her. He drew in a deep breath to regain his composure, so that he wouldn't kill this man outright. After all, he may prove useful, and killing him wouldn't serve any purpose other than to see his own ass thrown in lockup.

"Actually, we know that you have committed a very serious crime rather recently, but we're not interested in arresting you. We're here for information, and possibly to hire you ourselves, both of which—if provided satisfactorily—will keep you out of jail."

Gitano's face registered surprise, and he pursed his lips

thoughtfully, "What is this thing I do? It must not be so bad if you no want to lock me up. This I am curious for, but for you to hire me? This makes me more curious."

"Iliamna." Shreve said simply and nearly jumped across the table to wipe off the look of desire that flitted across Gitano's features, using his fists.

"Easy," Mitch whispered, placing a hand of restraint on Shreve's arm, and felt muscles tense with anger. "We know," he addressed Gitano, "that Iliamna's cousin, Alana, hired you to get rid of her." They actually didn't know any such thing, since all of their information was sheer gut instinct at this point; supposition based on the ramblings of a distraught mother, and information provided by Iliamna.

Gitano narrowed his gaze and sat back against his chair, wisely not speaking.

"Again, we're not here to arrest you..."

"Yet," Shreve amended.

"Yet," Mitch sighed.

Gitano's brow raised and he leaned forward again. He took a few deep breaths, placing his arms on the table, "I think Alana no say nothing to you, so for you to know this thing, you have spoken to Iliamna? You know where she is?"

"Where she *was*," Shreve amended.

"She get away from Red?" Gitano murmured. "I never know this thing to be possible."

"She had help," Shreve hissed, and Gitano looked him over more closely.

After a few minutes scrutiny, he grinned, "Yes, this I can see. You are good with a gun, I think, and you think to take Iliamna as your woman, which I no think Red could stop you to do. I understand. I, too, wished to take this woman as mine, but..."

It was that one word—"but"—that saved Gitano's life. Shreve didn't even hear the rest of what the man had to say because the resonating bells of rage were ringing too loudly in his ears. He closed his eyes and popped the kinks of tension from his neck, taking in several deep cleansing breaths.

"I can take this, if you want to wait outside," Mitch said, "especially since it looks like you are a mountain of TNT only moments from explosion."

Shreve continued breathing heavily from his nostrils, but shook his head, "I don't want to be here, but I need to be."

Mitch sighed, and then turned back to speak to Gitano, who was watching Shreve with a mixture of admiration and wariness.

"So, if you know I take Iliamna for money paid to me from Alana; and if you free her from Red," Gitano said, pointing his head at Shreve, "this is why you no arrest me?"

"After a fashion," Mitch said.

"So if you free her, why you need hire me? You find out Alana wish to hire me again?" He said, pulling a telegram from a pocket. "But how you know?" He continued, passing the telegram to Mitch, "Unless you have a man to watch me? But why you have a man to watch me?" His brow knitted as he tried to sort through what they wanted with him. He didn't succeed. "I think I maybe have more confusion."

Mitch forced his features to remain blank, not daring to reveal that Gitano had *him* in a state of confusion. As he reached down to pick up the telegram, he decided it best not to reveal what he knew to Gitano; or rather reveal their ignorance to this point. Gitano was giving them far more information than they'd hoped for—all with little-to-no prodding from either he or Shreve. As he read the telegram, his gaze widened slightly, and it took significant effort to keep the alarm from registering.

"I think you maybe see I picked this up only minutes before you come to find me; that maybe you were expecting it? But I know not why you think this..." He let the sentence trail off, his gaze questioning.

Neither Shreve nor Mitch disabused him of his speculation. "It doesn't say what the job is," Mitch observed.

"I do not think this is *necessario*. I not know Alana much time, but I know she not like beautiful woman."

"So someone has potentially stepped into her path that she feels threatened by," Mitch surmised.

"I can no think of Alana wishing to kill all beautiful woman. Just Iliamna. She hold much hatred for this woman, all because Iliamna is a beauty beyond compare, and Alana looks like a dog that lose a fight with a bigger dog, and that girl's voice—*¡ay Dios mío!, Santa María!*" He exclaimed, signifying his distress with the sign of the cross. "Still I already take Iliamna out of her sight, so…"

"Yes, but you took Iliamna to Texas; and we already ascertained that Alana is headed to Texas. It's not a far stretch to surmise that, since Alana went to Texas to meet Shreve, she's seen Iliamna at Shreve's ranch. Either that, or yet another beautiful woman has crossed paths with Alana en route, which is always probable also. The likely scenario is that she knows Iliamna is at your ranch."

"My ranch is a fair distance from Dawson Creek though. She would have had to leave here longer than stated by her mother in order to have reached my ranch, so it must be another woman, but who and why?"

"She is headed to Texas, so maybe she met up with someone who knows you…"

"This is all too convoluted," Shreve interrupted. "Too many ifs and unknowns. God, I need some air," Shreve declared and then stood and stormed from the saloon. He needed air to think.

"I think perhaps that he has *amor mucho por la mujer*, for this woman he has much love," Gitano said thoughtfully.

"Indeed, and it has angered him a great deal that you took her to a whorehouse."

"But can he no see this is a good thing? For he find her, no? Had I take her to Barbados like her cousin demand I do, he no ever find her."

"So, Alana has agreed to pay you three hundred dollars to do another job, which we all feel means that a beautiful woman has somehow interfered with some plan or other that she's made. Someone that she really despises, as we've also determined that she isn't in the habit of killing willy-nilly. Most likely Iliamna, but she hasn't been in Texas long enough to know that Iliamna is at Shreve's ranch…Shreve is right—this is too convoluted."

"I know very little, Señor. I know not why she hire me again."

"Well, there certainly is one way to find out—respond to her telegram."

"I take job?"

Mitch nodded.

Gitano expounded, "So I reply to telegram saying I take job. When I get to Texas, I meet Alana and she tell me who she wishes me to remove from her sight. Then we know for certain if it is Iliamna."

Mitch nodded again and sighed, "I can't help but harbor a deep curiosity over how she would have found out about Iliamna so soon after her departure from here. Still, if Alana *has* hired you to get rid of Iliamna again, you'll provide Alana with lots of assurances that—this time—if Iliamna returns, it will be as a ghost."

"You want I should kill her?"

Mitch shook his head, "No, you're only going to convince Alana of that. We need to keep Alana from making another attempt in the future. If she is convinced that her cousin has been dealt with decisively..."

Gitano pursed his lips thoughtfully, "She no hire me again, for which I would not be sad. That girl is *muy loca*. I do this thing because I like Iliamna. She stay mad at me for whole trip to whorehouse, but she never say one bad thing about me, to me. She is *una verdadera dama, una buena mujer.*"

"What does that mean?"

"It means that—in his opinion—Alana has bats in her belfry, and Iliamna is too good to kill," Shreve said with a sigh, wishing he'd seen her purity of heart before doubting her word, as Gitano did. "I think that we've spent too much time discussing this. We need to go."

Gitano nodded as the men stood and all three made their way out of the saloon. Impulsively, Gitano stepped up next to Shreve, "I know you wish kill me, but I give my word that I no harm her."

"You punched her in the face—twice," Shreve hissed, turning to face Gitano, again trying to rein in his anger.

Gitano shrugged, "This thing I do for it is needed," he explained. "She say this to you, did she not?"

Shreve shook his head and closed his eyes, drawing in deep breaths through his nostrils, "No, she didn't."

"This thing I must do, because is *necesario*. She very brave. Stand in front of me for me to do this thing, her chin up. As brave as is beautiful, no?"

"Easy, Shreve," Mitch said, noticing that every time Gitano even mentioned Iliamna's name, or merely mentioned her with that lustful tone, Shreve looked like a volcano about to erupt just so he could deliberately spew lava all over the top of the man. "Gitano has agreed to help us; to provide evidence against Alana. Killing him will hinder us. Keep that in mind."

"Why can't we just ride into town and arrest Alana? We know that she's hiring Gitano to do something illegal, so why do we have to go to all of the trouble..."

"Because I'm thinking logically. We're trying to not only stop Alana from harming someone else, but also trying to build a case against her. If we just arrest her, it's Gitano's word against Alana's. Not many judges would convict on that flimsy evidence; however..."

"If we catch Alana in the process of hiring a gunman, then it's our words against hers. I get it." Shreve sighed. "We'll just need to plan carefully."

The three men moved out of the doorway as several patrons filed out, and then headed for their horses.

"Exactly," Mitch continued. "We have to proceed as if Alana either knows it's Iliamna and knows where she is located, or that it's someone completely different. We'll know which better to plan for as soon as Gitano meets up with Alana."

The men mounted up, and then looked down at Gitano, standing there looking a little disconcerted.

"Where are you supposed to meet her?" Mitch asked. "I didn't see that information in the wire."

"She no tell me. I most likely find out as soon as I say yes to her offer."

"Then let's get over to the telegraph office and send your affirmation, now. Knowing you're willing and on your way, may deter her hiring someone else; may hold off any alternate attack she may

164

have been planning. You can send a wire to Iliamna at that time too, to ensure she knows just what a sorry..."

"I don't need it spelled out for me, Mitch," Shreve grumbled.

"Um, my horse," Gitano interrupted, "he is no available..."

Mitch looked at Shreve.

"He's not doubling up with me," Shreve snapped.

Mitch laughed, "Climb up behind me. We'll get you a mount to borrow until your horse *is* available."

After a few minutes, the men were again in Shreveport proper and headed for the telegraph office, "So Gitano, where are you sending your reply?"

"Some place in Texas with name of Twin Rivers, I think the telegraph man say."

Shreve moved nearer to Mitch's horse, and shook his head to clear his hearing, his eyes widening with dread, "Did you just say Twin Rivers?" He whispered in near panic.

"Sí, this is so," Gitano said cautiously.

"What? What am I missing?"

"There isn't any reason for Alana to be in Twin Rivers. It's not on the way to my ranch," he said, as the men dismounted, "unless she's getting help..."

"The lady at the whorehouse?" Mitch interjected.

"Oh my God, Red!"

# CHAPTER THIRTY-ONE

"Confirmation received!" Alana called, pushing through the saloon doors. She nearly fell when she missed the bottom step, and started muttering about the hazard of diffused lighting, as she latched onto a nearby chair and righted herself. She bent over and retrieved the telegram that had floated to the floor, when she'd lost her footing. With a sigh, she straightened her hair and spine, and maneuvered through the tables to the bar where Red sat, watching her with amusement. "Find something funny about me nearly breaking my neck—again?"

"A drunkard can manage those two steps with ease—coming and going—but you seem to miss that second step every time. Yes, I find it funny."

"Well I don't," Alana huffed. "You should replace those steps with a ramp or something."

"Since I like it as it is, I'll leave it as it is; so, what you got there? Did your hired gun agree to the job?"

"Yes. He'll be on tomorrow morning's train, so that should give you time to finish helping me master those womanly wiles we've been working on the better part of two days now."

Red sighed inwardly. This girl was an oaf who appeared to lack any feminine traits at all, which made Red doubt her ability to teach her how to beguile a man. She'd have greater success training Satan how to be good, than teaching this one to turn a man's head. Still, in order to see her revenge upon Shreve completed, she needed to maintain her agreement with this girl; so she straightened her spine in determination, slapped her hands upon her thighs, and slid from the stool, "Ok, we've been a might bit unsuccessful the past two days, so let's start with the very basics. The wiles of a sexy woman," she declared with enthusiasm, "lesson one. In order to find your motivation, you need to understand men."

Alana grinned and followed Red into the center of the room.

"You need to comprehend that men are animals with only sex on the brain; however—and this is very important—they may say they'll have sex with any female in a skirt, but they really are more particular than that. At least most are. Men have to be enticed. You have to get them to quit thinking with their brains and start reacting with their pecker. You have to get them so aroused, that they will overlook anything that may annoy them in favor of releasing that built up need. Understand?"

Alana nodded, her gaze trained on the sway of Red's hips as she sashayed between the tables. She hadn't actually heard much of what Red said; was, in fact, more intent on trying to get her body to do what Red's was doing. Red looked sexy—even in obesity—while Alana looked laughable.

When Red turned and spotted Alana's efforts, she sighed heavily. "You weren't listening, so perhaps I'd best explain without showing you how it's done first." Red walked back to a nearby table and pointed to a seat next to her. Alana bounded across the floor in a manner that reminded Red of a puppy dog, with its tail wagging in pleasure at anything new; any act of kindness. It made her feel somewhat sympathetic toward the girl; made her wonder how hard her life had been to create in her heartlessness so young. She closed her eyes and shook the bewilderment from her head. When Alana had finally settled, she sighed, "Ok, let's try this again, shall we?"

Alana nodded.

"Men like things that look and smell good, which is why someone came up with that saying, the way to a man's heart is through his stomach. Get the connection?"

"Food looks and smells good," Alana huffed, "I'm not a dolt, you know."

"Right. Of course," Red bit her lip. The girl had looked so ridiculous in her attempts to act sexy that Red had almost forgotten that she may not be a woman of wiles, but she was wily. "So, attributing that to sex, men prefer women who look good and smell good. Those two things make up parts one and two of three traits of sex appeal. The third trait is a woman's ability to use her body as a magnet. A woman can have a beautiful body, but if she doesn't know how to show it off or work it to her advantage, a man isn't likely to notice. Whereas a woman who is confident in her body, even if she's overweight, will attract a man's attention."

"Okay, so I sway my hips and, voilá, I get Shreve's attention."

"You keep swinging your hips like you were a minute ago and all you'll get is Shreve's laughter."

Alana pursed her lips and her cheeks reddened, but she had no rejoinder. Red was right—she didn't know how to use her body to her advantage. "Since you think I'm doing it wrong, teach me to do it right. That's what you said you'd do."

"Yeah, but I didn't know it would take a miracle," Red muttered beneath her breath, standing from her seat. "First things first, we need to dress you in something a little more provocative and teach you how to dress your face up also. If you feel sexier, you'll be more likely to act sexier. And," Red added beneath her breath, as she made her way toward the staircase, "if we can hide your face beneath mounds of makeup, you'll be less likely to scare men away."

"Why does this come naturally to some women?" Alana whined, following Red up the staircase. Alana's tone, more nasally than usual, caused Red to wince. She had to force herself to shut out the tone and hear only the words or she'd likely turn around and permanently seal the girl's lips shut. Red grinned, for the thought had merit. If the girl couldn't talk, her sex appeal would shoot up considerably.

"I don't know. I guess some women are closer relations to Eve, is all I can figure. That woman had so much sex appeal that she managed to persuade Adam to break God's law. Now *those* were some powerful wiles. And some women just got natural charm. They don't even know how sexy they are, they just are. They don't even have to try."

"Like my cousin," Alana said softly, her tone bitter.

"And like the whore Shreve took from me," Red added, nodding. "That girl was a true woman. She didn't need to do anything but walk into a room for a man to want her; which is why I want her back. She'll make me a fortune."

"Yeah, that sounds like my cousin too," Alana said, settling on the divan in front of Red's vanity. "She was desired and didn't even know it. Anytime we went to town, I could see men watching her and her completely unaware. It just doesn't seem right that some of us have to work at it."

Red pulled the pins free from Alana's hair and immediately

decided that, on top of needing to learn how to wear makeup, she needed a hair dye too. She shook her head—*No wonder no one wants her*, she thought; *she defines drab*. Red sighed again, reaching into a drawer, which held her stash of transforming products. She pulled out some rouge, lipstick, and powder, and sat them upon the vanity. "So, would you like to be a blonde, or would you really like to brighten your hair up and dye it red. I have Henna powder for either choice."

"Red? But that seems so crass. Mother always said that a true lady doesn't dare dye her hair," Alana huffed.

"Yes, but a true lady doesn't know how to be a woman in the bedroom either, which is what we're trying to teach you to be. As you look now," Red said, throwing her remainder of tact to the wind, "the only thing you'll ever entice is a mosquito, so stop pretending to be something you're not and open yourself up to the potential inside. The only way you're going to turn Shreve's head is to go for a complete overhaul."

Alana sat fuming, staring at her reflection in the mirror. She wanted to snap back at Red's unflattering assessment, but looking at her reflection only confirmed that assessment. "I think it might be better to go with blonde," she murmured after a time. "Red might be daring, but I don't think many men prefer redheads, and I don't want to turn Shreve away."

"Blonde it is," Red said, returning the red Henna to the drawer.

"Did you have to be so harsh?" Alana asked, as Red prepared the dye.

"It's time you faced some realities, girl," Red said. "You aren't exactly a gift to manhood. Your features are bland, your hair is drab, and your voice could grate cheese..." Red sighed, kneeling in front of Alana. "I'm sorry to sound so unsympathetic, but the reality is, you don't hold a candle to the woman that Shreve stole from me, nor to your cousin—if what you've said is true; and while I can work miracles with appearance, and can maybe teach you how to flaunt your...well, what *should* be God-given gifts...I'm not at all certain I can change your manner of speech or the sound of your laughter. Hasn't anyone ever indicated..."

"All of my life," Alana interrupted, her tone bitter.

Red sighed, "I'm sorry for that. You have gumption which makes up for some of your flaws, but...well... is there anyway you'd be willing to play the part of a mute—for the rest of your life?" Alana glared at Red. "I guess not," Red sighed again. "Well, let's start with the cosmetics, the Henna, and the sex appeal. Once we've mastered those, we'll see about changing your manner of speech."

"Do you think we'll be able to do it all in the next day or two?"

"I think it would take six months minimum, but since all we have is a couple of days, we'd better hope I become a miracle worker real fast."

# CHAPTER THIRTY-TWO

"Mrs. Red Fox?" A ranch hand knocked on the screen door and then, as if remembering, swiftly removed his hat, slapped the dust from the Stetson and then placed it on a peg by the door. He then stomped his feet to remove as much dirt from his boots as possible before pulling the screen door open and stepping into the house.

Iliamna just grinned. She appreciated the effort that the men went to, to keep the outdoors out of the house, but sometimes their exaggerated efforts were simply too laughable.

"What can I do for you, Johnny?" She asked, wiping the flour from her hands. Carmen had taken to her bed with a severe cold, which left her and Karan with the daily chores. After only a few days of trying to cook for the dozen ranch hands, cleaning the house, and tending to the baby, she was in awe of Carmen's abilities, especially since Carmen had done it all single-handedly for quite some time—before she and Karan had arrived to help.

"I went to pick up supplies in town, ma'am, and there was a telegram waiting for you," Johnny said shyly, his gaze on his stocking feet that continually shuffled about in nervous tension. He was just a few years older than Iliamna, and so smitten with her that he couldn't even look her in the eye. Carmen laughed when Iliamna mentioned this the first time, saying that, "the boy knows better. He don't dare look at you with desire in his eyes, or Shreve will kick his ass." She'd been joking, of course, but she wondered whether Johnny really worried over that happening. She couldn't imagine Shreve doing anything like that, although she didn't think he'd hesitate to use violence if her life were in danger—had already proven he was capable of taking a life in her defense; however, that was completely different than killing in a jealous rage. That she couldn't see him doing.

She took the telegram from Johnny, "Thank you Johnny. Oh, and would you mind letting the men know that lunch will be served in a quarter hour?"

"Yes ma'am," Johnny said, and then turned and fled the house.

Iliamna shook her head and then settled down at the table to read the telegram. Her hands shook mildly, for she knew that it was most likely from Shreve. She drew in a deep breath and then opened the folded paper, tears welling in her eyes at the brief message:

*Am such a fool. Forgive me?*

"Oh, Shreve," she whispered.

"Are you okay, ma'am," Karan asked, coming into the kitchen with Brendan on her hip.

Iliamna sniffled and rubbed the tears from her eyes. She planted a smile on her face, which quickly turned genuine when Brendan spotted her and smiled a big, toothless smile. She stood, slid the telegram in her pocket, and took the baby from Karan, hugging him firmly. "I'll feed him his bottle if you'll finish up the meal. I told Johnny it would be ready in about fifteen minutes."

"Yes ma'am. Will do."

"I'll only be a moment, little one," she murmured, placing Brendan in the bassinet near the back door. Renewed tears threatened as she thought about Shreve's words; words that expressed that he finally believed her. She closed her eyes for a moment, trying to control the rush of emotions that flooded her mind. Relief, joy—and anger.

"Ma'am, are you sure you're okay?" Karan asked, removing the bottle from the pot on the flame. She held it out for Iliamna, who stood staring at it, as if not even aware of its existence. It took Karan saying her name several more times for her to return from the musings in her mind back to the kitchen.

Iliamna shook her head and took the bottle from Karan's outstretched hand, "I'm sorry, Karan. I guess I'm just a little distracted."

"And missing your husband too, I'd wager," Karan said. "I know that if I was married, I'd miss my husband something fierce if he were to go away for a long time," she continued, throwing another batch of seasoned flour in the frying pan.

Iliamna smiled sadly, reaching down to pick Brendan up from the bassinet, "Yes, I guess I do miss him."

"Well, hopefully he'll conclude his business in a flash and you'll be back together with him soon."

Iliamna smiled, not certain how to feel about that prospect. He'd apologized, most humbly, so she would forgive him, but if she forgave him and decided to stay, would there be some future instance when her honor would again come into question? Could she live with him knowing that he was so mistrustful? Could she really leave little Brendan behind, a baby who was becoming more her own each passing day? "I think I'll feed Brendan on the front porch, Karan. It's such a beautiful day that I find it difficult to remain cooped up. Oh, and after the men have settled down, would you take Carmen some soup? I already prepared it."

"Yes ma'am."

"Thank you." Iliamna left to the sound of the maid singing the antiquated tune *I Leave my Heart with Thee*[8], which caused the tears to well in Iliamna's eyes again, for if she did leave Shreve, he would definitely keep her heart with him.

She settled onto the porch swing, and snuggled Brendan into the crook of her arm. No sooner had the baby started suckling on the bottle's nipple, than Iliamna's mind drifted again to Shreve and her circumstances. He was a very enigmatic man with the most magnetic personality. She only knew about him that which he'd revealed—which could be untrue, for all she really knew. She shook her head and sighed, for she found she was very nearly doing what she'd accused him of—being mistrustful and disbelieving. That knowledge jolted her down to her core. If at her young age, she could easily doubt someone, it suddenly was easy for her to see how a man Shreve's age—and a prosecutor by trade—could mistrust those around him. Moreover, if the infinitesimal amount of information he'd revealed about his past told her anything, it was that he had every reason not to trust people. She now felt very bad about her stubborn attitude towards his wary nature. That feeling was short-lived as Brendan chose that moment to remind her of his presence.

"Oh my," she muttered, placing the bottle on the little table and lifting Brendan from her lap, "it looks as if we're both going to need a wash and a change." She stood, holding the baby away from her, as

---

[8] *I Leave my Heart with Thee.* Written in the early 1800s. Music composed by James Hook.

she quickly made her way indoors and up the stairs. "I must say I'm looking forward to the day when you can talk. A nice warning now and again would be nice," she continued conversationally as she ran the bath water. "Nothing elaborate, mind. Just a simple "I have to tinkle" would be most helpful. Here, darling, you just lie down here while I peel these wet clothes off and then we'll both clean up, okay?" She laid Brendan onto the rug and then quickly shed her clothing, her nose crinkling as she lowered her skirt to the floor. "And that's another thing," she said, lifting Brendan and carefully stepping into the tub, "I simply haven't enough clothing yet for you to be spoiling them so quickly. Wash day is only once a week you know." She continued conversing with the little boy as she quickly washed away the stench of urine from both of their bodies. When she felt cleansed, she carefully moved from the tub to her adjoining bedroom. "You're just going to have to lie there a moment while I dress, and no messes on my bed, if you please." The baby gurgled which made Iliamna smile; a genuine smile that reached down and relief her heart of all doubt and anger. For the first time since arriving at the ranch, she felt at peace.

Barbara Woster

## CHAPTER THIRTY-THREE

"How we do this thing?" Gitano asked. The three men boarded the train for Texas the next morning, but none spoke until the conductor came through telling the passengers that they had crossed over the Texas line and would reach their first destination of Dawson Creek within a couple of hours. However, the three of them had decided they would remain on the train until Twin Rivers, since that was a closer ride to the whorehouse. This didn't exactly sit well with Shreve, since Twin Rivers was a further ride from his ranch.

"My first instinct is to go the ranch and take Iliamna to a safe location," Shreve replied. He'd been stewing most of the night and hadn't slept well, which made him cranky and far from gun shy.

"I would agree with you if we didn't need to move on Alana first thing," Mitch said. "If Alana doesn't pay Gitano and give him specific instructions, then we can't build a case against her."

"I understand that," Shreve snapped, "but what I don't understand is your reluctance to let me go remove Iliamna to safety. If all that's needed is for Gitano to accept Alana's money..."

"It may not be Alana who pays him," Mitch interrupted. "Remember what you said when you found out the telegram's origination?"

"Yeah," Shreve muttered.

"If this Red lady is now involved, then there is more to this than just arresting Alana."

"That still doesn't explain why we have to allow Iliamna to remain at the ranch; to remain unaware of what's going on," Shreve said, trying to hold tight to his temper.

Mitch sighed, "You know, there may not be a justifiable reason, Shreve, but bringing Iliamna into the mix just mixes things up more. To me, any additional cogs added to the wheel of our plans, may cause it to function incorrectly. Think like me for a minute, and not a man in love. First, if Alana has someone watching the ranch and we arrive there..."

"The person could notify Alana and we lose any hope of arresting her," Shreve concluded.

"Precisely, but there are too many more unknowns also. Let's look at all we're facing here. We have to plan this with every contingency in mind—whether those contingencies come into play or not. So, we have to assume the woman is Iliamna, since Alana made the trek to meet you. Then, we have to assume that Alana may have someone keeping an eye on your ranch to ensure Iliamna is there when Gitano arrives to kidnap or kill her. We already assume that Alana has gotten help from this Red lady, who is out for vengeance against you, which adds yet another unknown to our plan. For all we know, Alana isn't calling the shots anymore. It may be Red, which is another eventuality we have to prepare for. With that in mind, we have to assume that Red may have already recaptured Iliamna and taken her back to the whorehouse..."

"Which means heading to the ranch first could be wasting time," Shreve interjected.

Mitch nodded and continued, "In which case Red may be paying Gitano to act as executioner—for you or Iliamna. We simply don't know anything of value to be going off half-cocked. Too many variables to go mucking everything up with an act of love."

Shreve ran his hand along his stubbled jaw, sighing heavily, "Things would be so much easier if we could just shoot them both."

"Then that would make us the criminals," Mitch retorted.

"Yeah, but things would be far simpler."

"I only meet Alana the two times," Gitano interjected, "and as I tell you before, she *muy loca* and this make her *imprevisible.*"

Before Mitch could complain about his lack of comprehension, Shreve muttered, "She's crazy so we may not be able to predict what she's going to do."

"Ah."

"Anyway, I say this thing because I think Mitch he is right. It is best to know much everything and to do this I must go to meet her and take her money. This give me chance to ask much questions. If we know more, we plan better, yes? But this also hard thing to do for me because I tell Alana one time that I no wish to know nothing about any person who hire me, so if I ask too much question, she may have much *recelo*."

"She'll get suspicious," Shreve interpreted immediately.

"Sí, this is so."

"Are you certain your enthusiasm to assist doesn't stem from your love of money?" Shreve asked, suddenly suspicious of Gitano's eagerness to help.

"I have not lie about loving money," Gitano said with a shrug, "but I do this thing because I no like Alana wanting harm to Iliamna." Gitano turned back to Mitch, "I have one more thing to say for that you said is possible to happen."

"What's that?" Mitch asked, his brow furrowing over Gitano's thick-accented butchery of the English language. It appeared to Mitch that the more nervous he got, the less comprehensible he got.

"You say this Red person may stole Iliamna back to her place already, yes? Well, if this is so, how I tell you this thing for you to rescue her again? Alana may say to me to go kill Iliamna *inmediatamente*."

"He said..."

"I got that one," Mitch interjected. "And that's an unknown for which we definitely need a plan. If Red has Iliamna, and Alana hires Gitano to kill her straightaway, how are we to know and how are we to prevent it happening? Gitano can't shoot his way out of the whorehouse as you did, Shreve."

"There is one thing more that we have not think of," Gitano said, as if a thought suddenly struck him.

"Great," Shreve muttered, "yet another dilemma in this convoluted plan-making."

Gitano snorted, "*Sí, es posible*. Is only, what if Red she recognize me and make connection that it is me who bring Iliamna to her place. If this is so, she may speak of this..."

"Which may alert Alana that it's Iliamna at my ranch, if she doesn't already know," Shreve concluded. "Just great!"

Shreve glanced out of the window at the terrain, his brow knitted in worried contemplation. Mitch and Gitano also fell silent, each trying to determine a course of action based on the little they really knew. Shreve knew it would be far easier to execute a plan if Iliamna was still at the ranch, and Alana hadn't hired someone to act as lookout, but Mitch was right—it was better to be prepared for any eventuality. Being unprepared was worse than finding oneself with his pants down around the ankles in a gunfight.

"Okay. I propose that first," Shreve said after a time, "you keep your head down, Gitano. Try not to bring attention to yourself so that Red doesn't recognize you. She probably paid little attention to you, since it was just business. Next, Mitch and I could remain out of sight, a few miles from the whorehouse. If, for any reason, you do not come out of the building in a certain amount of time, Mitch and I can assume the worst and...what? Ride to the rescue with guns blazing?"

"But if he does emerge and meet up with us," Mitch continued, nodding, "we can assume that the target is elsewhere and we can discuss what to do then."

"So, it's gun blazing if he doesn't come out," Shreve confirmed, "and more planning if he does."

"That about sums it up," Mitch grinned sheepishly.

Shreve sighed heavily, "I'm feeling more confident by the mile," he said sardonically.

"There does appear to be too many unknowns at this juncture; too many possibilities to plan for. If only we knew ahead of time who Alana is gunning for and where that target is, we'd know what to do," Mitch added.

"Is only possible that we wait to see," Gitano said softly. "Sometimes things must be done with no plan."

Shreve sighed, "I still think it would be easier just to kill 'em," he whispered angrily.

"You might want to get some rest," Mitch said, "or you'll be threatening to kill everyone on this train next. You're too tired and too worked up."

"Yeah," He groused. "You happen to have a way for me to do that?"

"I could pistol whip you?"

"I wouldn't even recommend you try it," Shreve grinned thinly.

"I'll just try to lie down and close my eyes." He stood and pulled on a chord above their heads. A door opened, revealing a bed. He jumped up and laid down, his hands behind his head, his gaze glued to the ceiling, and his mind in turmoil.

Mitch shook his head and sighed.

"He very angry," Gitano said softly.

"He's got a lot of reasons to be," Mitch said, and then turned his attention to the barren landscape out the window. After a moment, he turned back to Gitano, "I have to admit, you've got me stumped."

"How I do this thing?" Gitano grinned.

"You kill people for money, but aren't much different than some normal folks I know. You don't even strike me as a man who has the temper to kill. Even Shreve seems more of a hothead."

"I heard that," Shreve said.

"I know," Mitch replied, and then turned back to Gitano, "Anyway, I've arrested my share of killers and not one of them was on an even keel. There was just something not right about them. But you..."

"I am normal man?"

"Yeah, I guess. So, if you're so normal, why kill?"

"I love money," Gitano said simply.

"That's it? You love money?" Mitch shook his head.

"Sí this is so, and killing pays much money."

"Like I said, in my experience it takes a special kind of person to kill another person; someone that's a little more than crazy; but I can't see crazy in you."

Gitano grinned, and replied softly, "Is there. I hide it well."

"I guess you do." Mitch shook his head in bemusement. He leaned his head against the headrest and lowered his Stetson over his eyes. After a moment, he spoke again, almost as an afterthought, "You know, now that I know who you are, I'll be arresting you one day."

"I not think this to be so," Gitano whispered confidently, and then turned to look out at the passing landscape.

## CHAPTER THIRTY-FOUR

"So, Butcher," Red said, trying to maintain a positive tone of voice as Alana sashayed about the room, "do you think Alana has mastered allure?"

Red speared him with an irritated look when he didn't immediately respond; a look which said, *I paid you $10, so you better make it good.*

"I definitely want to take her upstairs and have my way with her," Butcher exclaimed in, what he hoped, was sufficient enthusiasm.

"Well, you can't have me," Alana purred, and Red and Butcher closed their eyes to hide the effect the sound had on their hearing. "I'm Shreve's woman."

"He can have you," Butcher whispered beneath his breath, and Red shot him another disgruntled look. Butcher straightened his shoulders and said, "Well, you are certainly easy on the eyes, which should make that half-, I mean, Shreve, a happy man." He concluded with a look at Red, which fairly pleaded with her to let him off the hook now. As far as he was concerned, he'd earned his ten dollars just by compulsion of hearing that voice. Red may have improved this girl's outward appearance considerably over a few days ago; but as far as he was concerned, she was still just above a Desert Mole Rat on the scale of attractiveness.

Red nodded at Butcher, who bolted up the staircase. She shook her head and sighed, and then turned to look at Alana again, still sashaying comically across the floor. A once-over of her appearance and she had to admit that Alana was far easier on the eyes than before she'd completed her overhaul. The makeup served to hide most of the pits in her skin, the mascara brought attention to her eyes, which were normally easily overlooked amid the blotchy face. The lip color defined a normally too narrow mouth, and the rouge added needed color to a pale complexion.

Her voice however, was still a major problem. The high nasally sound could peel the skin off a snake. On top of that, she'd accomplished little toward instilling womanly wiles into the girl, which still astonished her. In all her years of transforming women into whores, she considered herself an expert; however, this girl seemed above instruction. That too surprised her, as she didn't lack intellect; albeit that intellect appeared more suited to being deceptive than being womanly. Red sighed again.

She could only hope that Shreve's honor would float to the surface and he'd take her on when he realized that this was his mail order intended and not her whore. If she were in Shreve's shoes, she'd be hard-pressed to be persuaded of the benefits of this girl over the other. She sighed heavily, which brought Alana's attention to bear on her.

"Am I not doing it right?" She whined, plopping down into a nearby chair.

"You *look* fine," Red said, taking a seat opposite. Alana didn't miss the emphasis on the word "look" and scowled.

"I am not certain what you expect me to do about how I talk. It's not like I do it on purpose," Alana whined.

"I'm just not at all convinced that God wasn't laughing when you were born. After messing with your looks, He could have spared you in the vocal region; but *no*, He had to make you a walking joke."

"You really can be cruel, you know that? I thought that bar owners were supposed to be a sympathetic lot."

"We are—normally—but someone has to tell you the truth of the matter, girl," Red retorted, "and the truth is that you don't have what men want—no matter how we dress you up; and that has me mighty concerned over how we're going to talk Shreve into taking you, when he's got that gorgeous whore of mine as a replacement."

"We'll just have to make certain that he sees only me; and if he happens to be grieving too..." Alana let the sentence hang, looking at Red to see if she caught her meaning.

"You want me to kill the girl," Red said softly, easily reading the girl's expression. Once again, she was astonished at how evil this girl was. Red wasn't above killing, but it was an inclination she'd developed late in life as a survival mechanism; a means by which to keep afloat in an era when men ruled. Never had killing crossed her mind at this girl's age; an age when the only thing that should preoccupy the mind is cotillions and romance. She looked over to where Alana sat nodding, an over-eager expression on her face, which made Red shake her head with a sigh. Sometimes she forgot how deep malevolence ran in the girl's veins, because she seemed so naïve and childish at times. It made her wonder if her youth is what made her so dangerous. After all, maturity aided a person in thinking logically and prevented irrational action—more times than not.

Red shook her head again and settled at the table, "You seem to forget that I want my girl back—alive. She will make me a lot of money, so I'm not inclined to dispose of a profitable asset. That would be stupid, and stupid I'm not."

Alana deflated, "Then what do you propose we do. I want Shreve and Shreve wants your whore; a whore I can't compete with, according to you."

"Well since you're unwilling to play the part of a mute, I suppose we could make Shreve *think* his woman is dead. A sort of compromise, wouldn't you say? And as I said before, I certainly don't want Shreve coming back here searching for her."

"And you've said you'd be unwilling to pay the extra two hundred for Gitano to do away with the girl," Alana added, with a twinge of anticipation in her voice; a hope that Red would suddenly be willing to change her mind. Red's expression said otherwise, and Alana sighed, "Well then, I suppose we could always have him do with her the same as I had him do with my cousin—ship her off to Barbados."

"I want my girl *back*," Red reiterated in a tone that defied Alana to continue with plans of permanent removal. "I agree that it would be better if your man were to possibly keep her out of sight for a while—until Shreve is convinced she isn't here—but then I want her returned. That's what I am paying for."

Alana huffed, "Fine! But I'm telling you that keeping her alive might not be wise."

"After what Shreve and I went through with my whore, I doubt that he'll grace my doorstep again—once he's satisfied that his whore isn't here anymore. So, there shouldn't be a concern of him finding out about her. And even if he should discover she's back here, I'll have her so used up in so short a time that any beauty that attracted

182

him to her in the first place will have diminished considerably, so that she'll be as unappealing as..."

"Me," Alana concluded.

Red nodded.

"So what do we do while we wait for Gitano to arrive?" Alana asked after a prolonged silence.

"We work on your voice," Red said.

## CHAPTER THIRTY-FIVE

"Ok, we'll wait for your arrival here," Mitch said with a heavy sigh indicating doubt in their plans. That had Shreve sighing also. "It'll be okay, Shreve," Mitch reassured, placing his hand on his friend's shoulder. "If Gitano is delayed more than half hour, we'll go in and get your girl, because we can then assume that she's been brought back here. And remember, Gitano, if they do tell you to kill the girl right then, stall using every tactic in your arsenal. We'll be along within half hour of your arrival at the whorehouse. And if it doesn't happen to be Iliamna, then at least we know that we'll have Alana and Red in custody with enough charges to put them in jail for the remainder of their life, so Iliamna will be safe from any further attempts against her—or you, Shreve."

Shreve nodded, hoping all went accordingly and that, if Iliamna was back at the whorehouse, she hadn't been hurt already. He closed his eyes against the thought, "Just get going, Gitano. The sooner you get there, the sooner we can put this behind us and I can stop worrying over whether Iliamna is safe."

"Sí, this is so. I go now."

"It'll be okay," Mitch reassured Shreve as they watched Gitano gallop away.

"I sure hope so," Shreve said, staring at his pocket watch, each minute ticking away far too slowly.

\* \* \* \* \* \* \* \* \*

Gitano dismounted and crossed himself as he pushed through the saloon doors, saying several prayers at once; hoping that God heard the prayers of hired killers; especially since his prayers weren't selfish ones. He prayed that Red didn't recognize him, that Iliamna wasn't there, and, if she was, that they didn't ask him to kill her. Of course, they hadn't sent enough money for him to kill anyone, so that gave him a modicum of hope, and a method by which to stall if killing was requested. He'd simply haggle over pricing for half hour.

He stood there a moment, allowing his gaze to adjust from the bright sunlight outdoors to the smoky, dimly lit room. He was just about to move further into the room when a familiar voice stopped him in mid step, "*¡Dios mío, Santo Maria!*" He hissed, closing his eyes against the onslaught, "That voice!"

"I knew you'd take the job," Alana exclaimed, taking his hand and pulling him along toward the bar, "I told Red that you were the man to get the job done," she continued chattering like the young girl she was. "She wanted to hire someone else, but I wouldn't hear of it." She led him over to the bar and then started away, "Wait here. I'll go get Red." Gitano sighed in relief that he was spared her voice for a few minutes longer. He crossed himself again as he heard the two women approaching his position, praying again that Red wouldn't remember him. God must not have heard after all, for the minute he turned, recognition dawned in Red's eyes.

"You brought me the girl," she said simply. Gitano nodded, eyeing the two guards that approached with the two women, double pistols hanging from the gun belts strapped to their waists. He suddenly felt under protected with his one .38 caliber tucked into his waistband.

Alana stiffened, "You know him? And what girl?" Her eyes widened as she rapidly put two-and-two together, and then she sucked in a deep breath between her bared teeth, "You didn't take Iliamna to Barbados, did you?" She whispered in an angry hiss. "You said you knew of a Texas whorehouse...*this* whorehouse."

"That's right," Red nodded, "That was the girl's name. Iliamna. Good God! That was your cousin? No wonder you wanted her gone. You don't hold a candle to that girl!"

Alana snarled.

Gitano suddenly felt ill at ease, faced with a hostile child, a known-vicious bartender, and two hired guns. He lifted his chin and affected an arrogant air, "Is correct. I bring her here. I tell you when you hire me, I no listen to where you want her gone. Where she go is my decision, and I know this place pay *mucho dinero* for beautiful girl."

"And I did, and I want her back."

"Sí, I see this is so," Gitano replied, falling back on his professional detachment. In the corner of his vision, he could see Alana's hostile expression aimed at him, but he couldn't afford to worry over the petulance of a child. "And since you will pay me

185

much money," he continued, "I just need know where girl is. Why she no here no more?"

"Someone took her from me. I'll tell you where she is," Red said.

Gitano nodded, "And then I bring her back here?"

"No," Red interjected quickly, "I'm paying you to keep her away from here, but only for the next two weeks. By then, Shreve should be convinced that she's no longer in my possession and stop searching for her here. In two week's time, you'll bring her back. Unscathed."

"Two weeks is long time. If you want I should keep her, it take much money for me to feed her..."

"I sent you three hundred to get you here, which means I'm more than willing to pay what it takes. I want that girl back." Red reached into her reticule and pulled out some bills, "I am giving you half of your total payment up front..."

It was as far as she got when the sound of a gun firing startled her into dropping the hundred and fifty dollars. She spun around to see her startled gunman gaping at his empty holster and a furious Alana pointing his .38 at her chest.

"You'll tell *me* where Shreve's ranch is," Alana hissed, pulling back on the hammer.

Red glanced down at the hole in the center of Gitano's chest, "You've made a mess of my property," she said abstractedly, astonished at the girl's ability with a gun. Most women of her acquaintance didn't have the strength to pull a trigger on a .22, much less on a .38. She'd definitely underestimated this girl. She knew she was evil enough to *hire* a gun, but never fathomed her ability to use one.

"Tell me," Alana hissed.

"I want her alive," Red said firmly, stalling. Hoping that her guards would take action, but both seemed more like timid jackrabbits than gunmen. She sighed.

"And I want her dead," Alana snapped, steadying the gun with her other hand. "Who do you think is going to get what they want now?"

"Well now, I can't see as I have much option," Red said, preferring life over a whore, even one as special as Iliamna. Of course, she could just send this girl on a wild goose chase, and try to retrieve her whore before she gets wise...or not. This girl would figure it out quickly and then come back to shoot her. It was better to just let it go. "Just follow the primary path north for three days. You'll run into Shreve's ranch just north of a big lake..." It was as far as she got before Alana started inching toward the saloon doors.

"Shreve will kill you if you touch Iliamna. You know that, don't you?"

"He'll forgive me when he finds out that Iliamna isn't who he thinks she is."

Red snorted, "You don't get it, do you? Shreve won't want you. He'll put you on a train back east if he doesn't arrest you for having Iliamna kidnapped in the first place. You don't think that Iliamna hasn't told him everything by now?"

"He won't believe her."

"You're a naïve..." The shot whizzed past her ear and shattered the mirror behind her. She ducked and her gaze came into contact with the hole in the middle of Gitano's chest. She'd been lucky, she realized, to still have a head. By the time she looked up from the corpse at her side, Alana was gone. A few seconds later, she heard the pounding of hooves from the side of the building. She looked at the saloon doors just as Alana galloped by on one of her best mares. She shook her head and sighed heavily.

Butcher came running downstairs and for a moment, she thought to send him after the girl, but she wasn't certain he could take on the devil and win; especially when the little twit managed to disarm one of her men without so much as a hint of a warning. "Get someone to clean this mess up," she snapped, and started for her office. She wasn't happy that she'd lost Iliamna, but it was better than losing her life and more of her men. In a way she couldn't explain, she was relieved that her collaboration with Alana had come to an end. She somehow felt cleaner in her soul without the presence of the girl in her saloon and that made her want to spread some of the cheer along to her patrons, "Butcher!" She called as she settled in behind her desk. The bouncer appeared a few minutes later.

"Yeah, boss?"

"When we open in a few hours, tell our patrons that we're having a two-for-one special, both on drinks and girls."

Butcher arched his brow in question, but Red merely waved him from the office. As soon as he closed the door behind him, Red laid her head down on her arms on her desk. She was suddenly very tired and emotionally drained.

# CHAPTER THIRTY-SIX

Shreve snapped his watch closed, "It's been half an hour and there's no sign of Gitano. Let's go."

Mitch nodded, "I just hope we placed our trust exactingly," he said as they headed to where they left their horses munching peacefully in a nearby field.

"A little late to worry over that. Besides, he may take the money and run—eventually—but I really think he likes Iliamna too much to run before seeing her safe."

"*If* Iliamna's the job," Mitch said, freeing the lead rope, "We were prepared for the fact that it could be someone else altogether."

"Which could be why he didn't show. If it wasn't Iliamna, he may have decided to take the job, and has already left in search of his quarry."

"Yeah, but I kind of hoped he wouldn't," Mitch said, as they mounted. With a kick on the horses' haunches, both men spurred their horses into a gallop. Within ten minutes, the small no-name town came into view, "Very quiet," Mitch called as they galloped down the hill.

"The only noise that ever comes from around here—I've noticed—is at the saloon, and I believe that it's currently closed at this hour," Shreve replied.

"I take it that this used to be a regular haunt for you?" Mitch said as they slowed their mounts.

Shreve nodded, dismounting in one fluid motion from his saddle. He immediately pulled both pistols from the holster, pulled back the hammers, and sprinted to the side of the saloon doors. He was ready this time.

He and Mitch took up position on either side of the doors. Even though the place was currently closed, the main doors were open, making it easier for them to see inside over the top of the swinging doors.

Quiet. The only activity inside were two men scrubbing the floor near the bar. Shreve looked over at Mitch who nodded. They pushed through the swinging doors simultaneously.

"We're closed," a voice called from a corner table.

"I don't see any signs of Gitano, Red, or Alana," Mitch said, while keeping his guns aimed on the men at the bar. Both dropped their sponges at their entrance and sat watching them warily. Butcher looked up from his drink at Mitch's comment, and immediately went for his gun. Shreve grinned, and fired.

The bullet slammed into Butcher's thigh, knocking him to his knees. Shreve took a step toward him, but Mitch placed a hand on his upper arm, restraining him, "We aren't here to murder," he reiterated.

"I missed his heart by a mile, or didn't you notice?" Shreve said, a smile evident in his tone.

Mitch grinned, "Yeah, I noticed. I also noticed that you are more than ready to fire again."

"Only if he doesn't prove docile now," Shreve said.

"What's going on?" A feminine voice called from the upper landing, and Mitch immediately ran for the stairs, taking them two at a time.

"Don't move," Shreve said, but Butcher ignored his warning, so he fired another warning shot that struck Butcher's gun arm; an arm that now lay useless by his side.

Mitch hit the upper landing at the same time, and spotted the obese redhead leaning over the railing, gaping at the goings on below. She was so preoccupied, that she didn't readily notice him heading in her direction. When she did, she made the mistake of drawing on him. He fired, and she fell backward with a thud, gripping her upper arm with a loud groan. "I wouldn't recommend picking up that little pea shooter again. Now get up, and let's head on downstairs. We need to be conversing about a number of serious matters."

"And why should I listen to murdering scum like you?" Red hissed, squeezing her eyes tight against the pain radiating through her upper arm.

Mitch rolled his eyes, "Stop being so dramatic. It's just a small flesh wound. Besides, we haven't killed anyone, although as a lawman I am well within my rights to if someone draws down on me—which you did. So," he continued, as Red pulled herself up from the floor—with effort—"I'd say you are fortunate to still be breathing." He waved the gun at her as she passed, indicating that she precede him down the staircase. When she spotted Shreve, his gun moving from her gunmen to Butcher, she lifted her skirts, sprinted the rest of the way down the stairs, and made a beeline for him—like a freight train with too much coal in its firebox.

It took a moment for Mitch and Shreve to register her intent, but by the time they did, she was already barreling into Shreve, knocking him to the floor. The two gunmen took advantage of Shreve's incapacitation, and stood, drawing their weapons. Neither got them fully from their holsters before Mitch fired, knocking both against the bar; a bullet hole in one man's gut, the other with a hole in the forehead.

The moment Mitch ascertained that he'd eliminated the threat, he ran across the floor, skidding to a halt, where Red sat atop Shreve's stomach, pounding on his chest with her fists, screaming in rage, completely oblivious to Shreve's fists pounding on her upper arms, trying to dislodge her.

Mitch placed the barrel of his gun against the back of her head. "I won't hesitate," he said simply, pulling back on the hammer. Red froze and then slid sideways onto the floor. Shreve groaned.

"You okay?"

Shreve moaned, and slowly slid to a sitting position. He nodded and winced, "I'm going to have a sore chest for a few days, but I'll live. Damn, Red, but you might consider losing a few pounds," He said offhandedly, stretching his back.

"How dare you show your face in here again, Shreve," Red huffed, her face as red as her hair, her breathing haggard.

"Where's Gitano?" Mitch asked, getting to the point quickly.

"Who?" Red asked, but the slight widening of her gaze and the flare of her nostrils gave her away.

"She knows," Shreve said simply. "She has the same expression she had when I showed her Iliamna's picture. She was lying then, as she's lying now."

Red remained quiet.

"Gitano is working for us, so we know he came in here," Shreve said. "So where is he, or do we need to take a few more shots at you to help with your recollection?" He aimed his gun at her other arm.

Red's jaw clenched, and when she finally answered, the level of hostility in the two little words was intense, "He's dead." She nodded to where the two men lie against the bar, their blood mingling with the blood already soaking the wood floor. At their looks of disbelief, she snapped, "Don't believe me? The body is out back."

"Why kill him if he came to do a job for you?" Mitch asked.

Red's gaze narrowed, "I didn't kill him. Alana did."

The mention of Alana's name jarred the men, and they suddenly realized that Alana hadn't put in an appearance yet, "Where is she?"

Red's gaze narrowed again. When she'd mentioned Alana, she had expected them to ask who that was, not recognize the name, "You know about her?"

"She's the main reason we're here," Shreve said, scanning the upper landing.

"I don't understand," Red said, pushing herself upright with her good hand. She made her way over to a nearby table and settled into a chair, laying her injured arm on the tabletop, "what would lead you to believe that she would be here with me?"

Mitch glanced at Shreve, wondering how much they should reveal. Shreve nodded as if comprehending the glance, which gave Mitch the go ahead, "We put two-and-two together," he replied finally. "We just happened to be speaking with Gitano when he got your telegram."

"I didn't send him a telegram," Red countered, her countenance getting smugger.

"No, Alana did, but you both were responsible for hiring him, and we all know *why* you wanted to hire him—to get Iliamna back. We connected you to Alana because of where the telegram originated. There's only one person close to Twin Rivers that has a grudge against me, and that's you."

"You can't prove I had any involvement..."

"We have Gitano's body out back—according to your own admission. That's enough to charge you with accessory to murder;

and enough to shut this place down permanently. We're putting you away, Red—for good," Mitch said.

Red wasn't certain if they had enough to really hurt her, but she didn't like the fact that they were ready to try, "I give you Alana, and you forget about me. Deal?"

"Not a chance," Shreve said. "Where is she?"

Red remained stubbornly mute.

"I'd call this an uncooperative witness," Shreve said, holstering his gun.

"I'd say she's closer to hostile," Mitch said, rubbing his thumb along his jaw line thoughtfully.

"How do you propose to convince her to talk?" Shreve asked, nonchalant, "Because if you leave it up to me, Alana's location will be the last bit of information she'll divulge to anyone—ever." He concluded his threat by pulling a knife from a scabbard attached to his belt.

"She took off more than half hour before you came in shooting up my place," Red said.

"Where?" Mitch demanded.

When Red remained quiet, Mitch placed his hands on the tabletop and leaned down toward her, "Don't make me keep asking things twice."

"She's gone after Iliamna," Red said in a whisper. "Took off outta here like a bat outta hell."

"Damn. I should've seen that coming. How are we going to transport Red to jail and go after Alana too?" Shreve asked, desperation in his tone. "We leave her loose and she'll take off on us, which means she'll remain a threat. On top of that, it's a three day ride to my ranch, and Alana's got a good head start on us."

"Get up," Mitch snapped at Red. "Shreve, see if you can't find something to paint an out of business notice on the doors and then be ready to shut this place up tight. I'll take Red upstairs to her office, handcuff her to her desk and then let the girls out. They can make their way to Twin Rivers."

"We got time for all of that?"

"I think our mounts can catch Alana's without too much

difficulty. We'll get to her long before she reaches your ranch; but you're right—we have to ensure that Red and her bodyguard are taken into custody or they'll remain a thorn in your side. We leave without giving the local menfolk a reason as to why this place is shut down, and they'll come to investigate; possibly free Red before the sheriff can get back here..."

"I got it," Shreve said, moving toward the back of the saloon in search of supplies.

Mitch reached over and latched onto Red's arm, hauling her toward the staircase.

"You can't leave me here locked up!" Red screeched, digging her heels in.

"And what about me?" Butcher called from the corner, "I need me a doctor."

All gazes turned to where Butcher still lie, writhing in pain from the gunshot to his thigh and arm, temporarily forgotten in the hubbub.

"I'll tie you both up, and as soon as a nearby sheriff gets my note, someone will come and haul you both off to jail. Now move, Red. Shreve," he called, "find a couple of cloths to gag 'em with first. We don't need them drawing attention."

"I'm not going," Red retorted stubbornly.

"Fine," Mitch replied, and then kicked at the back of Red's knees. She collapsed on the stairs with a loud shout of pain. "I'll just handcuff you here then."

Shreve returned five minutes later and helped Mitch gag the two very disobliging prisoners, who spat and jerked about—anything to keep the rag from their mouths. In the end though, Mitch had both firmly bound and gagged.

"I'll get the girls dressed and out the door, you get the notification posted," Mitch said, heading upstairs again. "They'll most likely be sleeping right now. I only hope there aren't any patrons with 'em."

"You'd think that anybody up there would have come to investigate the shooting," Shreve shouted, scrawling *Out of Business* on several pieces of paper.

"Possible that the girls are too scared to make an appearance," Mitch called back, and then pushed open a door to one of the rooms. It was empty. He quirked a brow questioningly and then checked another room. Empty. "Do you know where she kept her girls?" He called over the landing at Shreve.

He had to call out twice for Shreve to hear over his hammering.

"Check the room closest to Red's office. Other end of the landing."

"Right," Mitch said, heading down the corridor. Shreve resumed hammering the signs up on the doors and outside walls.

Mitch reached the end room and opened the door. He scanned the room and finally found about a dozen women, all dressed in their skivvies, huddled against a far wall, alarm in their gazes. "I'm Marshall Crowell," he said. "I need you to get dressed and leave here now. This establishment is closed for business."

"But where are we to go?" One of the women whispered.

"There's bound to be some horses tied out back. Take them and ride for Twin Rivers. Locate the sheriff there. He'll help you ladies find a way back to your homes. Now let's go. I need you to hurry please. We need to get going, and need to see you ladies on your way before we do." He pulled out his pocket watch, and sighed. If Alana left when Red said, she had nearly two hours head start on them. He'd told Shreve they could easily catch up to her, but now he worried that they'd have difficulty doing so, unless she stopped for the night. He shook his head—he couldn't think about that right now; right now, he needed to prod these girls into moving quicker.

It was another half hour before all of the women were sufficiently clothed and mounted, some two to a horse. "Just keep heading west. Any doubts as to which way is west? Just keep an eye on the sun. It rises in the east and sets in the west. That way is west," he added, pointing. "Twin Rivers is no more than a day's ride. When you get there, locate the sheriff and hand him this note. He'll come back and deal with the two inside. Now go. You need to be well on your way before the local towns folks notice something going on." They'd been fortunate thus far that no one had risen to investigate the shooting, but then again, the menfolk in this small no-account town were probably accustomed to gunfire at all hours of the day and night.

"Mitch," Shreve called, leading Mitch's stallion toward the marshal, "We really need to get moving."

"Right." Mitch mounted, and then addressed the girls one more time, "Remember, head west, and make certain the sheriff gets that note. When the women nodded, both men spurred their horses into a gallop, determined to close the distance between Alana and themselves quickly.

## CHAPTER THIRTY-SEVEN

Alana refused to slow or stop, despite the sinking sun. Instead, the setting sun seemed to spark a fire of greater determination within her. She would not allow anything to deter her from her destination, including the inky blackness. She'd simply give the horse the lead, and keep it motivated to maintain a gallop. Her anger was providing enough fuel to keep moving, and she intended to transfer that fuming urgency to her mount.

Red's estimation was a three-day ride, but Alana figured she could cut that in half if she rode night and day, which she fully intended to. Come Hell or high water, she'd get to Iliamna and make her and everyone pay for her Hell of an existence. If she could keep her mount in motion, she would reach Shreve's ranch by suppertime the following evening.

As the horse continued to race across the Texas terrain throughout the night, without incidence, Alana took it as a sign that fate was on her side. She was tired, and the intensifying snorting from her horse's nostrils bespoke of its increasing exhaustion, but she wouldn't afford it time to rest. If she wasn't going to rest, then she wasn't going to allow the mare to rest.

No matter her determination, she was tense with nervousness at traveling across a terrain unseeing; not knowing whether her horse would stumble in a gopher hole and send her tumbling. So, when the sun began to rise on the horizon, she started laughing softly, in gratitude to whatever higher being kept her on track. Apparently, someone somewhere was on her side, for the first time in her life.

As the sun rose higher, and the temperature increased, she ignored the profusion of sweat glistening on the mare's hide and the perspiration coating her skin. She couldn't afford to bend to discomfort; couldn't afford to feel anything for the horse pounding the ground beneath her body. It was a mere tool to get her where she needed to go—nothing more.

Noon came and went, and the horse began to slow its pace, despite her shrill protestations; but she grew quiet immediately, when she spotted the sun reflecting off water in the distance, and knew that it must be the lake Red said was near Shreve's place. She would rest for a very short time there, allow her horse to drink and recuperate, so that it could take her the final leg of her journey.

She pulled the timepiece from around her neck and grinned. She'd reach her destination even sooner than anticipated. Far ahead of Red's three-day estimate and her own day and a half approximation. That is, if her mare didn't drop dead when they stopped.

* * * * * * * * *

Her mare dropped dead when she stopped. She had just enough time to clear the mare's back, when it snorted and toppled over, convulsing briefly before its eyes glazed over. She stomped her foot in anger, but then relief flooded her when she saw two men approaching on horseback.

She wasn't certain if she could talk either into loaning her his mount; however, she thought it might be possible to convince one or the other that it may be in his best interest to do so. She slid her hand into her skirt pocket and gripped the butt of the gun, prepared to pull it out and use it, if either of these men proved unchivalrous.

After several deep breaths, she affected an air of a damsel in distress, waving at the approaching men frantically. The mounts slowed and turned in her direction, and she laughed briefly. She'd gotten their attention. Now she just needed to get one of their horses. As they drew nearer, a thought struck her and she changed her plans. After all, she'd need her bullets for more worthy adversaries, so she'd only use it if these men didn't turn out to be the gentlemanly sort.

"Ma'am, what are you doing way out here?" One of the riders asked.

"And what happened to your horse?" The other eyed the horse in shock, wondering how it managed to be ridden to its death—by a woman.

"I'm so glad you came along," she said softly, in a near whisper, hoping to hide her retch-causing voice from these men. "I am visiting my cousin at her ranch. You may know her husband, Shreve Red Fox?"

"Ah, yes. Iliamna. Now that's a woman," the one man said

without thinking, and then cleared his throat, "Sorry, Miss. I didn't mean no disrespect, but how did you end up out here?" Alana took a few deep breaths through her nostrils and tried not to allow his reaction to her cousin to rile her. She needed their help and wouldn't get it if she acted deranged. As she began her explanation, one of the men dismounted and went to check over her horse.

"I went riding and got lost. Yesterday morning. I got frantic and started galloping around, not knowing where I was going. I'm afraid I drove my poor horse to death. Must have been ill to begin with. Now I have no way of returning to the ranch. Is there any way…"

"We happen to work for Shreve, ma'am, and don't recollect your visiting. When did you arrive?"

"We've been in Dawson Creek for the past week and a half, Mason," the other rider piped up. "She could have come at anytime whilst we were away. The mare certainly is a goner," he said, standing and returning to his mount.

"That's right. I only just arrived two days ago. I'm Alana Dearborn," she introduced, walking nearer. Thus far, she felt relieved that her whispering had worked in preventing their cringing at her speech. Perhaps that was the answer to her problem—not to play the part of a mute, rather learn to whisper the rest of her life.

"If you won't feel too discomfited ma'am, I can let you mount up behind me," the second man said.

"I just want to get back to the ranch quickly. Poor Iliamna must be near panicked at my disappearance; and I'm absolutely exhausted and hungry also. Do you think we could ride quickly?"

"We wouldn't want you to get too jarred, Miss," Mason said, as his partner assisted Alana in mounting.

"Oh, I'd preferred to be jarred than to be out here in the heat much longer."

"We did want to get back before the evening meal was laid out," Spencer said, pulling himself up in front of Alana. "And as long as the lady is obliged to allow us to race home, I say we do just that."

"How far out is it?" Alana queried, wrapping her arms around Spencer's waist. "How far did I wander?"

"We should be at the ranch inside three hours," Spencer said.

"Now hold on tight, Miss. I wouldn't want you taking a tumble."

The men spurred their mounts into a gallop and Alana laid her head against Spencer's back. Despite the jarring, she soon found herself dozing off.

# CHAPTER THIRTY-EIGHT

"It's a mare," Shreve said, kneeling beside the carcass of the horse. "I can't say whether it's the one Alana was riding, but it's definitely not one of mine, and I don't see a brand to place it as one of my neighbors."

"Think she's desperate enough to keep moving on foot?"

"I don't know the woman personally, but I think we discovered enough about her from other sources to conclude she's mentally imbalanced, and capable of anything—including trying to get at Iliamna anyway possible. If that means running the rest of the way to the ranch, I wouldn't put it past her," Shreve said, mounting again. "Either way, we need to keep pushing on. If she is on foot, we'll likely overtake her. If she's veered off the main path, we may make it ahead of her, and may get lucky enough to apprehend her when she arrives."

"*If* she arrives. A woman on foot doesn't stand a chance out here."

"So much the better. The desert critters can have her. I won't be shedding any tears if she meets her demise out here, that's for damned sure. Let's go."

## CHAPTER THIRTY-NINE

"We'll drop you off here, Miss Alana," Spencer said, helping her dismount in front of the back door leading to the kitchen.

"At a servant's entrance?" Alana's eyes widened in outrage, and she nearly forgot to maintain her damsel in distress ruse. She'd not been this insulted since Red's comments about her person last week. So offended was she, that she nearly pulled her gun out to shoot these two between the eyes.

"As you know, we don't have a big staff miss, and since it's close to meal time, you're likely to find someone in the kitchen who can get you settled and fed. Of course, if you'd rather, you can mount back up, and we can ride you around to the front..."

"No, I understand perfectly," Alana sighed, and then grinned. These two hadn't realized just how close they'd come to being buzzard food. Plus, they'd unknowingly placed Iliamna right into her path, which was ideal, since Alana hadn't really planned out her scheme, and could have wandered a house this size for a while in search of her prey; possibly encountered difficulties that would have hindered her plans. Her grin widened.

"We'd see you in, but we really need to get ourselves bathed for dinner. We'll see you around though."

"I certainly appreciate both of your assistance, and will let Iliamna and Shreve know how grateful I am. Perhaps you will see a small bonus in your next check," Iliamna whispered airily.

"That would be mighty nice," Mason said, and then tipped his hat and trotted away, followed closely by Spencer. Alana watched them go, took a deep breath, and reached for the doorknob. She stopped. What was she supposed to do now that she was here? Her relief at having found a ride to the ranch had consumed her for the entire trip, and now she was here, only a door separating her from Iliamna. And then her hand brushed up against her skirt pocket and she recalled the .38 tucked away in the depths. She slipped her hand in her pocket and grinned. As she stood there fingering the warm metal, an idea formed. Initially she thought to shoot Iliamna on sight, but as she stood there—one hand on the gun, and the other on the doorknob—a different idea formed, one that widened her grin maniacally.

She opened the door and slipped inside, quietly.

An elderly woman stood at the stove, stirring something. The only person in sight; but then she heard a gurgle and looked over to her left.

A baby!

The initial idea that had formed while standing outside the door, fled her mind, and a new idea took shape. She reached down and hefted the baby, cradling it in her arms. She looked at it curiously, wondering whether this could be Iliamna's child, but after doing some quick mental calculations realized that it would be impossible. Still, it was someone's child, and if Iliamna cared for it at all...

"Can I help you?"

The sound of the voice startled Alana from her musings, but she retained control of her reaction, instead lifting her gaze to meet the curious gaze of the elder woman across the room. She smiled sweetly and moved forward, so she could be heard using her newly discovered whispering technique.

"One of the cowhands told me to come in through the rear, as I was more likely to encounter someone in here so close to mealtime," She continued softly. "I'm Alana Dearborn," she said, stretching out to shake the woman's hand while cradling Brendan in her other, "I'm Iliamna's cousin. When she wrote and told me that she'd moved here to Texas—well, I live about a day's ride west of here, so I decided to come on and pay her a visit. She did invite me after all."

"Oh my," Carmen whispered, "Well, welcome then. I'm Carmen, the housekeeper here. You look like you rode hard and fast, if I might say so. Perhaps you'd like to bathe before supper is served? I can set you up in the spare bedroom, and draw a nice bath."

"That sounds absolutely divine," Alana purred.

Just then, Iliamna walked into the kitchen, and Alana dashed over to greet her before she ruined her current plans.

"Cousin dear, I'm here!" She exclaimed, and threw her arms around Iliamna's neck. In her ear she whispered, "If you want

Carmen and this precious baby boy to live, don't fight me." When she pulled back, she noticed the look of horror on Iliamna's features and grinned. "I decided to take you up on your offer of a visit," she said cheerily, "and Carmen was kind enough to offer to draw me a bath. Oh goodness, do wipe the look of revulsion off of your face, Cousin," Alana whispered dramatically, "I don't smell all that wretched." She teetered softly, and then Iliamna blinked several times. She drew in a deep breath and then looked down at Brendan.

"Here, let me take little Brendan from you. It's time for his bottle," Iliamna said stiffly.

"Oh, do please let me feed him, while I wait for Carmen to draw that bath. It has been absolutely ages since I held a newborn."

Carmen watched the exchange in wonder, curious as to Iliamna's reaction to her cousin; wondering whether she was simply tired from working so hard throughout the day. The girl did like to pitch in and assist, giving everything her all. Still, her lack of enthusiasm was apparent, especially if she'd invited her cousin for a visit. Of course, her cousin could have been fibbing, and had simply dropped in unannounced, which may explain Iliamna's shock.

The other thing that made Carmen curious was the vast difference between the two. How could Iliamna be so beautiful and genteel and the other so horrid looking? Still, it wasn't for her to judge others.

"Will you see to that bath now, Carmen?" Alana asked, taking Brendan's bottle and settling at the kitchen table.

"Of course, Miss Alana." Carmen left the kitchen and Iliamna immediately moved toward Alana, preparing to snatch Brendan from her grasp, until Alana dropped the bottle on the table and retrieved the .38 from her pocket. She placed the muzzle near the baby's temple, and Iliamna froze midstride. Alana stood and smiled.

"Imagine my surprise, when I discovered Gitano had delivered you to a whorehouse instead of hauling you off to the coast and forcing you on a boat to Barbados, as I'd instructed; or selling you to a tribe up north somewhere. Imagine my greater surprise, when I discovered that my intended—Shreve—paid a visit to that whorehouse and whisked you away to live with him here."

Iliamna blanched. She was so immobilized with fear for little

Brendan, that she could barely draw breath, much less speak.

"So, in order to ensure my plans don't get mucked with again," Alana continued, "I decided to take matters into my own hands, instead of relying upon the hired help. So, pick up Brendan's bottle, and follow me."

Alana headed for the door, but when she turned, Iliamna remained rooted, "Unless you would like me to replace his head with a bloodied mass, you'll do as instructed."

Iliamna quickly bent and retrieved the bottle, and nearly sprinted the short distance to the back door. "Don't hurt him. I implore you."

"He's just coming along to ensure your compliance. Do what I say, and he'll survive to marry someone in the future; and since I'll be taking your place in Shreve's household, I'll do my best to ensure he marries a proper woman. Now let's go."

"Go where? Where are we going?" Iliamna asked, reluctantly stepping from the kitchen into the yard.

"I'll let you know when we get there. Now, where is the barn?" She said rhetorically, scanning the area. "Ah, there it is. You're going to have someone hitch us up a buggy. If you give any hint as to your current state of distress, I'll kill all three of us, starting with Brendan. Do you understand me?"

Iliamna nodded, raising her chin and striding off toward the barn, "Good evening, Charles," she greeted stiffly. "This is my cousin, Alana."

"Hello, Miss Alana. Nice to meet you."

"Likewise," Alana whispered.

"Could you please hitch a buggy for me? I need to collect the men for dinner, but since Alana is here for a visit, I didn't want to subject her to my normal mode of walking."

"Sure 'nough, Mrs. Iliamna. I'll have that done in a jif."

Iliamna sighed and turned away, swiping at the tears that threatened to fall. Alana saw her emotional struggle and patted the pocket holding the gun—a reminder that she needed to keep it contained. She kept breathing deeply the entire time Charles bustled about the barn, readying the horses. When he completed the task, he led the horses from the stable and helped the two women climb aboard the buggy.

"Head north," Alana whispered, waving cheerily to Charles who stood watching them depart.

"That will take us directly in the path of the field hands," Iliamna said.

"Good, then things will seem normal when you tell them it's suppertime. Only we won't be joining them. Just make certain you don't give anything away. I'm just aching to kill you."

"Then why don't you already?" Iliamna hissed. "You offered Gitano money to kill me, so now that you have a gun, why not just finish what you wanted him to do? Why go through with this charade?"

"Because, as much as I despise you, I wouldn't be able to insinuate myself into Shreve's life if I murdered his former whore; and also, I always wanted your life to be full of abject misery, so what fun will my life be if I killed you? I wouldn't be able to love your former lover, and gloat every day of my life if you were simply rotting away in some shallow grave. But," she exclaimed, raising a finger as if raising a point, "if I managed to take you away somewhere where you'd never be found and your life was guaranteed miserable; a life I directly affected...well, as I said, I can gloat."

"Afternoon, ma'am. Miss."

"Rod, isn't it?" Iliamna asked sweetly.

"Yes ma'am. Looks like you're finally getting our names right." Rod looked at Alana curiously. Iliamna caught the hint, "Rod, this is my cousin, Alana," she introduced. "She's visiting from Louisiana."

"Right nice pleasure to make your acquaintance, Miss," Rod said politely. "Is that why you're riding the buggy to fetch the men for dinner?"

Iliamna nodded, "I didn't want to bother Alana with my normal routine of taking a long walk, especially since she insisted on bringing Brendan along."

"Want me to let the rest of the men know, so you can head on back? It'll be dark soon."

"Are the rest of the men too much further north?"

"Not too far."

"Well then, I'll shoo them along, as always. You head on, and let Carmen know we'll be back soon."

Rod tipped his hat, hefted his gear, and headed toward the ranch.

"You're good under pressure," Alana complimented, as Iliamna clucked her tongue to get the horses moving again. "I never would have even guessed that you were fretful over Brendan's survival. And here I thought that I was a smooth liar."

Iliamna raised her chin a notch and refused to reply. After fifteen minutes, she spotted the final group of ranch hands and headed toward them. The sun was moving lower on the horizon, and her concern was mounting. Once these men moved on toward the house, she would lose all contact with anyone at Shreve's ranch. Her future would be entirely in Alana's hand. Her eyes misted over before she could prevent it, and one of the ranch hands noticed.

"Is everything okay, ma'am?"

"Having me here for a visit has been emotional for her. We haven't seen each other in forever," Alana responded. "I'm Alana Dearborn, Iliamna's cousin. She's been spouting tears off and on since I arrived."

Iliamna sniffed loudly and wiped the tears from her eyes, "I didn't mean to alarm you, Jeb," Iliamna told the foreman, her voice thick with emotion.

"It's okay, ma'am," he said, but couldn't erase the concern knitting his brow. "Is it time for supper then?"

Iliamna nodded.

"Want I should take the reins and see you two ladies safely returned?" He asked.

"No, no," Alana answered quickly, but then calmed her nerves, "We have so much catching up to do, we'd like to mosey back at our leisure. Just have Carmen put our dinner aside, please."

"It isn't safe out here at night, ma'am," Jeb said, the hairs on the back of his neck raising—at her explanation, her tone of voice, and her stiffening spine. Maybe it was the attorney in him, but something was off; only he couldn't put a finger on what it was. Perhaps the visitor's voice caused his weird response. She seemed to be affecting an airy tone purposely, but it didn't do much to alleviate the horrible nasally pitch that caused his skin to crawl. No wonder the lady of the house was having a hard time keeping her body relaxed. He'd stiffen too if he had to listen to that cousin of hers talk too much.

"Are you sure, ma'am," he asked, addressing Iliamna.

"Thank you, Jeb, but I don't think I'll have any trouble finding the house. I just want to show Alana a bit more of the ranch." Before he could respond again, she clucked her tongue and the buggy jarred forward.

"Keep the horses pointed north. I'll let you know when we'll shift direction again." Alana looked over her shoulder, and wasn't pleased to see that the foreman was still standing there, watching them. She smiled widely and waved. He waved back automatically and then turned toward the house. Alana grinned, and then straightened in her seat. Things were going precisely as she wanted. Iliamna was once again beneath her control. She looked down at the baby, sleeping soundly in her arms after finishing off his bottle. *I'll have to find a place to dump you before too much longer*, she thought, glancing out at the landscape.

# CHAPTER FORTY

It was well after nine in the evening when Mitch and Shreve made it to the ranch, and the first thing that Shreve noticed as they passed beneath the front gate, was that nearly every light in the house was on and that there were at least a dozen horses tied up front.

As Mitch and he dismounted, Mitch shot him a worried look, which Shreve returned. They bolted up the front steps and banged open the front door.

"Iliamna!" Shreve yelled, bounding up the stairs to the master bedroom. Empty. He ran the length of the upstairs and then bolted down the stairwell again when he didn't find her up there. He was halfway down, when he came to a sudden stop.

Over a dozen people, including Sheriff Barkley, had converged on the foyer and were standing there with Mitch, each wearing their emotions clearly on their faces; looks ranging from dismal gloom to blazing fury. Carmen was wringing her hands, sniffing loudly, while another woman, with whom Shreve was unfamiliar, attempted to console her, ineffectively.

"Shreve," The sheriff said simply.

Shreve sank to the step. His breathing came in heaving gasps as if he were starting to hyperventilate, and tears stung his eyes, "Is she dead then?" He whispered after a few minutes.

"Not that we're aware of," the sheriff said, and Shreve's head shot up.

"You mean..."

"We haven't found a body, but we did locate little Brendan. He was left beside a boulder some half hour ride north of here."

"Oh my God! Is he okay?" Shreve asked, leaping to his feet and finishing the distance to the foyer. "Is he hurt?"

"He's okay, thanks to Jeb," the sheriff replied.

Shreve turned his gaze toward Jeb, who quickly picked up the explanation, "Something just felt off. I can't quite place my finger on it, but Mrs. Iliamna seemed tense. Still, I came on back for dinner.

Then Carmen expressed concern over how the two women had left even though Miss Alana had asked that a bath be drawn, so, I decided to ride back out to the north pasture. Thought perhaps the buggy had lost a wheel, or that outlaws may have waylaid the women. That's when I heard a baby squalling, and spotted little Brendan's flailing arms and legs, but there weren't no sign of the women or their buggy. I wanted to go after them straightaway, but couldn't take Brendan out with me, so I brought him back here, turned him over to Carmen, and immediately sent Bobby over to fetch the sheriff. By the time the sheriff got here, it was too dark to go after the women."

Shreve sank to his knees, "Alana has Iliamna?"

Mitch moved over to kneel beside his friend, "That doesn't mean harm has come to her. We have to remain focused on the positive, Shreve. Jeb said there wasn't a body, so we have to move forward under the assumption that she's still alive."

The sheriff stepped up, "Why would y'all think that something untowards has befallen Miss Iliamna, and why would you think her cousin was behind it, is what I want to know? Are you saying that our discussions about *rescuing* the women at sunup has turned into something different?"

Shreve looked up, a tortured expression on his face, "There's so much more," he whispered, and then pushed himself from the floor. He straightened his spine and lifted his chin, "In fact, I think it's about time I explained everything that's been happening over the past several weeks. Let's move to the living room."

"Karan and I will make some more refreshments," Carmen offered, her voice a mere whisper.

"No, Carmen," Shreve said, placing a hand on her arm, "let... Karan, is it?"

Karan nodded, and Shreve continued, "Let Karan take care of it. I need you to hear this. You can get the refreshments, Karan?"

"Yes, sir," Karan snapped dutifully. She was intrigued by the master of the house, and all of the goings on of the past couple of hours, and wanted to be included in the meeting, but she was too new in the home, and not yet privy to private conversations.

She bustled off and everyone else moved the conversation into the living room. Shreve closed the door behind them and then settled onto a chair near the window. He glanced out at the darkness for a few minutes, hoping to see a sign of a returning buggy, but there would be no buggy returning, he knew. He sighed deeply.

"Do you want me to explain?" Mitch asked, concerned for his friend. Shreve nodded.

Mitch stood, "Let me start by introducing myself. I'm Marshall Mitchell Crowell. Mitch, for short. Shreve and I go way back, so when he came to Louisiana in search of help, I was the first person he came to see."

"It's a pleasure to make your acquaintance, Marshall Crowell. I'm Sheriff Tom Barkley." The sheriff reached out a hand and the two shook, and then Tom asked abruptly, "Does this have to do with how Miss Iliamna ended up in a Texas whorehouse and that Red woman that tried to have you arrested for murder?"

The outburst that followed took several minutes to die down, but only with a little help when Shreve shouted to cool it, "Everyone settle," Shreve snapped. "It has everything to do with it, Sheriff," Shreve said. To his employees he said, "Anything that we say in here, better stay in here. Is that understood?"

Everyone nodded, eyes wide with curiosity.

"Good, then I'm ready to take it from here, Mitch."

Mitch nodded and settled on a nearby chair. Shreve went to stand beside the fireplace and then launched into everything that had taken place in the previous weeks—from his placing an ad for a mail-order bride, to visiting the whorehouse and finding Iliamna; to not believing her story and going off in search of evidence—concluding with their confirmed suspicions that Alana had arrived at the ranch to finish what she hired Gitano to do. It took more than half hour to recount every detail, and not one person interrupted. When he finished they all remained seated in stunned silence.

That's how Karan found everyone when she entered bearing a tray full of sandwiches.

"Thank you, Karan," Shreve said.

"I'll return with a pitcher of tea shortly," she said softly, her gaze moving around the room. "Is everyone alright, sir?"

"Just fine, thank you. Run along and get the tea. I'd wager that by the time you return, everyone will have recovered from this dazed state."

"Very good, sir."

Karan had no sooner left the room than Carmen whispered, "What a fantastical accounting."

Shreve nodded. "Why do you think I wanted corroboration of some sort? Iliamna's story seemed too fantastical, but I was just stubborn enough to overlook the obvious signs that she was telling me the truth—like the bruise lining her jaw when I met her. It took me too long to realize that she hasn't a deceitful bone in her body. Too long."

"And now that woman," Carmen hissed, "has taken her away from us; to God only knows where. She was such a dear girl, and so marvelous with Brendan."

"We have to try not to speak of her in the past tense," Mitch encouraged. "We'll strike out in the morning and begin an extensive search. We'll find her—alive."

However, after a ten day exhaustive search, everyone's hope vanished, much as Alana had with Iliamna, and not a trace remained.

# CHAPTER FORTY-ONE

"Shreve! Shreve!" Mitch rode across the north pasture at breakneck speed, continuing to yell Shreve's name, leading a horse behind him. The men heard, and gave chase on foot, but it took another few minutes before Shreve realized that someone was screaming at him, so deep in thought was he.

He lifted his head and stared at the horses barreling toward him, and willed one of them to run over the top of him; and then shook his head and sighed. He had to snap out of his doldrums if he was going to keep his ranch afloat. He had an obligation to his ranch hands and to Jeb not to wallow in self-pity. It had only been two weeks since he'd lost Iliamna, and during that time he was at risk of losing himself. Only the support of his friends kept him going. Even Mitch had remained at the ranch, telling Shreve that he needed a vacation and that he trusted his deputies to keep everything under control in Shreveport.

Everyone around him understood only too well his anguish and afforded him his grieving period; but also pushed him into working—anything to keep his mind out of the abyss. That's what he'd been doing today—working his fingers to the bone in the north pasture.

Mitch skid his horse to a halt and leapt to the ground, dashing over to where Shreve stood, waiting. As Mitch approached, his concern for his friend intensified. He wasn't sleeping well, and the dark circles beneath his eyes grew more prominent with each passing day; but now, he had news to impart.

"A ranch hand has spotted the buggy returning from the south. It's headed here."

Shreve didn't so much as blink at the news, "It could be any buggy, not necessarily ours. Is unlikely to be ours if it's coming in from the south," he replied dully. "Alana headed north, remember?"

"It bears the crest of the Double Heart Ranch on the door," Mitch said, trying to keep his glee tamped down; especially as it may not mean anything.

Shreve sighed, "Someone probably found the buggy and is returning it. If the ranch hand suspected it was Iliamna," Shreve drew in a sharp breath and closed his eyes for a minute to steady himself. He hadn't spoken her name in six days, because of this very reason—it was simply too painful. After a moment, he continued, "If the ranch hand had reason to believe that she was returning, why didn't he approach the buggy and find out who was driving it, instead of sending you along to notify me with only partial news? No, it's not Iliamna. It can't be." Shreve turned and started to walk away, but Mitch stopped him.

"There was a woman driving," Mitch said, "and the ranch hand said that he was so excited by what he saw, that he immediately rode back here to tell someone. He wasn't thinking Shreve. That's why he didn't ride out to check. None of us have been thinking straight—stop walking away, damn you! It could be her!"

Shreve did stop, but when he turned back to respond, Mitch was taken aback by the utter defeat in his friend's gaze, "We both know it isn't her, Mitch, so why don't you stop trying to convince me of that fact."

"Come back to the house with me, Shreve. Even if it isn't Iliamna, the person bringing the buggy back may have some information that could lead us to where Alana took her. We owe Iliamna that much—not to give up on her..."

Shreve stomped over to his friend and stopped just shy of punching his lights out, "You don't think," he whispered harshly, "that I didn't give it everything I had? That I didn't put forth every effort to locate the woman I love? You think I just gave up on her," the tears filling Shreve's gaze contradicted the flushed anger in his cheeks. "If I thought for a minute that the person headed this way was Iliamna or someone that could help find her, I'd..." he stopped. His shoulders slumped and the tears fell.

"Come with me," Mitch whispered. "The buggy will arrive inside half an hour." Mitch wrapped his arm around Shreve's shoulder and led him toward the extra mount he'd brought. "You men head on back to the house. We may need to form another search party quickly."

Every man took off at a dead run back toward the house. Even if the person returning with the buggy turned out to be another dead end in their search, their curiosity was still well aroused. Everyone's but Shreve's.

"I can ride a horse, Mitch," Shreve snapped when Mitch took the lead rope instead of handing the reins to Shreve.

"Yeah, but I want to get back now, not tomorrow."

"Smart ass."

"That I am," Mitch replied glibly, and spurred both horses on toward the house. It didn't take long to arrive, so Mitch wasn't surprised that they'd arrived ahead of the buggy. He was surprised, however, at how quickly every ranch hand had assembled—waiting on the front porch. "You men head on back to the ranch house. We'll come get you if we need to head out," he called.

The men reluctantly dispersed, but instead of going inside the ranch house, they settled on the ground outside the building—waiting, anticipating. Each hoping that—for their boss's sake—it was Iliamna returning.

"You want to wash up before our guest arrives?" Mitch asked, as he and Shreve headed up the steps.

Shreve shook his head and simply headed into the living room. He took a seat by the window and just as quickly stood and moved away. He didn't want to see who it was; didn't want to hope anymore.

Mitch moved into the room and poured a tumbler of whiskey, "Can I get you one?"

Shreve shook his head, settling in a chair near the fireplace. Just as quickly, he stood and began pacing the room. Despite his need not to hope, hope slowly began to invade his heart and mind, and by the time he heard the buggy coming up the drive, he had all but convinced himself that Iliamna was alive.

He closed his eyes when he heard the front door open and the faint sound of voices drift to his ears.

"Want to go out there and..."

"No," Shreve interjected. "I can't."

The door to the living room opened and Carmen stepped in. The alarm on her face was palpable, and when she stepped aside to admit their visitor, both men understood why.

## CHAPTER FORTY-TWO

"No!" Shreve yelled and barreled across the room, unaware of the danger his actions were putting him in; but Mitch saw and moved to intercept him. He knocked Shreve to the floor, wrestling with him, trying ineffectually to pin him down.

"Get off me!" He yelled repeatedly, but Mitch refused to relent.

"She'll kill you," he said simply, hoping his words would break through Shreve's anguished haze. "She'll kill you." He repeated.

"I don't care."

"You should, since there's a good chance she can lead us to Iliamna."

That stopped Shreve's struggles and he lie there breathing heavily, trying to regain composure over his anger.

Neither man had met Alana in person, didn't know what she looked like; but the .38 she held out in front of her as she entered the room, the fact that she'd arrived in one of Shreve's buggies, and the horrified look on Carmen's face, was all of the information either man needed to determine who had entered Shreve's home. And her next words only confirmed it.

"Well, that doesn't seem an appropriate way to greet one's fiancé," Alana huffed as the display of testosterone began to settle. "So, which one of you two is my intended?" She asked, and both men cringed. "It's so hard to tell, since neither of you look like a half-breed; of course," she continued, moving further into the room and placing a bundle of letters on a nearby table, "if I had to guess, I'd say it was the one that nearly went berserk at my arrival." She speared Shreve with a look that made him blanch, leaving him feeling cold and filthy inside. "Ah, now I see the likeness," she said, after reaching into her reticule and pulling out the picture Shreve sent to the woman he believed to be Iliamna.

A shudder of repulsion crept along Shreve's spine and he looked away. His gaze landed on Carmen, inching her way toward the living room door, and he felt renewed hope, which made him want to grin. However, he restrained himself. He'd held out hope too many times and been disappointed an equal number of times. Hope still managed to creep in a small bit, as he quickly calculated the odds. Although this woman had a gun aimed at Mitch and him, and had proven her ability to shoot it with deadly accuracy—if Red were to be believed— it didn't hold enough bullets to take out every man on his ranch— which, he was certain, was where Carmen was sneaking off—to get his men. That gave Shreve more hope than he'd felt in weeks.

"I'm okay now," Shreve said, and Mitch rolled away, allowing him to stand. Both men moved cautiously toward the fireplace, as far away from Alana as the room allowed, each watching her warily, as she strolled around the room stroking pieces of sculpture with possessiveness. She seemed to have forgotten their presence as quickly as she'd noticed it and they took advantage of her sudden inattentiveness to try to formulate a strategy.

"You know she's not stable-minded," Mitch whispered, watching the gun swing loosely in her hand.

Shreve snorted derisively, "Really? What drew you to that conclusion?"

"Oh, a lot of little things really," Mitch retorted sarcastically, "Primarily her demeanor right now...well, that, and the fact that she had Gitano kidnap her cousin and then put a bullet in his chest without blinking when she thought he double-crossed her—if Red is to be believed."

Shreve rubbed his hand along his jaw, "If we get near her again, she'll shoot us," He observed unnecessarily.

Mitch shook his head, "I got that much."

"We need answers."

"You think she's going to willingly supply them?"

"I told you we should have shot them all instead of trying to bring them to justice, didn't I?"

"Now isn't the time for that, Shreve. You're not a killer."

"Want to place a bet on that?"

"The only killer in this room is wandering about right now as if she's queen of the manor; and she'll kill *you* if you reject her. You know that."

"She really thinks I'll have her after what she did to Iliamna."

"Yeah, I got that feeling readily enough," Mitch sighed. "You realize the absurdity of all of this, right? Us conversing calmly with each other, while a madwoman traipses about the room in complete oblivion?"

"What I realize is that if Carmen returns with the men, someone is bound to get shot, and possibly killed, before we can wrestle that gun away from her."

"You two whispering over there is a display of poor manners," Alana interrupted, turning to face Mitch and Shreve.

"She's back," Mitch whispered.

"What you should do is offer me some refreshments and ask me to sit, so we can discuss marriage arrangements. Still, mother always said that people out here were backwards." She sighed, "Well, I'll just have to work hard to make certain our home is a proper place, run as a well-managed eastern home is run. I'll make your home the envy of everyone in this indecorous state, Shreve."

"Dear God, don't say my name!"

"Easy Shreve," Mitch whispered.

Alana affected a pouty expression, "Is that anyway to speak to the woman with whom you promised to marry?" Alana stroked at the bundle of letters affectionately, as if reminding Shreve of who she was would change his disposition towards her. "Certainly the man who wrote such beautiful prose wouldn't speak to me in such a manner; oh, and I absolutely love the home you built for me."

"I'm going to kill her," he whispered and Mitch had to place a hand on his arm to prevent him barreling across the room again. Just then, both men caught sight of a gun barrel slipping through the living room door. It opened a bit further and Jeb slipped his head in. He took in the scene and then moved further into the room, taking aim at Alana.

"Don't shoot her!" Shreve yelled, just as a pistol discharged.

# CHAPTER FORTY-THREE

Jeb hit the ground and rolled away just as Alana swung on him and fired. He'd been fortunate that he was alert to the potential danger, or her shot could've proved his end. What he wanted to do was return fire, but Shreve's command that he not shoot had his hands tied, so he took cover behind the sofa.

Another man stuck his head around the door, and yelled as wood splinters struck him in the cheek from the bullet slamming into the doorjamb.

"Can you get behind her?" Shreve whispered to Mitch, both men kneeling behind the love seat.

Mitch peered around the side, "No. She's perfectly positioned in that corner. She can see everything and everybody; and she doesn't appear stupid enough to just expend bullets on a whim."

"Expend bullets," Shreve said thoughtfully.

"What are you thinking?"

"She's fired off two shots, which means she's potentially got four left. Jeb?"

Jeb stuck his head near the edge of the sofa, "Yeah."

"Think you can get her to…" Shreve's request was cut short by the sound of mewling, which caught all of the men off guard.

"Shreve," Alana was crying, "where are you?"

Shreve and Mitch looked quizzically at each other, and then peered over the top of the loveseat. Alana had slid to her bottom and was hugging her knees to her chest.

"I really don't think she'll shoot you now," Mitch said, and Shreve readily caught his meaning. He sighed deeply and carefully maneuvered around to the front of the chair, remaining crouched. Slowly, so as not to startle her, he moved toward Alana.

When he was within a few feet, she lifted her head and Shreve felt a twinge of guilt over wanting to kill her, as her tear-filled gaze was so full of innocence.

"I'm right here, Alana," he said softly, comfortingly.

"There was a man with a gun," Alana said in a childlike voice that had Shreve shaking his head. He didn't need a reminder of her age, nor did he want to feel sorry for her. He shook his head harder to dislodge any feelings of sympathy and then took a deep breath.

"He won't hurt you. We just can't have you waving a gun around. You're going to hurt someone. Maybe even yourself."

"You care about me hurting myself?"

Shreve's eyes widened, "I don't want you to get hurt, no." Of course, he wouldn't reveal *why* he didn't want her hurt. He needed answers from her.

Alana sniffled loudly and swiped at her nose, but she still held her finger on the trigger of the gun, which made Shreve very uncomfortable. "You wanted to talk, so how about you consider giving me your gun..."

The innocent girl was gone that fast, her gaze suddenly heated and guarded, "You don't want to marry me!" She said angrily, nonsensically.

*Where did* that *outburst come from?* Shreve wondered. The second thing he wondered was how he was supposed to reason with someone whose brain was emotionally unpredictable, followed closely by the realization that he was completely exposed. If she got angry enough, his life would be over as quickly as her mood shifts. He had no experience dealing with mental instability—or did he?

He suddenly realized that he had dealt with the insane all of the time when he'd been a prosecutor. Mitch had even told Gitano on the train, that it took a special kind of person to kill. Well, he'd interviewed those special kinds of people on a regular basis; extracted answers that they didn't want to let go of. If he could converse calmly with those people, he could converse sanely with Alana.

Shreve sat watching the girl; the prosecutor in him coming to the forefront of his mind—viewing things clearly for the first time since the damaging whirlwind, involving this woman, began a month prior. Questioning. Searching for answers. Were her mood shifts an act? A way to gain sympathy in the hopes he'd forget what she'd done to Iliamna? The thought of Iliamna started his pulse to racing.

Was she still alive? It was clear that the girl was capable of murder, but had she murdered her cousin? If she wanted Iliamna dead, why hire Gitano to take her away? Of course, she *had* offered him more money to kill her at one time, but it hadn't been sufficient. So, if she wanted her dead, why take her away from the ranch? Why not just show up and shoot her dead on sight?

*She's alive*, he finally concluded, and felt relief flood through him, but that didn't resolve his current predicament. He needed to find her, and this girl was his only hope to do so.

"Alana," he whispered softly, in what he hoped was a caring tone, "I saw the letters you brought with you, and I saw you looking at the picture, so I know you're the woman I was supposed to marry."

Alana smiled, her gaze softening.

"Do you think maybe we could sit down with some refreshments and talk?"

Alana smiled widely, and slowly moved to stand, but Shreve didn't miss that she refused to relinquish her weapon, "I'm glad you can see reason, Shreve," Alana cooed.

Shreve reached out his hand, but it took a moment for Alana to stop eyeing it suspiciously, and to place her free hand in his, "Let's sit over here at the table," he said, leading her to a seat that faced away from the sofa. He glanced over at Jeb and nodded slightly, and then moved to sit opposite her.

Alana laid the gun on the table, without taking her finger off the trigger. She smiled shyly at Shreve and Shreve cringed inwardly. He'd said for them to talk, felt confident he could get her to open up; but suddenly his tongue felt like lead. What was he to say? How was he to get her to relinquish Iliamna's whereabouts? He knew that if he even mentioned her name, she'd put a bullet in his head.

He decided to wait—either for her to speak, or for Jeb to make his move.

"I think we should send for the preacher today," Alana said abruptly.

Shreve's gaze widened and his brow arched, "Oh, um, well, wouldn't you like to sew some fancy new gown..."

"I brought one with me," Alana interrupted.

"You did?"

"Of course, silly," Alana tittered.

She was saying something else, but Shreve had stopped listening. Still, he forced his features to show interest in what he didn't hear; willed his gaze not to shift to the movement to Alana's rear. Suddenly realized that he'd sat Alana to where she would see any movement reflected in the window opposite.

"Crouch," he said loudly, startling Alana.

"I beg your pardon," she snapped, her hand flying to her chest. "Why would you scare me like that?"

"I'm sorry, dear," Shreve said impulsively, breathing a sigh of thanks that Jeb understood, and immediately dropped into a crouch as he rounded the end of the couch. "I'm afraid there's something you should know about me."

Alana's gaze narrowed, and she eyed Shreve with renewed suspicion.

Shreve affected an innocent expression and then blurted, "I have a propensity to...um...shout things out inexplicably. Like just now. I thought you should know. It's...um...well, why I've not married before now."

"Oh, I thought it was because you were half Indian," Alana said offhandedly. "Well, no matter," she continued, waving her hand in dismissal, "if you're willing to overlook my flaws, I can certainly work to overlook yours."

Shreve closed his eyes and took in a deep breath, *I may have flaws, girl,* he thought, *but you have serious defects.*

He was relieved when Jeb reached up and snared Alana around the upper chest, pinioning her to the chair, putting an end to this particular conversation. Every time she whispered something at him, his head would inexplicably hurt.

Her gun hand was still free however, and she jerked it up and fired over her head, attempting to shoot Jeb in the head. Jeb ducked and held fast, which wasn't easy to do, since Alana had started bucking wildly; swinging the gun around, ready to fire at anyone who might come into sight.

Shreve had thrown himself from the chair the minute Jeb grabbed hold, and immediately ducked under the table in the hopes of coming up and latching onto her arm. His ribs got assaulted by her flailing feet, but he refused to be averted. He glanced over the edge of the table cautiously, and realized he had little to worry about, as Alana couldn't see him over Jeb's arms. He slipped his hand up and snagged Alana's gun hand. Alana let go a yelp when Shreve twisted the gun free, and then fell still; affecting a blank stare.

He tossed the gun aside and stood, looking down at a little girl who appeared to have mentally left the room. Something told him not to trust this apparent psychological lapse; that she was too wily by far to allow capture to finish her. She was playing a game, and he knew just how to snap her out of her self-imposed mental exile.

"So now that we've got her subdued, how do we get her to get her to tell us where she took Iliamna?" Mitch asked, as he stood and walked over to where Jeb was still holding tight to the girl.

"Go and let everyone know that we've got everything under control in here, and have someone fetch a rope, will you?" Shreve replied instead.

Mitch nodded.

Soon after, the room filled with curious ranch hands and an irate housekeeper.

"Tie her wrists and feet," Shreve instructed to the one who'd brought in the rope.

Once she was trussed up tight, Shreve moved a chair in front of her and sat down, eyeing the blank expression curiously, "So, Mitch, you wanted to know how we get her to tell us where Alana is?"

"Yeah, but from the looks of her, she won't be doing much talking," Mitch said. "It's like her brain finally gave up on her."

Shreve grinned. He knew she was still in there, and very much alert. "Well, if she can't help us," he said, "we could always go to Twin Rivers to question Red," Shreve offered. "Alana is bound to have confided in the woman who was acting as accomplice."

Alana's lip curled in disdain, "She won't reveal anything."

Shreve smiled thinly and replied sarcastically, "Welcome back from your little hiatus. I didn't think you'd be gone long."

Alana huffed in derision, "You think you're so smart, don't you?"

"Smart enough to know you were faking a mental break, and smart enough to know that mentioning Red would snap you out of it."

"Red despises you Shreve Red Fox; she wants you to suffer even more than I want Iliamna to suffer, so if you think she will tell you anything, you're sadly mistaken," Alana grinned, but it held no humor.

Shreve smiled shrewdly, "But I can offer her something of value," he continued.

"There's nothing you have that she wants. You took what she wanted already—something that I took away from you," she retorted smugly.

"I can offer her immunity from prosecution."

Alana's snarl slipped, replaced by confusion, "What does that mean?"

"It means that, if she cooperates, *she* won't go to jail."

Alana's brow knitted and she fell quiet, deep in thought. After a short bit, she looked at Shreve again and he was taken aback by who now sat before him. Gone was the shrewd murderer, replaced by a little girl, an expression of vulnerability on her face. "So," she said softly, "if I cooperate, *I* won't go to jail?" Her voice was so unsure, so inexperienced, that Shreve almost forgot again how monstrous she could be.

"You won't go to jail," Shreve confirmed, his tone calming and assured.

"Shreve?" Mitch whispered. "That's not your call. You can't offer her or Red immunity from..."

"She tells us where Iliamna is and she doesn't go to jail," Shreve reiterated adamantly, a twinge to his voice that had Mitch tilting his head in question. Shreve just looked at him in return, his gaze saying "trust me."

After a few minutes, Mitch confirmed, "She won't go to jail, but in order to see that happen, Iliamna must be found alive. Agreed?"

"She's alive," Alana said, her tone suddenly eager to please.

"Where?" Shreve asked with bated breath.

"I took her to the coast. Sold her to a sea captain who said he'd take her to one of the sugar plantations on Barbados," she revealed swiftly. "That's where I wanted Gitano to take her; where he should have taken her. Had he done as I asked, no one would have found her and I could have married you as we planned. Oh, can't you see, it was for the best? Now she's gone and there isn't any reason why you and I can't be happy. I can make you happy, Shreve..."

"Someone shut her up. I've heard her talk enough," Shreve snapped, leaving the living room with alacrity, the color drained from his skin. Mitch leapt to his feet and followed.

"Barbados," Shreve whispered. "It may as well be the moon. How are we going to get to her before harm befalls her?"

"We just have to try. We'll get her back. Now that we know she's alive, we'll get her back," Mitch reassured his friend, "but I need to know what you're gaze was trying to convey in there. You aren't really intending to allow Alana to get away with every crime she committed are you? Immunity?"

Shreve shook his head, "No, I have special plans for that one. Jail is too good for her."

\* \* \* \* \* \* \* \* \*

"Jeb, I can't say when we'll be returning, so I'm counting on you to keep things running until we get back," Shreve said the next morning, as the men and Carmen loaded supplies onto one of the buckboards. It wasn't the more comfortable—or modern—methods of transport, but it would hold three people and enough food stores for an extended journey.

"You can count on it, Shreve. By the time you get back, the men and I should have seen to the harvest and be preparing to take the cattle to market."

"I should be helping with it all," Shreve sighed, feeling uncomfortable at having to rely so heavily on his men.

"No," Jeb countered, "you should be seeing to the rescue of your fair maiden." He smiled at his exaggerated British accent, and laughed at the look that crossed Shreve's features. He felt better knowing that he'd assisted in making his friend smile, even if it was just a small smile and short lived.

"Yeah, I guess I can't do both."

"Just bring the Missus home."

Shreve nodded.

"Why do I have to go? What can't I just stay here? I've told you where you can find her," Alana whined from her seat against the back of the buckboard.

"Because if you've lied to us, we'll know it right away, in which case, we'll dump you at the first jail we come across with instructions to lock you away forever."

"I didn't lie, I promise," Alana whined again as the men climbed aboard and Shreve clucked his tongue to start the horses moving.

"And I believe you," he replied sarcastically.

Alana fell into a pout, but it didn't take long before she started droning on again, "Even if you don't believe me, it doesn't mean you have to keep me tied up back here like a common criminal."

"You *are* a common criminal," Mitch snapped, "and if you don't stop your incessant mewling, I'm going to have Shreve tie a lead rope and make you walk the whole way."

Shreve shook his head to relieve the ringing in his ears, "I don't know how anyone's managed to spend any time in the company of this girl without wanting to cut her tongue out."

"It was a little more tolerable when she was whispering every word, but this high-pitched wailing noise is enough to grate a man raw."

"How long before we reach our first stop?" Shreve asked, as Alana started complaining about the bouncing jarring her butt.

"Too long," Mitch sighed, placing his hands over his ears.

## CHAPTER FORTY-FOUR

"Where are we?" Alana asked for the thousandth time, as Shreve turned the team up a long drive four days later, toward a massive building in the distance.

"San Antonio," he replied curtly, seriously considering gagging the girl. After four days in her company, listening to her whiny tone was rubbing his nerves raw. One look at Mitch said that he was at his wits end as well. "We're here," he reassured his friend, who merely smiled with relief.

"Not a minute too soon. I swear I was tempted at least a dozen times, to slit her throat and toss her carcass to the buzzards."

"You and me both."

"Y'all are just heartless," Alana cried, and then launched into a tirade on how men—and her parents—had treated her poorly all of her life, so it wasn't precisely her fault that she'd turned out the way she had.

Shreve clucked at the horses to move them along at a swifter pace, and was more than ready to leap from the buckboard when they slowed to a stop. He and Mitch jumped at the same time, nearly running up the front steps.

"Hey, what about me?" Alana called, and then fell into a sulk when neither responded; nor returned to retrieve her.

Half an hour later, Mitch and Shreve returned, followed by several men, and Alana immediately lit into both for leaving her bound and alone, "You heartless cads; the both of you..." but neither was listening.

"Remember to use caution. She may not look as if she's capable of murder, but she will slit your throat if given the chance," Mitch was saying. "If she hadn't proven to be completely insane, we'd have simply locked her away in a jail somewhere for the rest of her life."

"You're the marshal," the man with the spectacles replied, "so I would be insane myself not to listen to your words of wisdom."

The men approached the back of the wagon, where Alana had

fallen silent again, a quizzical expression on her face. "Where are we?" She asked when no one seemed ready to explain anything to her.

"Welcome to Southwestern Insane Asylum, San Antonio, Texas. Your new—permanent—home. I'm Doctor Barnaby. I'll be your attending physician."

Alana turned her gaze to Shreve, "You said no jail," she shrieked, causing the doctor and two attendants to wince.

Shreve tried to keep his grin at bay, "This isn't jail," he replied. "Didn't you hear your doctor? It's an insane asylum. Did you really think there would be no consequences? You lied, deceived, manipulated, conned, and killed. There were bound to be consequences."

"I am not crazy, and I'll be damned if I'm going to let you get away with this. You're not going to lock me away in a crazy house, full of crazy people..."

"You might want to get that straight jacket ready that you brought out with you," Mitch said calmly, while Alana continued to rail at him and Shreve.

The two attendants boarded the back of the wagon, stepping carefully over the supplies, but keeping their balance wasn't easy, as Alana hurled her body side-to-side—in an attempt to free herself, or hurl the attendants over the side, no one could decide precisely which was her intent. When they reached for her, she started scratching at them, hissing and spitting as a wild cat cornered. Shreve may have bound her wrists, but she was still capable of inflicting injury with her nails, as one of the men discovered, swiping at the bloody scratch on his cheek.

Both men took a step back, heaving, "We may have to bring the tranquilizer out, doctor," one of the attendants huffed. "We can't get close enough to get this straight jacket on her, and we aren't going to be able to get her out of the wagon without the straight jacket on."

"Want to lend a hand, Shreve?" Mitch asked, eyeing the wild woman Alana had become, warily.

"You might want to leave me out of it, because if I crawl up there, I'm going to hit a woman for the first time in my life," Shreve said, and Mitch could tell that he wasn't joking.

"I'll lend a hand," Mitch said, slapping Shreve on the back. He leapt up onto the back of the buckboard, which sent Alana into another round of bounding wildly back and forth.

"Get away from me," she squealed, kicking her legs in the air.

"Maybe we should just let her wear herself out," one of the attendants offered. "Surely she can't keep up that level of hysterics forever."

"I don't have forever," Shreve snapped. "I want her out now."

The attendants sent Mitch a look of longsuffering, who shrugged, "I'll grab her legs, and then maybe one of you might just be able to latch onto her arms."

It took several more minutes, but Mitch latched onto her legs. He held on tight while one of the attendants moved toward Alana's arms. She was still hissing and spitting, but with her legs subdued, it was easier to latch onto her wrists. "Undo the rope so we can get the straightjacket on her," the one man called to the other. Several more minutes and a massive struggle later, they had Alana trussed up like a Thanksgiving Day turkey, being carried into the asylum, squirming and screeching wildly.

"Well, Marshall, I have to say I'm impressed that you two managed to bring her all of this way in a passive manner. How did you manage, anyway?"

"We lied to her," Shreve said simply.

"Well I won't be doing that, but we have medicines that will subdue her just as well as a lying tongue. Have a safe trip home, gentlemen. We'll tend to her from here."

"Just never let your guard down around her, doctor," Mitch reminded, as he and Shreve boarded the buckboard, "because she won't hesitate to kill you and your men in a bid for freedom."

"She'll be so full of our special blend of medicinal plants that she won't even recall what brought her here after a while. Guess we learned a thing or two from our native allies after all. Safe journey."

The doctor turned and headed back inside, and Mitch took up the reins; both men were relieved that none of them would have to deal with Alana's machinations any longer. Of course, disposing of Alana had been the easy part. Now came the hard part—locating

Iliamna.

# CHAPTER FORTY-FIVE

It was another two and a half days before Shreve and Mitch reached the Gulf of Mexico, exhaustion clinging to them like a death shroud. Half a dozen ships, ranging in size from small fishing vessels, to larger trading vessels, moored just offshore.

"She wasn't likely sold to the captain of a fishing vessel," Mitch said, seeing the look of hopelessness lining Shreve's features, "and some of these boats don't appear seaworthy enough for a long voyage, so they are probably short-distance traders. What we're looking for is a stout, sizable vessel capable of making the trek to Barbados and back regularly. There can't be too many of those."

"Trying to cheer me with your knowledge of ships?" Shreve asked sardonically.

"Yeah." Mitch laughed, pink tinting his cheeks. "Is it working?"

Shreve shook his head in bemusement, "I appreciate the effort. I only hope someone recognizes the drawing of Iliamna that I brought along, and can tell me which captain bought her. If we can hone in on the exact ship, then we can pinpoint Iliamna's location better, instead of just barging onto the first vessel headed to Barbados."

"Right. After all, the captain may have decided not to sell her. May have decided to keep her...sorry."

Shreve sighed deeply, "Let's just hope that Alana told us the truth about where she brought her..."

"Don't start doubting the information now, Shreve. She really believed that she'd get a fair shake if she told the truth. She may be insane, but I didn't judge her to be stupid. And remember, she returned from the south, so that acts as a sort of corroboration to her story, right? Let's start circulating the picture at the saloon over there." At Shreve's continued look of doubt, Mitch added, "Hey, listen—if anyone knows anything about Iliamna, they are going to be around here, and it won't take us long to find it out. This doesn't exactly appear to be a major seaport with hundreds of ships coming and going, okay?"

Shreve nodded and turned his team toward the saloon. It

reminded him of the area of Louisiana where they'd located Gitano—the men eyeing them with as much wariness as they had there. What was it about them that shouted *law*? He voiced his thoughts aloud to Mitch, who replied, "We just don't look as if we belong here. We may be tough, but we haven't been hardened by life the way these men have."

"Speak for yourself," Shreve grinned edgily, and then dismounted in front of the saloon. "How do you want to do this?" He quipped, remembering the last time they'd gone in search of information.

"Want I should pull my badge out and pin it to my vest?" Mitch retorted as they moved to stand just inside the door.

"Might draw attention," Shreve replied.

"Yeah, but you know that I have a bit of an ego."

"And this conversation sounds vaguely familiar," Shreve replied. "Let's head on to the bar. I promise that I'll keep my wits about me, not down half the stock from stress, or kill anyone who doesn't answer my questions the way I want them to."

"That's good to hear, especially as you sound only half-joking."

"I swear, Mitch, I have had run the gamut of emotions more this past month than in my entire life. I even think I've cried more than when I was an infant. I've certainly been more angry. You know, when I was a prosecutor, fighting to put away some of the worst criminals in Louisiana, I didn't get as angry as I have over the crimes committed by Alana."

"That's because those crimes didn't directly affect you, so you could remain detached."

"True, but I surely will be mighty pleased when I can get back to my normal self, I tell ya."

"Preferably with Iliamna by your side?"

"Sure shootin."

"Get you gentlemen a drink?"

"Two whiskeys," Mitch said, "and we'd like to ask you whether you recall seeing this woman. She would have been around the area nearly a month past."

"I can only help with getting the whiskey," the bartender said and then moved away. They received nearly the same rejection of help from everyone they approached. It was as though there were a code among dockworkers that prevented them ratting on a ship's captain. Perhaps because they were worried that they'd not be able to find work if they did.

When they'd been at it for a couple of hours, they determined a change in tactic was in order, so they waited and watched for someone who'd imbibed a few drinks—but not too many to be drunk—and would possibly appreciate the offer of a bottle on them.

It took another quarter of an hour, but they located someone just enough in his cups to start spilling his guts.

"I don't recall that beauty," he said, tapping his finger on the picture, "but there was a girl in here quite a number of weeks back that didn't belong; said she had a parcel to sell to the right buyer. She kept hawking her wares, until she found someone interested in what she had to sell. Captain Avery of the ship *Golden Dawn* sat and conversed with her a short spell and then followed her out of here. Can't say what transpired after that. That help you fine gentlemen enough to buy me that bottle of whiskey you promised?"

Mitch reached into his vest pocket and pulled out four bits, "You've been more than helpful, but I'll throw in an extra two bits if you can tell me whether the good Captain is currently in port."

"I haven't seen him in here for a week or more, but if anyone would know when he's expected, it would be the dock master," the man replied in a tone that fairly begged for the additional coin. Mitch pulled the added coin from his pocket and tossed it on the table, "Go get your bottle." When the man departed, Mitch stood from the table, "Let's go try to locate Captain Avery. If he didn't purchase Iliamna, he may have information as to who did."

"At least we know that Alana was here; that she was telling the truth."

"It has definitely lifted my hopes considerably. Hope that we're one step closer to finding your woman safe and sound."

"I'll be happy to find her in one piece. I only hope she'll willingly forgive me for all that I put her through."

Mitch stopped walking and speared Shreve with a look of incredulity, "You aren't going to start carrying the burden of guilt around over what that madwoman did to Iliamna, are you? Because you had absolutely nothing to do with what happened to her. If anything, you saved her from a horrible fate on at least one occasion—or did you anticipate that she'd have remained a virgin in a whorehouse? And, need I remind you that you are currently doing your utmost to rescue her again as we speak."

Shreve nodded, his countenance grim, "I know all of that, but I gave her my word that she'd be safe while I traveled to Louisiana. If only I'd just taken her at face value; hadn't doubted her word."

"Had you remained at the ranch, it wouldn't have changed a thing. God, Shreve, but you can be thick. Being at the ranch wouldn't have prevented Alana from coming to Texas and attempting to do away with Iliamna. It may have prevented the trouble with Red, but not with Alana—and Alana has been the greatest danger to us all since this whole thing started. Now do you think you can stop dwelling on what might have been, and start focusing on what will be?"

Shreve nodded, sighing heavily, "I just want her back, Mitch, and I want her to forgive me for doubting her word."

"I think she'll be so happy to see you that she won't even remember that you doubted her word at all."

"I sure in Hell hope so. So, what say we find that dock master and see about obtaining information on the Captain of the *Golden Dawn*."

"If we have to wait for him to arrive, we'll need to find a couple of rooms followed by a decent meal. No offense, Shreve, but I'm sick to death of reeking like the dead, and eating hardtack and gruel."

Shreve snorted, "You and I both, and the horses would probably appreciate a good rubdown and some hay, so we'll need to find boarding for them too—if we're delayed."

Mitch nodded, "Well, we'll find out in a minute." He pointed up at a sign that read *Dock Master*. They jumped back off the buckboard and climbed the worn, wooden steps.

"Help you gentlemen?" An elderly man called as they stepped inside.

"Yes, sir," Mitch replied, "we're here to inquire about the *Golden*

*Dawn.*"

"Passage or work has to be arranged with the Captain, not here," he replied curtly.

"We aren't passengers, or dockworkers," Shreve replied, his tone terse and professional. "This here is Marshall Mitchell Crowell, and I'm Louisiana State Prosecutor, Shreve Red Fox. We need to ask the Captain—Avery, I believe his name is—a few questions about a missing woman."

That caught the elder man's attention, and he lowered his spectacles to the table, along with his pen, "Well now, that must be a mighty special lady to bring a Marshall and a Prosecutor chasing after her across state lines."

"She's my wife," Shreve said, and had to prevent shaking his head to dislodge memories of a conversation he'd had with Iliamna about his propensity to prevaricate of late.

Mitch had to know he was lying, but to his credit, he didn't even blink.

"Well now, that begs the question as to why a married woman would end up from beneath the shelter of her husband—unless she was running away from that husband?"

Shreve drew a deep breath in through his nostrils and took a step toward the older man, who merely grinned.

"I can only assure you, sir," Mitch interjected, placing a hand on Shreve's arm in restraint—a habit of late, "that this woman was taken against her will as an act of retribution against Shreve, who, as a prosecuting attorney, has made his fair share of enemies. Fortunately, we were able to apprehend the person behind the abduction, which led us here in search of the good captain—who may be completely unaware that he purchased someone's wife."

"Hmm," the elder man huffed, and reached for a book. He flipped it open and turned the pages for a short bit until he reached the page he was searching for, "The *Golden Dawn* under the command of Captain Jonathan Avery, set sail for Barbados over three weeks ago, and is scheduled to return to port at the end of this week. So, gentlemen, it looks as if you have a few days to wait on the good captain's return."

Both men sighed simultaneously.

"Can you point us toward decent stables for our horses?"

"And even better accommodations for ourselves?" Mitch added.

## CHAPTER FORTY-SIX

"You aren't going to pace the entire time that we wait, are you? We're in a good place to spot the return of the ship. At least you are. Your window overlooks the bay."

"I know, I just hate the waiting. What if he sold her to a plantation owner, and we then have to procure passage on board his vessel. That will be another two weeks waiting, while in the company of the very man who bought and sold Iliamna; two weeks more of not knowing if anything untoward has befallen her?"

"Do you ever look on the bright side?"

Shreve stopped pacing and sat down on the bed, "I used to. Now all I do is fret."

"You have every reason to worry, Shreve, but don't let that worry incapacitate you. We need to be prepared for what happens next, including...well, I think you know where I'm going with this."

Shreve nodded, "Including the fact that Iliamna may very well not be a virgin any longer. I know. Now who's being the pessimist?" Shreve placed his face in his hands and lowered his head, "God, the waiting, the not knowing anything, is killing me," he muttered.

"I know, old friend, but do try to remember that we are closer now to finding her than we were three weeks ago, when we all thought her dead."

Shreve nodded, and then jerked when a knock sounded at the door. He was about to stand, but Mitch beat him to it.

"Our baths have arrived. Indulge in a good long soak and I'll meet you downstairs for dinner in an hour." He pulled several dollars from his vest pocket and distributed it among the porters who had delivered their bath water, and then retreated to his own room to soak away the worry and stress of the last few weeks.

Shreve shed his clothes and set about washing the grime away from his body. The soak felt so good that he was unable to keep his eyes open, and before long, he drifted off into a restless sleep, his mind recalling pieces of his conversations with Iliamna; and just as he witnessed the horror of her circumstances haunting her in her dreams, anyone watching him would see memories of the last month haunting his.

*"I guess it's a good thing that we aren't really getting married,"*

*"Why's that?"*

*"Because if you can't trust the woman you're to marry, then...well, let's just say that the starting foundation is going to be set on some mighty unbalanced stones."*

*"Good point. I guess it is a good thing we aren't planning to marry; but just so you know—I do like you, Iliamna, despite everything, or I wouldn't be trying to prove your innocence."*

*"...the attorney in me needs answers that one person's word can't supply."*

*"Shreve?"*

*"Yes, Iliamna?"*

*"Why did you tell the sheriff that we're planning to wed? More prevaricating?"*

*"I don't rightly know. Does it bother you?"*

*"A little, yes."*

*"Why?"*

*"Because we're not, that's why?"*

*"I'm not so sure anymore, Iliamna. I'll admit I've grown rather fond of you."*

*"But you still don't believe me, or have you suddenly changed your mind about going to Louisiana?"*

*"No, I haven't changed my mind."*

*"Because the lawyer in you still has unanswered questions about me."*

*"Don't you see that I couldn't marry you with doubts hanging over my head? I wish I didn't have such a suspicious nature, but I do. I don't trust very easily, I'm afraid."*

*"And I've already said that there cannot be a marriage without a foundation of trust."*

The hand on his shoulder startled Shreve and he shot to his feet.

"I'm sorry, Shreve," Mitch said, moving to sit on the bed, "but when I knock repeatedly and don't receive a reply from a man whose been teetering on the abyss of depression of late—well, you can see why I'd let myself in to ensure he's safe. Naked, but safe. Bad dreams?"

Shreve looked down at his glistening nudity and reached for a towel thrown over the back of a nearby chair. He stepped from the tub and started toweling himself dry, "Yeah, bad dreams."

"Looked like it," Mitch replied, tapping his foot impatiently while he waited for Shreve to dress.

"Hungry?"

"Yeah, a bit," Mitch replied. "The proprietor told me about a place down at the other end of the avenue that ain't much to look at, but serves a decent meal."

"Okay, well then let's head out. I could put a dent in this empty pit of mine too. Mind if we walk though? I could do with a leg stretch. Been sitting too long of late."

Mitch stifled a yawn, "Me too."

It took fifteen minutes, but they finally located the dilapidated café of which the proprietor spoke. He hadn't been joking about the exterior, which had been aged prematurely from the constant spray of sea salt, much as the sailors and dockworkers they'd passed on route. The interior however, though old, was kept scrubbed clean, which was a pleasant surprise, until they saw the owner of the establishment issuing instructions in an authoritative bark. She was a rotund Russian woman who ran the place as if she were in charge of an army regimen. Those not serving or cooking were made to scrub every surface. It was quite an impressive sight to behold.

"Two for dinner," a scruffy man said a minute or two after they entered. "Find a table."

They did as instructed and soon someone was bringing by a plate with a steak, baked potato, and pole beans.

"Um, we didn't place an order," Shreve said.

"We only serve the one thing. If you came in and took a seat, this is what you get. That'll be four bits each," The man said, extending his hand. He collected their coin and then shuffled off.

"At least the proprietor was right about the food being good. At least it looks good. I say we dig in."

"Well I definitely can't complain," Shreve said, leaning back against the chair after he downed his last bite. "That was some mighty fine eatin'."

Mitch lifted the mug of beer, brought shortly after the meal, and tipped it, downing the last bit with a satisfied sigh, "Definitely can't complain."

Within minutes, their dishes were cleared away; a fresh mug placed in front of them along with two plates with a slice of apple pie the size of their combined fists.

"Lordy, but this place sure does know how to feed a man," Mitch exclaimed, cutting a piece of the pie and groaning with pleasure at it slid down his throat and landed in his belly. "Mm, mm, mm, delicious."

"I'm maybe thinking that we should have ridden in the buckboard, because it's going to take a mighty big effort to walk back."

"Yeah, but we would have had to wait too long for the buckboard to be re-hitched, and we were too hungry for that," Shreve said, finishing off his pie. He stopped short of picking up the plate and licking it clean. "This place is run better than a tip-top crew of seamen."

"Better, I'd say," Mitch laughed.

Another man came over and removed their plates, "Have a nice day, gentlemen," he said, and though the words were pleasant, the tone was brusque, indicating that they clear out so that the next men waiting could eat.

"Whew," Shreve exclaimed as they stepped out into the evening air. "I think a walk will certainly help at this point."

"Well, if nothing else, that meal helped to lift my spirits a bit." There were halfway back to their hotel when Mitch reached over and smacked Shreve on the arm, "Look!"

Moored offshore a ways was a sizable vessel; the words *Golden Dawn* emblazoned in a sunset orange across the bow, but that's not what caught Shreve's eyes. Two deckhands had lowered a boat into the water and the rower was currently pulling on the oars, bringing it toward shore. Still, that's not what sent Shreve into a tear across the avenue, down to the shoreline, and halfway into the surf. It was the parasol.

"Iliamna!" He yelled, but the woman in the boat, features obscured partially by the parasol and by the setting sun, did not react. Her backbone was rigid, and her face remained transfixed on the buildings behind him. His heart dropped a bit. "Please be her," he whispered and then yelled again, "Iliamna! Iliamna!"

Mitch joined him in the surf and started shouting in unison. As the boat drew nearer, Shreve noticed a shift in the woman's demeanor. No longer was her gaze transfixed, it was searching; and no longer was the parasol obscuring her features; she'd lowered it and was actively searching the shoreline. There was no doubt any longer in Shreve's mind as to whether he'd found his woman. She was there in front of him, sitting on a small skiff, headed straight for him.

Then she spotted him and her countenance went from rigid to shock. He saw her mouth, "Shreve," and then buried her face in her hands. Only the shaking of her shoulders bespoke of the intensity of her tears.

The man rowing stopped, replaced the oars, and leaned over, placing a hand in comfort on her shoulder. She jerked away and lifted her gaze, her mouth moving animatedly, her finger pointing toward Shreve.

Shreve shifted his gaze to the man operating the oars. He was a burly man with broad shoulders, bronzed skin, and blonde hair, which fell in waves below his shoulder. He was also looking over his shoulder at Shreve and Mitch. Shreve saw his lips purse, but then he turned back, picked up the oars, and returned to his rowing.

It seemed to take forever for that boat to near shore. Iliamna kept gazing over the side of the boat, for reasons Shreve couldn't quite fathom, until he saw her lift her gaze, smile at him, and leap. She hit the water, slipped, fell face first; and then came up sputtering, soaked, and laughing her head off. She finally gained her footing in the shallow water and began trudging toward Shreve, the captain shouting at her to wait.

Shreve headed further into the surf, and met her partway. When

241

he reached her, he immediately wrapped her into his embrace and kissed her for all he was worth.

"Excuse me," a voice said near Shreve's ear. Shreve reluctantly released Iliamna, turned toward the voice, and landed a solid punch across the man's jaw.

"Shreve, no!" Iliamna cried, pulling on Shreve's arm, as he moved to attack the captain again. "He didn't harm me," she said, and Shreve looked at her, set to question her veracity again. After all, for a woman of her beauty to be in the company of a seaman for two weeks and come out of it unscathed...*No!* His mind shouted.

"I believe you," he whispered, stroking her cheek with his thumb. He lowered his lips and kissed her gently, wrapping his arm around her waist again and drawing her tightly against him. "I love you," he whispered against her lips.

"Oh Shreve," she cried, "I love you too. Oh, I've missed you. I never thought to see you again." This time it was Iliamna that wrapped her arms around Shreve's neck and kissed him, all of the fear of the past month releasing in mere minutes. She felt safe again.

"Is it safe for me to get up now?" the Captain asked. "Especially since the water is lapping at my chin sitting here like this."

Mitch bent and offered the captain a hand up.

"Who are you?" Iliamna asked softly.

"Marshal Mitchell Crowell, Miss Iliamna," Mitch introduced, deliberately emphasizing the *marshal*. "I'm a friend of Shreve's. We've spent the better part of a month searching for you."

"We never gave up," Shreve whispered.

"If we can get out of the water, I'd be appreciative. I prefer life atop the water, not immersed in it," The captain quipped.

"Right, and I certainly hope you're not planning to contest ownership over this woman," Mitch asked, his tone authoritative.

"Actually, I was planning on returning her," the captain said with a grin, "but why don't we find somewhere more suitable for holding this conversation."

"We have a room down the avenue," Shreve said. "Mitch can loan you some dry clothes while yours dry. Then perhaps you two can fill us in on everything that's happened?"

Both Iliamna and the captain nodded, and all four trudged back to shore and down the avenue, amused gazes following them all the way back to the hotel.

The proprietor must have heard they were coming, because his wife ran out to meet them, carrying an armful of towels, "Please dry off as much as possible, otherwise you'll ruin my freshly scrubbed hardwood floors."

"You said you were bringing her back," Shreve said, while the four of them worked as much water out of their clothing as was possible.

The captain nodded, removing his coat and squeezing the water out, "I would have done sooner, but every time I, or another of my men, attempted to get near her cabin, she'd start throwing everything in sight. I decided it best to wait to approach her until she'd had time to cool down. Once she did, and I was able to converse with her at length, she explained everything. How her cousin, who was jealous, forced her from her home and transported her here to be rid of her. After meeting with her cousin, it was easy to see the truth of her story. She probably would have been able to tell me that before I'd purchased and boarded her, but she was unconscious at the time."

Shreve immediately stopped drying and took Iliamna's face in his hand, searching for any signs of bruises.

"Back of the head this time," Iliamna whispered, tears stinging her eyes.

"Oh, God, baby. My poor darling girl." Shreve wrapped Iliamna in his embrace again, and this time Iliamna began to cry, huge rib-rattling sobs that tore at each man's heart.

"I feel real sorry for what happened to her," the captain said. "I'm just glad I didn't have to travel through half of Texas to get her back to you."

Iliamna's tears subsided, and she sniffed repeatedly. Suddenly her head shot up and her eyes widened in fear, "Oh my God, Brendan..."

"He's fine. Jeb got worried when you didn't come back for dinner, so went in search. Found Brendan where Alana left him."

"And Alana?"

"She's where she belongs, and where she'll never harm you, or anyone else, ever again."

"I can't say that I'm not relieved. I never imagined when I ended up in Shreveport, that I'd become the subject of someone's vindictiveness. Surely she must have known that there would be consequences to her actions; that eventually someone would discover her deceit."

"Apparently not," Mitch said as they entered the lobby, "but what surprises me, Captain, is your willingness to purchase a girl in the first place."

"A lot of times, the women come to me freely. They're on the run or homeless. Figure they'd do better in the islands, working for a rich plantation owner. I bought this girl because...well, frankly, I thought she'd fare better in my care than the woman selling her. Turns out, my intuition was correct."

"In that case, Captain, I owe you a debt I can never repay," Shreve said, stopping and extending his hand. The captain reached out and clasped it, shaking it firmly.

"You're a lucky man," he said, smiling at Iliamna. She blushed, and Shreve pulled her closer to his side, "and yes, I know—she's taken."

They entered Shreve's room and Iliamna immediately moved to the bed. It was a difficult trek from shore to hotel in a heavy dress. She was exhausted, and it showed on her face.

"You gentleman head next door and get changed. I'll assist Iliamna and get changed myself. I'll meet you over there in a short while. And Mitch, don't come looking for me this time. If I'm not over there before morning, it simply means I—we—were too exhausted and went to bed."

Mitch laughed and gave Iliamna a tip from an imaginary hat. The door closed behind them, leaving Shreve standing there, staring at Iliamna. She couldn't prevent the color seeping into her cheeks, "Shreve, please don't stare."

"I'm just scared that if I take my eyes off of you, you'll vanish, as if you're but a dream." He moved slowly toward her, and then lifted his hand to stroke her cheek. When he'd satisfied himself that she was real, he lowered his head, and kissed her slowly and thoroughly.

"I can't tell you how happy I am that you're not a dream," he whispered.

Iliamna smiled wistful.

"Stand up," he commanded softly. "We both need to get out of our wet clothing before we catch our deaths, and I have a feeling we aren't going to be able to do it without assisting each other. These wet things are going to stick to us like glued paper."

"Will you marry me, Shreve?"

Shreve stopped moving, his shirt half over his head. He slowly peeled it the remainder of the way off, and laid it across the back of the chair before turning to face Iliamna. When he finally looked at her, her gaze shifted downward quickly.

"Care to repeat that?" he asked softly, moving to stand before her.

She couldn't find her voice; was too discombobulated standing before a half-dressed man. She'd never seen a man's naked chest before, and if he answered her question in the positive, was most likely to see a completely naked man. She needed to get control of her emotions.

Shreve was flabbergasted, but simultaneously intrigued. Had she really just asked him to marry her? He placed a finger gently beneath her chin and lifted her face. He grinned when he noticed that her eyes were squeezed tight. *Embarrassed*, he thought, smiling. "Care to repeat what you just asked me, Iliamna?"

He heard her sigh. He knew she liked him to say her name, so he obliged, "Iliamna," he whispered, placing a light kiss on the side of her mouth.

She sighed again, "Say you'll marry me, Shreve," she breathed, and he pulled back. He had heard her correctly. She was proposing to *him*. That definitely intrigued him.

"I'll marry you, Iliamna," he replied, and she finally opened her eyes. They misted over with tears, and she smiled. "Would you like to explain what possessed you to ask?"

"We're about to undress each other," she replied in a voice barely audible, "and if you want me half as much as I do you..." she couldn't continue; only hoped he didn't think her a shameless hussy.

245

He laughed.

"Oh darling, I'd say I want you just as much as you apparently do me, but are you saying what I think you are?"

She nodded, "I want you to make love to me, Shreve."

"Oh, it will be my greatest pleasure, Miss, but I can wait until after we say our vows if you prefer."

She shook her head and speared him with a look that could melt butter, "No! Now." She answered and began to unbutton her dress. She didn't have a clue if what she was doing was going to excite him or anger him, since she was simply following her gut instincts, but she hoped it didn't anger him. She continued unbuttoning her dress, and noticed his gaze followed her movements with interest. *Definitely not angry*, she thought gleefully, and felt her pulse quicken.

When she went to slip it over her shoulders, the material clung fast to her arms. She was stuck.

She giggled lightly, "I think I may need your assistance, sir."

Shreve's breathing was unsteady as he moved to stand next to her. He slipped his hands along her shoulders and beneath the material, pushing downward slowly and firmly.

He watched her eyes flutter closed and her lips part slightly, releasing short gasps of desire. It took longer than either cared for, but eventually the dress slid over her hands and dropped at her feet. The only thing remaining was a pair of lacy panties.

"May I?" He asked softly and Iliamna's breath caught in her throat. She looked into his eyes and nodded. The gaze in his eyes reminded her of the first time he'd seen her unclothed; the comment he made about not being able to stop him if he wanted her. She knew that to be true now. He was going to make love to her, even if she hadn't brazenly asked for it.

He slipped his hands beneath the lacy material of her panties, the palm of his hands flat against her hips, burning her with the heat radiating from them. He slowly moved them down, squatting as he moved, so he didn't have to break contact with her skin. When he was kneeling before her, he released her panties, and slid his hands up the back of her thighs and then reached around to cup her buttocks, pulling her abdomen into contact with his lips. The heat seared her skin and she cried out, nearly collapsing into him. He gripped her hips and held her firm, reining kisses along every inch of her skin, from her abdomen upward, until her reached her breasts.

By the time he'd kissed each in turn, she was squirming wildly and whimpering in need. He stood and scooped her into his embrace, laying her across the bed.

"I'll be right back," he said softly with a grin that sent shivers racing along her body. He stood and unbuckled his pants, hoping they didn't cling stubbornly to him, or he'd have to make love to her with his pants stuck around his knees. He seriously thought that might be the case, when he got to his knees and the pants held fast. He let out a string of curses in his head, but then it was his turn to hold his breath, as Iliamna sat up, reached out and slid her hands beneath the jean material, much as he'd done with her dress.

"Oh," he breathed, as she pushed downward firmly. The pants gave way, and she finished pushing them to the floor, holding them in place so that he could step out of the legs.

He was about to move toward the bed, but she slipped to her knees, and as he'd done with her, and slowly ran her hands along his legs, reining kisses along his abdomen and upward to his chest. He quivered and his *other* brain came even more alert. She slipped a hand around the side of his hip, but stopped short of touching him.

"Please," he whispered, guiding her hand around to the front and wrapping it firmly around his shaft. Her breath left her in a whoosh, while the pulsing beneath her hand fascinated her.

After a moment, long before she could appease her curiosity fully, Shreve pried her hand away, and pulled her up by her elbows and flush against his naked body, holding her tightly, kissing her with every ounce of energy in his body. Iliamna clung on for dear life, barely able to breathe, only knowing she wanted more.

He slipped his arms beneath her legs without breaking the kiss, and lifted her into his arms again, depositing her on the bed. He slid between her legs, pushing them apart with his knees, never once taking his mouth from hers. He needed her and he couldn't wait any longer. He only hoped that his kisses would distract her from the pain to come.

He took his erection and guided it toward her vagina, slowly pushing against the warmth until he felt her grow wetter and the tension release from her lower body, making access easier. He slid in a little and withdrew, trying to maintain control over his own need—growing more desperate by the moment.

She started squirming again, and moaning against his mouth. He kept her mouth imprisoned, knowing that when he pushed in she'd be tempted to cry out, and he wouldn't risk someone in another room hearing her deflowering. He wouldn't allow her to suffer that level of humiliation.

He slowly slid in and she immediately stopped squirming, instead, she moved her hips toward him, slowly lifting upward. The naïve compliance was his undoing and he slid all the way in, breathing in sharply through his nostrils when he felt her innocence give way. He expected her to jerk, to moan loudly, to display some sort of protest—even if mild.

Instead, she reacted as if they'd made love a hundred times before; sliding her arms along his side, stroking his back, kissing him with increased ardor, moving her hips in unison with his. His thrusts intensified, and he finally released her lips, lowering his head into the crook of her neck, breathing heavily. He heard her moan loudly and felt her muscles contract. She was nearing her release. With a final thrust, he pushed deeply and felt his own release.

He shuddered and then lowered himself against her. He needed to move away, was worried his weight would be too much for her, but his limbs were too weak. Still, he started to make an effort only to have her arms tighten around his waist, "Please stay," she breathed near his ear.

"I don't want to hurt you," he breathed back.

"You can't," she replied in a whisper, and then her eyes fluttered closed and her arms loosened.

He understood the need she had to remain close to him, after all, it had been her first time; but he also knew he could hurt her, especially if he fell asleep atop her. He waited until she was breathing steadily, and then slowly slid to the side, pulling her against him. He reached down and carefully drew the blankets to cover them, and then fell asleep—the stress from the entire month finally dissolved, as quickly and fully as a lump of sugar left out in the rain.

# CHAPTER FORTY-SEVEN

"Would you mind then?" Shreve asked, as the four of them settled down to dine at the café that Mitch and Shreve ate at the previous evening.

The only thing that differed between the service this morning and that of last night, was the food. The moment that they seated themselves, a server brought around four glasses of freshly squeezed orange juice, and plates piled high with scrambled eggs, bacon, ham, and toast with freshly-churned butter. It was a meal fit for a king and designed for a hearty appetite, which Iliamna and Shreve definitely worked up during their evening together, and again in the wee hours of the morning before the sun managed to peer through the slit in the heavy curtains hanging over the window in their room.

"Are you certain that's what you want? I mean, wouldn't you prefer a fancy wedding with your family..."

"I haven't any family to speak of," Iliamna interrupted. "Shreve is all I have; he's all I want. But didn't we say that we'd invite the sheriff? And what about Carmen and Jeb, shouldn't they be here?"

"We'll marry here, and then have a party when we get back. That way, my friends can help us celebrate. Fair compromise? Because I'm telling you right now, Miss Iliamna Dearborn, I would much prefer to marry you now than wait another week until we get home."

Iliamna smiled, "I wouldn't prefer to wait either, so yes, fair compromise."

"Good. Captain?"

Captain Avery nodded and took another bite of his breakfast, "Well then," he said after swallowing and then taking a sip of his juice, "if you are both certain that this is what you want and the method in which you want to take care of it—I am certainly able and willing to perform your nuptials. Either you can file your marriage license with the county clerk in the nearest county, or you can take your license back to your home and file it there. You'll need to do it quickly or the state won't recognize your marriage as legal—which as a prosecutor, you would probably know."

"Does it matter if it's filed here?" Iliamna asked

"Not at all. What matters is that it's filed, and the license I give you is signed by the clerk who records it. That's what makes you legal."

"Well, if you don't object, sweetheart," Shreve said, "if we can locate a clerk around here, I say we go ahead and see it legalized sooner rather than waiting the six or so days until we get back home."

"I think that's the best thing to do, yes," Iliamna smiled.

"After breakfast then?" The captain asked.

"Preferably immediately following," Shreve said. "I don't mean to sound like I'm rushing things, but we need to start back as soon as we get the license taken care of. I've already been away from the ranch far too long, and Mitch, you've been away from your duties in Shreveport even longer. It's time we get back to some normalcy."

"And I miss everyone so very much. Little Brendan especially."

"He'll be happy to see you," Shreve said, leaning over and placing a kiss on her cheek. "That's something else I want to ask you about. Would you be willing for us to adopt Brendan; make him legally ours?"

"Quite frankly, I already think of him as mine," Iliamna said.

"I'm glad. Although, that's more paperwork we get to see to when we get back, which is another good reason to finalize our marriage while we're here."

The server came by and removed the dishes, "Have a nice day," he said in that brusque way that was kind, but clearly indicated the party of four needed to clear out. They smiled at each other, stood, and made their way over to the captain's skiff.

"I hope neither of you get sea sick, because a marriage ceremony performed by the captain of a ship is only legal if performed aboard ship."

"Oh, I'll be just fine," Mitch quipped, "as long as you don't plan to weigh anchor and leave port."

"No, that wouldn't be part of the requirement," the captain laughed.

The four of them chitchatted while the captain rowed the little boat over to his trading vessel. With care, Iliamna latched onto the latticework and climbed aboard, followed by the men, whose struggle with their footing on the rope was comical.

"Not a word," Shreve said when he stumbled onto deck and saw Iliamna grinning at him.

"Very good," the captain grinned, "we're all aboard. Let's proceed to my cabin, shall we?"

The captain pulled out a Bible; it's binding cracked and worn. "Is there a particular verse you'd like me to read? Or would like to keep this short and sweet."

"Short and sweet, please Captain," Iliamna said.

"Okay, short and sweet it is. Now, let's see," he pulled out a document from a file in his desk. At the top were the words Marriage License in a beautiful, flowing script. "Let's start with you, Iliamna. I need your full name for the paperwork."

"Iliamna Adina Dearborn."

"Adina?" Shreve whispered near her ear.

"Yes."

"It's as beautiful as your first name."

"Thank you."

Shreve smiled.

"Now your full name, Shreve," the captain said.

"Shreve David Aguistin Red Fox."

"You have two middle names? One is very unique," Iliamna giggled.

"Yes ma'am. My father may have been Choctaw, but my mother was as Irish the Isle is green."

"Well, I'll be a leprechaun with a pot of gold!" Iliamna quipped, and everyone laughed, but then she realized that she knew next to nothing about this man she was marrying. "We have quite a bit to learn about each other, don't we?"

"Indeed, but look at it this way—we have the rest of our lives to do it; and there will always be something to discover that's new."

"I want it always to be that way."

"If that is what you want, then we shall make it so," Shreve said, wrapping an arm about her shoulder. "I will always endeavor to surprise you with something new on a regular basis."

# CHAPTER FORTY-EIGHT

March 15, 1917

"Karan, would you please get Aleia's bottle from Carmen? She's not going to allow me to finish setting up for Brendan's birthday party without feeding her first," Iliamna said, retrieving her crying eight-month-old daughter from the bassinet next to the front door.

"Yes, ma'am, and don't worry about the party, Carmen and I will make sure everything is ready long before Shreve and the men get back for meal time."

"Thanks Karan." Iliamna settled onto her favorite rocking chair, a gift from Shreve the summer before, and rocked her baby girl, cooing gently to keep her calm while she waited on Karan. "Brendan, darling, do try not to get too dusty. You won't be able to eat cake if dirt is flying off your clothes every time you move. You don't want dirty cake, do you?"

Brendan giggled and shook his head, and then toddled away, "And stay where I can see you, please," Iliamna called as Karan came outside.

"Do you want me to keep an eye on him, ma'am?" She asked politely.

"Maybe you can get him to help with his party setup. Then we don't have to worry so much about his getting into mischief."

"He *is* a handful, that one."

"What do you expect, he's my son," Shreve laughed, coming around the side of the house carrying an upside down wriggling Brendan. "Looking for this?" He laughed, depositing the boy at Iliamna's feet.

Brendan scrambled upright and started to toddle down the front steps again, but Shreve snared him by his collar, "Oh no you don't," he scowled in mock displeasure, "you've given these women enough trouble for one day. Now go and help Karan carry something to the table, or you won't be getting cake today."

Iliamna grinned as Brendan scooted after Karan, and then she turned back to Shreve, who was leaning against the railing, watching her and Aleia.

"And how are my two best girls today?"

Iliamna smiled, "Busy and hungry. I thought you weren't due back for the party for another hour," she asked, and then her eyes widened, "I'm not *that* late in my preparations, am I? Goodness, but it's so easy to lose track of time nowadays."

"Relax, sweetheart, we came back early. Finished up, so I told the men to go get cleaned up. We want to look nice to celebrate our son's second birthday, after all. I'm headed to the washroom now. Want to join me?" He grinned mischievously, which made Iliamna blush.

"As tempting as you are, darling, I have a baby to finish feeding and a party to finish preparing for, as well you know. You know it isn't nice to tease me so when you know I can't take you up on your offer." Iliamna affected a pout and Shreve laughed. He walked over and planted a kiss on her lips.

"We can make plans for later, when the children are in bed," he whispered next to her lips.

"Sounds lovely."

"I'll be out in a bit. Then I'll help with anything remaining, okay?"

"Thank you, darling."

Shreve made his way to the front door and was halfway across the foyer when he heard Iliamna call his name. He grinned and turned back toward the porch.

"Forget something, sweetheart?"

Iliamna smiled, "No, there's a rider approaching. I think it's Sheriff Barkley."

"I'm not surprised. Didn't you invite him to Brendan's birthday party?"

"No," Iliamna blushed at the oversight and then sighed, "but we will be inviting him now."

Shreve grinned, "I'll make certain he knows he's welcomed."

"He is, of course," Iliamna whispered, her embarrassment

heightening. "I'm not really so forgetful..."

"No you're not. I love you, and I know you have your plate full, so you're entitled to forget a hell of a lot more than you do."

"Thank you."

"Howdy Shreve, Mrs. Iliamna," Sheriff Barkley called as he approached the porch.

"Sheriff. Haven't seen you in a while. Here for Brendan's birthday cake?" Shreve quipped.

"You know how much I love Carmen's cakes. I hope you don't mind that I showed up."

"Hell, no. You know you're on the list of people who'll always be invited to our children's birthday parties."

The sheriff tossed the reins of his stallion over the hitching post, dismounted, slapped the dust from his hat and clothes, and then moved onto the front porch. "And how is little Aleia faring?" He asked, leaning over to look at the eight month old, nursing in her mother's arms. "She looks like an angel, just like her momma."

Iliamna blushed, "Thank you, Sheriff. Can I have Karan bring you some lemonade?"

"That's something else I'll never say no to," the sheriff said, settling on the porch railing. Iliamna started to stand, but Shreve placed a hand on her shoulder.

"I'll tell her."

A few minutes later, Shreve returned, "Lemonade will be out in a minute."

"So, do we have time to talk before the party?" The sheriff said without preamble.

Shreve's brow quirked and he settled on the porch swing, his curiosity piqued, "Certainly, pull up a chair."

The sheriff pulled a chair over from the opposite side of the porch and then settled near Iliamna.

"Do you need me to go inside?" she asked.

"No ma'am. This concerns you too. Nothing bad, mind you, just information you might be interested in knowing," the sheriff amended quickly, when he saw the looks of concern flit across their faces. "A couple of things. First off, I got word last week from the marshal down San Antonio way. The doctor at the crazy house down that away didn't have any way of contacting you directly, so he sent word the roundabout way."

"About Alana?"

The sheriff nodded, "I don't want to be upsetting you, ma'am, but your cousin passed on in January."

Iliamna's gaze widened and her back stiffened, but other than that, she showed no sign that the news had upset her, "What happened? Did the marshal say?"

"Well, the long and short of it is, Alana wasn't taking to the herbal medicines that the doctor was using to keep her subdued; and her bids for freedom were accompanied by escalating violent episodes. In January, she attacked an orderly. Somehow managed to gouge out his eye. I guess that the doctor was at his wits end with her, and decided to increase her dosage. Apparently, her body didn't take kindly to the increase, and it killed her."

Iliamna nodded, solemn, "She brought this down upon herself. There's always consequences to our actions."

"She chose her lot in life and it proved fatal," Shreve added quietly. "I'm sorry that things ended up the way they did because she wasn't dealt a fair hand at the onset, but she could have chosen not to let it defeat her. I can't say that I'll be mourning her loss."

"Nor I," Iliamna whispered. "Thank you for bringing us the news, sheriff."

"Well, now, that's not the only news I've got to impart."

"Is there news about Red too?" Shreve asked.

The sheriff shook his head, "No, Red is safely tucked away in a jail cell and won't see the light of day until that red hair of hers turns gray. No, this has to do with the war going on across the way. I take it y'all done heard tell of what's going on?"

"Bits and pieces. We're fairly isolated out here, as well you know," Shreve said.

The sheriff pulled a folded up poster from his vest pocket and handed it over to Shreve.

Iliamna stood, "I'll be back in a moment. I want to turn Aleia over to Carmen. I can hear this too, can't I? I know how fickle you men can be when it comes to conversing about certain things in front of us women."

Shreve laughed, "Absolutely, darling. We'll wait until you get back."

Iliamna returned posthaste, and Shreve immediately handed her the poster.

It was brilliantly crafted, displaying a bald eagle—the symbol of their nation—combating a darker vulture-looking bird in mid-air, with very commanding wording beneath.

JOIN THE ARMY AIR SERVICE
BE AN AMERICAN EAGLE!

She looked at the sheriff quizzically, who sat back with a sigh, "Apparently, our men are joining the fight, some of whom will be training right here in Texas. Those men are on their way as we speak."[9]

"So why are you telling us this, sheriff?" Shreve asked. "Not out recruiting men for the fight, are you?"

The sheriff shook his head, "No," he sighed, pulling a telegram from his coat pocket. "I was in the telegraph office when this came in for you. Told Harvey I'd ride it on out to you, since I was headed this way anyway."

"Whose it from?" Shreve asked, reaching over to retrieve the telegram.

"Your friend, Marshal Crowell. It came about a week after this letter arrived for you, also from your friend. As you hadn't been to town recently, I was going to bring the letter out to you today.

Shreve's brow knitted and he looked at the letter and the telegram, wondering which he should read first. Iliamna seemed to read his mind, "The letter arrived first, so start with that."

Shreve smiled and opened the letter.

*February 25, 1917*

---

[9] American forces joined WWI beginning April 6, 1917, three years after the war began, and only a year-and-a-half from the war's end. The war claimed over 37 million lives, both military and civilian, and is still ranked as one of the deadliest conflict in human history (pbs.org).

*My Dear Friend –*

*I hope this letter finds you and your family thriving and happy. I have good news to impart. I, too, have finally located a suitable mate, and we hope to wed...well, soon. The delay in our nuptials brings me to the purpose of this letter.*

*News from Washington has convinced many that the war in Europe will soon make its way to our shores, if we do nothing to stop the Germans. So many men have lost their lives to date in this European War[10] that more help is needed to subdue the evil forces at work there. While I am hesitant to get involved in the business of others, I see so many men of my acquaintance enlisting for this fight; and so many of our women stepping up to take the reins in our workforce, that I find myself shamed into enlisting also.*

*This letter is to make a request of you—that you allow my darling Rose to take up residence with you and yours while I am away. She is a strong woman, and brave, and will do everything possible to help with the running of your ranch; and I must confess that I do not wish her to become one of those women hardened by work in our factories, although I am certain that the work is a noble one and much needed.*

*I will be leaving for Texas in a few week's time, and await word of your decision. I will wire you prior to my arrival in the event that this letter doesn't reach you in a timely manner.*

*Your friend,*

*Mitch*

Shreve shook his head, handed the letter over to Iliamna and then opened the telegram.

*Arriving Brendan's birthday.*

Shreve looked up at the drive, half expecting to see Mitch riding up at that very minute.

"What is it?" Iliamna asked.

He handed over the telegram. Iliamna sighed, "Well, I best be letting Carmen know to expect two more for the party. Sheriff, I'm glad you could be here today. If you'll excuse me, there is plenty more to do before lunch is served."

---

[10] WWI began late July 1914 and was termed many different things: The Great War, The First World War, the World War, and in America, the European War. Over nine million people lost their lives in this conflict started with the assassination of Archduke Franz Ferdinand of Austria.

The sheriff stood, "Yes, ma'am." The minute Iliamna entered the house, the sheriff turned back to Shreve, "You going to join your friend and enlist?"

Shreve shook his head slowly, "I don't know."

"Well, this is only my opinion, but I don't think he's coming here just to drop off his fiancé; I think he's coming to talk you into enlisting with him. Most times, things go easier in battle when you got a friend watching your back."

"Experience talking?"

The sheriff nodded, "My brother and I served in the Spanish-American war, back in '98[11]. Because of him, I'm alive today."

Shreve nodded, "Thanks for bringing the news, sheriff. I'll leave you to enjoy your lemonade, but I promised Iliamna that I'd help finalize the party setup and I haven't even bathed yet."

"I understand. I'll just stay here in the shade and enjoy the view until lunch is served."

Shreve smiled briefly and headed into the house. His mind was suddenly heavy with thoughts of his friend going off to war, and what his duty to his friend and his country should be. He wanted to punch the wall as a sudden bout of anger struck him. He should be celebrating his boy's second birthday unfettered by troubles, but that didn't look as if it would happen today. He waited until he reached the bathroom and then punched the doorjamb, hissing sharply as the pain radiated up his arm. He slid down against the door and cradled his hand. He closed his eyes against the pain in his hand and his heart and waited for both to abate before he could go on with his day.

After a few minutes, he forced himself to wash, building determination with each swipe of the cloth not to allow anything to interfere with the joy of this day.

---

[11] The Spanish-American War took place just nineteen years prior to WWI. On February 15, 1898, an explosion occurred on the USS Maine that caused the deaths of over 250 American sailors. Although accidental, it was believed to be sabotage by Spaniards (about.com).

## CHAPTER FORTY-NINE

"So, when are you leaving?" Shreve asked, as he and Mitch settled into the living room after the evening meal. The party had gone off without a hitch, and all of the guests had departed several hours prior, leaving Iliamna and Shreve to play host to Mitch and Rose only.

Shreve looked over to where Iliamna was conversing with Rose, and sighed heavily, at the same time that Mitch let loose his own sigh.

"Those men enlisting need to be at Travis Army base by month's end, so I'll be heading out by the end of next week," Mitch said softly, lowering his head. "You know what I'm going to ask, don't you?"

Shreve nodded, leaning on his knees, his head hung low. He took a deep breath. "I've got to have a damned good reason to go off and fight another man's war, if I'm going to be leaving my wife and kids to fend for themselves. You know that right?"

"Yeah, I said the same thing—minus the wife and kids part."

Shreve laughed shortly, "And what were you told that made up your mind in favor of?"

"You know we were going to stay out of it, right? The President didn't want us getting involved?"

Shreve shook his head, "No, like I told the sheriff—news to these parts travels slowly, so we barely knew there was a war going on."

"Well, Germany has decided to make it personal."

"How so?"

"German submarines are attacking American vessels. Killing our own people now."

Shreve's brow knitted, "No, I didn't know that."

"I heard tell from a friend of mine, that the President is ready to make American involvement official, which is why men are being recruited."

"I see," Shreve said softly, his gaze drifting over to Iliamna again. "How did Rose take the news?"

"She cried."

Shreve closed his eyes.

"We want to get married this week, before I leave. I requested the preacher come out here on Wednesday. We want you and Iliamna to stand in as witnesses."

Shreve nodded again.

"And I want you to think about coming with me when I leave. There's a great need for good men to fight."

Shreve raised his hand to stop Mitch's speech, "I'm sure there is, Mitch, but this isn't something to be taken lightly. If I say I'm enlisting, then some of my ranch hands are likely to follow. How is my ranch supposed to stay afloat, if the men are off fighting a war?"

It was Mitch's turn to nod his understanding, "I won't bother you anymore about it. If you ride out with me...well...I'll have my answer. In the meantime, the women keep looking over here with worried gazes. I think Rose may have told Iliamna what I'm asking you about."

"Yeah, and Iliamna's look says she's none too happy about it."

# CHAPTER FIFTY

"Are you leaving us then?" Iliamna asked as she lay against Shreve's side. She knew the burden that weighed on his mind was immense because he took great pains to please her long and slow this night, as if he wanted her to remember his lovemaking for a long while to come.

Shreve hugged her tight and sighed, but didn't say anything.

Iliamna felt tears prick her eyes. She had her answer. "How will we ever get on without you?"

After what seemed an interminable silence, Shreve finally whispered a response, "You are the bravest woman I know." He pulled back and slid onto his side, gently swiping her hair away from her face. "You managed to survive being kidnapped—not once, but twice. Any woman who can live through that can live through anything."

Iliamna had no response. She felt her life teetering on the edge of a cliff and could do no more than cry.

Shreve pulled her back into his embrace and held her until he felt the tears subside, and sleep claim her. Then his own tears began.

EPILOGUE

July 5, 1918

Iliamna settled onto the bed and clung to the telegram, the words tossing about in her mind repeatedly. With a heavy sigh, she lifted the parchment to her lips and placed a soft kiss upon the wording, and then lay it down on the bed next to her, smoothing out the edges with a gentleness that belied the turmoil welling in her mind.

A tear escaped and she swiped it away swiftly. There was no room for tears in her world now, only strength of mind. She stood and moved to the little dresser beside the bed, and opened the drawer, retrieving a beautifully bound journal decorated with bluebirds flying amidst trees. It was a gift from Shreve nearly a year-and-a-half prior on the morning of his departure with Mitch to enlist in the Army.

*"I want you to have a way to communicate your heart, while I'm away,"* he'd told her, as he held her in his arms. *"A way to speak to me, as if I were here."* It had proven therapeutic; a way to pull her thoughts from her mind without losing them. It also provided a good place to store his letters to her, letters that arrived monthly. Letters she removed carefully and lay on the bed next to the telegram so that she could write her next entry.

She thumbed through the pages in order to locate the next blank sheet, but as she flipped each page, and her gaze took in some of the words, her movements slowed and she closed it, reopening it to the very first pages.

Her first entry took up nearly three pages, an entry lamenting her loneliness and desperation at having to fend for herself. As the year progressed and life settled into a routine, the entries, she noticed, were more to do with the day-to-day running of their small ranch—

*August 8, 1917. We've hired ten hands, some of them women, to expand the ranch back to its original size, since nearly half the ranch hands went off to war with you. I discovered, on a trip to Dawson Creek, that there is a serious need for food stores, and so have decided to expand our ranch and open a business of sorts, to offer food to nearby families. Perhaps expand it one day. After a visit back east to Tennessee recently, Jeb said that there is a new self-serve grocer called Piggly Wiggly[12], of all things, which is what gave me the idea. Well, Shreve, we'll discuss it when you arrive home.*

The tone was encouraging, the idea to relay the hope that they'd survive and thrive. Toward the end of the year, the entries encompassed less than half a page, sometimes holding only a few words full of sadness and longing:

*February 21, 1918. I miss you, Shreve.*

Today's entry would be something altogether different. She looked at the telegram, lifted her fountain pen, and flipped to that blank page.

*July 5, 1918. Today I learned that I would forever remain alone. Those first five words of the telegram I received, written in so cold a voice—"We regret to inform you..." splintered my heart into a million pieces, so much so that I cannot even cry. Shreve, my husband, I will endeavor not to hold against you, your broken promise, for we now know you'll not return. I will also move forward on the plans of opening a grocer's shop, a legacy of sorts for our children.*

"Iliamna?"

The whispered voice startled her and she dropped her pen. She glanced up at Jeb standing in the doorway, and then bent to retrieve the pen.

"I'm sorry to bother you, but the vet is here to assist in delivery of the calf."

Iliamna nodded, "How's Bertha doing? Does the vet think she'll make it?"

"She seems to have her mother's spunk," Jeb said, recalling the day when Iliamna had arrived at the ranch, and momma Betsy had gone into premature labor.

Iliamna recalled it also and smiled thinly, "Well, let's hope that Bertha fares as well as her momma did. We need her." She sighed, "Tell the vet I'll be along in a moment."

When he'd departed, she made her final note in the journal.

*I am now in a position of having to relay the news of your...I can't even say*

---

[12] Piggly Wiggly was founded by Clarence Saunders on September 6, 1916 in Memphis, Tennessee.

*it, but still I must express to your children how brave their daddy was to fight against evil men, even if it meant laying down his life. They are so young and I'm not certain they will really comprehend, but in time, they will know.*

*And I must also tell those who worked with pride to keep the Double Heart running while you were away, that you will not be returning. I must give them a reason to keep moving forward, as I must learn to move on without you. I can only tell you, that I will do all I can to make you proud.*

Iliamna closed the journal, for the last time, knowing she would never write in it again, nor read what she'd written. She must look forward now, never back. She returned the book to the drawer of her nightstand, and closed it; finalizing that part of her life.

It would be a difficult road to travel alone, she knew, as she made her way toward the barn, but as she watched Brandon and Aleia playing chase in the front yard, she knew that she must survive—for her children's sake.